DARK DESIRE

The Leah Brooke Collection
Desire, Oklahoma 5

Leah Brooke

EVERLASTING CLASSIC

Siren Publishing, Inc.
www.SirenPublishing.com

A SIREN PUBLISHING BOOK
IMPRINT: Everlasting Classic

DARK DESIRE
Copyright © 2010 by Leah Brooke

ISBN-10: 1-60601-880-9
ISBN-13: 978-1-60601-880-4

First Printing: September 2010

Cover design by Les Byerley
All art and logo copyright © 2010 by Siren Publishing, Inc.

Printed in the U.S.A.

PUBLISHER
Siren Publishing, Inc.
www.SirenPublishing.com

DEDICATION

To all of the wonderful readers for your comments and emails. Thank you all so much.

DARK DESIRE

Desire, Oklahoma 5

LEAH BROOKE
Copyright © 2010

Chapter One

Ace Tyler carefully schooled his features into a look of faint amusement, willing his cock to behave as Hope's soft laughter stirred it as effectively as a stroke. Hoping the sunglasses he wore in deference to the bright sunlight would hide what he didn't want her to see, he kept his eyes averted, watching his town and trying his best to close out the sound of her voice.

Standing outside Lady Desire, the club Hope Sanderson and her sister, Charity, opened only weeks earlier, he blocked out most of the conversation going on several feet away, trying to quell his fantasies involving the petite fireball keeping order inside.

Several of the men stood talking on the sidewalk in front of the club after seeing their wives safely inside where the women hold a baby shower for Rachel Jackson. That the men enjoyed each other's company was apparent, and no one appeared to be in a hurry to leave.

Boone Jackson peeked inside. "We already bought a shitload of stuff for the baby. Why the hell would Erin feel the need to throw a baby shower for Rachel? I don't get it. What more could a little baby need? What the hell did we miss?"

Just then a collective "Awwww" came from inside as the women fussed over clothing too tiny to believe.

Jared Preston, Boone and Chase's brother-in-law and one of Erin's husbands folded his arms across his chest and smiled, lifting a brow. "Then you go in there and tell them that their party's a stupid idea."

Boone shook his head, waving his hands and, to Ace's amusement, even took a few steps backward. "No way. I'm not going in there. Look at them. They'd lynch me." He shot a glance at his brother.

Chase backed away, too, shaking his head. "Don't look at me. I'm not messing with Rachel *or* Erin over this. Rachel could pop at any moment, and she's grouchy as hell."

Feeling for Boone and Chase and amused at their reluctance to tangle with the women, Ace touched Chase's shoulder. "I know you're worried about Rachel, but the doc's watching her closely."

Boone grimaced. "So are we, and it's making her crazy. She's uncomfortable all the time now. Erin's the only one of us brave enough to go toe-to-toe with her and make her rest. We're scared to death of making her go into labor or hurting her feelings. Everything makes her cry lately. I'm glad Erin doesn't seem to blame us for it."

Jared touched his shoulder. "Erin knows you're good husbands. She's trying her best to run interference for you. She feels bad that she didn't trust you to take care of Rachel. She knows Rachel's grouchy lately and says that if she could get her through her teenage years, she can get her through this, too. She's having trouble letting go. Just bear with her."

Duncan glanced inside, an unholy grin spreading on his face. "We'll do our best to keep Erin occupied. Don't worry, Rachel will be fine. With all of us watching her, nothing will have a chance to go wrong. We won't let it."

Ace looked up as Clay and Rio Erickson approached, carrying two large boxes and wearing huge grins.

Clay laughed softly. "You're not going to try to keep us out of the club, are you, Ace? Those women inside will have your hide, especially my wife."

Ace nodded, sensing Hope's approach from behind him. The tingling at the back of his neck accompanied the stirring in his groin anytime she got close. Turning slightly, he caught sight of her out of the corner of his eye as he spoke to Clay.

"Jesse already told me to expect you with the stuff for the games they'll be playing."

Rio, Clay's brother and Jesse's other husband, grinned. "Yeah, Jesse and Kelly donated the prizes. They've been working on lube you wouldn't believe. How long do you think this thing's gonna last? I got a few of my own games in mind for my wife a little later."

Hope came to the doorway, stopping beside Ace and giving him a tantalizing scent of vanilla, a scent that now never failed to stir him. "Hello, gentlemen. Thank you, Clay and Rio, for bringing the prizes. Would you mind taking them inside? Jesse will show you where to put them." Moving aside to let them pass, she brushed against Ace, and he automatically put a hand at her back to steady her, his cock hardening more when she shivered.

Clay and Rio grinned and strode inside, Clay winking at Hope over his shoulder. "It gives me a chance to steal a kiss from Jesse."

Boone whipped his head around. "Hell with this. I'm going in, too. I can steal a kiss and make sure Rachel's okay."

Ace forced a smile, reluctantly dropping his hand from Hope's back and taking a step away. He watched as the other men standing outside followed suit, each anxious to be with their wives again. They'd also be checking out the club, since most of them had never been inside before.

Ace had lived in this town most of his life, and it still warmed his heart to see how seriously people took their relationships and how madly in love his friends were.

Wondering for the thousandth time why he had to fall for someone so young, so damned naïve, he purposely avoided looking at Hope, satisfying himself by breathing in deeply and filling his lungs with her scent.

Left alone standing out front with her, Ace fought the stirring in his groin, and watched the people who walked up and down the street in an effort to keep from looking at her. He'd managed to avoid her as much as possible since she'd come back to town several months earlier, but she kept making it harder to do. She was high-spirited and impulsive, and he itched to try to tame her. What a fucking challenge that would be. Trying to get rid of the mental image of bending her over and fucking her from behind, Ace cleared his throat.

"Having fun at the party?"

Hope smiled up at him, showing her dimples. "Yes, it's nice. Rachel's so excited about the baby. She said Boone and Chase barely let her do anything and they're always hovering." Sighing, she shuffled her feet. "She loves both of them so much."

Ace nodded, his gaze constantly drawn back to her no matter how hard he tried not to look at her. The mental picture of her carrying a baby he'd planted inside her tightened his groin even more. "And they love her. It certainly took them long enough to get together."

Her jaw clenched as she looked away. "Yeah, well, some men are a little slower than others."

Raising a brow, he turned to face her fully, satisfaction burning in his stomach when she turned a becoming pink. He wondered how red she'd be if he told her everything he wanted to do to her.

But then again, what would be the point?

"Yeah, well, some men know what's good for them and what isn't." He knew it would piss her off if she knew just how easily he could tell what she was thinking. Being sheriff of Desire, Oklahoma, he'd had to learn to read people. Reading Hope, however, had nothing at all to do with being sheriff and everything to do with being a man.

A man who loved her, who wanted her more every day. A man who knew the best thing he could do for her would be to stay away from her. He couldn't bear to see her face when he shattered all of her illusions. Lately, though, it just got harder and harder. He wanted her so badly he hadn't slept an entire night through since she came back to town. Dreaming of her, he woke sweating and aroused every damned night.

Hope looked over her shoulder, a wistful look on her face as she watched the others. "And some men are just too stupid to know a good thing when they see it." She turned to glare at him, her eyes holding a hint of sadness, before spinning to walk away.

He reached out and grabbed her arm before he could stop himself, knowing damned well the best thing to do would be to let her go. Pulling her out of the doorway, he lifted her to her toes and still stood a foot taller. "And some women don't know when they're trying to bite off more than they can chew. Christ, you're so tiny I could break you in half."

Narrowing her eyes, she grabbed the front of his shirt in her small fist. "You try it, Sheriff."

"Hell." Dropping her back to her feet, he backed away, fighting the urge to throw her over his shoulder and head home with her. "With that mouth of yours, I keep forgetting how damned small you are. You're a little girl playing at being a grown-up. I've already told you I'm no good for you. You couldn't begin to handle what I want from a woman, and I'm too damned rough and mean for someone like you. Just leave it alone, Hope, before someone gets hurt."

She would rip his heart out if he let her.

She surprised the hell out of him by rearing back and punching him in the stomach. "I'm going to hurt *you*. I'm tired of you telling me I'm a damned child. Just because I'm smaller than you doesn't mean I can't handle anything you dish out. Hell, most of the world's smaller than you, you big lug."

Folding his arms across his chest, he glared down at her. "You just assaulted a police officer. You know you can go to jail for that?"

The impudent little brat grinned. "You gonna frisk me, Sheriff? You want to handcuff me?" She stuck her hands behind her back, the action pushing her small breasts out, her pebbled nipples poking at the front of her shirt and making his mouth water. "I've had a fantasy about those handcuffs of yours for a long time."

His cock jumped. Just picturing her hands cuffed together behind her back while she stood naked in front of him, his hands moving over her body to explore every one of her secrets, had his cock rock hard in an instant. Turning away, he scraped a hand over his face.

How the hell did she churn him up so easily?

"I already told you. I take women to bed, not stubborn brats." He turned back to her again, bending down to her level, purposely keeping his features hard and cold. "Women who are mature enough to know what they want. Women who know the score. Women who like it hot and rough and can take whatever I give to them and not throw a fit when they don't get what they want. Not a little girl who races all over town, risking her life trying to get my damned attention by driving too damned fast. If my woman risked herself that way or threw a fucking tantrum, she'd be over my knee so fast she wouldn't know what hit her."

Hope folded her arms across her chest and took a step back while lifting her chin, the mixed signals of submission and defiance making him ravenous to have her.

She drove him nuts.

Looking up at him from beneath her lashes, she glanced inside before whispering. "I know what I need. I know what you need. I'm not stupid. I want it wild and rough and so hot it burns the sheets." She looked away, her face coloring. "I…I know that I need what you want in a woman."

"Do you?" He lifted a brow and waited. To his great amusement, the silence stretched. He'd never known Hope to be at a loss for words.

She glanced at him before looking away again, her face turning redder by the moment, fascinating him. "I guess I just need to push back."

Raising a brow, he straightened, shaking his head. "You like to play games. Like with speeding. I told you when you got the tickets you needed a damned good spanking. If you were my woman, your ass would have been bright red every fucking time you got a ticket."

Just the thought of putting her naked ass over his lap, running his hands over the soft globes, and spanking her until her juices ran down her legs made his balls ache.

She would be the death of him.

Hope cocked a hip, running a hand down his chest and grinning impishly. "I hear you like to spank bad girls."

Yeah, she would kill him for sure. It still drove him crazy that she knew about his need to be dominant in bed, but in a town like Desire, few things ever remained secret. "I do. Until they scream for release. You'd never be able to handle it, little girl, so just stop pushing me."

Hope grinned, but her face turned bright red, the combination stirring his lust to new heights. "That's what happens to the men who come here. Their mistresses show us how to get them so aroused they end up begging to come. They don't care who's watching or what anyone else is doing. They're so caught up in their mistresses and their need that they don't even see or hear anything else."

Ace clenched his jaw as he did every time he thought about Hope being around naked men, especially submissive ones who allowed the women to do whatever they wanted to do with them. Someone as daring and brazen as Hope would have a hard time walking away from that.

She and her sister, Charity, opened this club when they returned home from college, much to the surprise of everyone in town. The club was for women only, a counterpart for the men's club, Club Desire, that had been part of the town for years. Lady Desire hosted various meetings where the women could get together and offer or request advice on relationships. In a town where ménages and dominant-submissive relationships abounded, the women of Desire had embraced the club wholeheartedly.

The club also had lingerie and body lotion parties as well as self-defense and belly dancing classes. Mistresses came in with their subs to answer questions and to show women how to give their men the most pleasure.

The men in town seemed to be happy with the benefits of Lady Desire, enjoying what their women learned and glad they had the support they needed, but they kept a close watch just the same. Anything involving the women would be under constant scrutiny in a town such as this one.

As in Club Desire, only those still single could participate or touch those involved in any demonstration. It went outside the rules of the town for a married person, male or female, to touch anyone else in any sexual way, and the clubs had to abide by those rules.

As sheriff, it was his responsibility to make sure that no one broke those rules.

So, unknown to the women, he checked himself.

Boone and Chase had been the ones who turned a vacant building into the club for the women, and after discovering what the women wanted to use the space for, they rigged something in the electrical box and somehow convinced Hope that she had a problem. With the women kept out of the way, they made an access panel outside that had a padlock. They painted it a dull gray, making it look like something the women would just ignore. It worked. Neither Hope nor Charity had ever expressed any curiosity about it.

Ace had one of the keys and looked in regularly.

He tried to convince himself that he did it as sheriff, but deep down he knew the tiny bit of femininity standing in front of him and her sassy attitude were the main reasons. He couldn't figure out why she opened a club like this one, and the possibilities ate at him. If she touched one of the men who came in here, he would beat her ass so badly she wouldn't be able to sit down. He didn't give a damn what the rules said about being single.

The fact that he didn't have the right to do a fucking thing about it wouldn't stop him. She'd be over his lap so fast...

"I want you to do that to me."

Ace whipped his head around. Lost in thought, he'd forgotten what they'd been talking about. "What did you say?"

Hope blushed again, her big brown eyes downcast. "I want you to make me so crazy with need that I'd do anything you want." She shrugged and looked up, tucking a loose stand of hair behind her ear, surprising him to notice that her hand shook. "I know you think I don't know anything about any of this, but you're wrong. I've done it before, but it wasn't you. I want it with you."

Knots formed in his stomach as the implications of her claim set in. He ground his teeth together so hard it hurt and he had to relax his jaw before he could speak. "You've done *what* before?" Why the hell had he asked? He really didn't want to hear this. Hell, he'd go nuts if he knew what she'd done. He'd go nuts if he didn't. Damn it. She was going to drive him insane.

Lifting her chin, her eyes sparkled with defiance even as she wrapped her arms around herself. "I've been with dominant men before. I'd always fantasized about it and knew that you would expect nothing less. I fantasized about it. I tried it. I like it. A lot. But I could never really let myself go. I didn't feel…special, the way I know I'd feel with you." Her voice lowered, and he had to strain to hear her. "I dream about it."

Reaching out, he grabbed her arm, trying to ignore how soft her skin felt or how wonderful she smelled. "What the hell did you let them do to you?"

Hope pushed his hand away, and turned toward where the men approached from inside the club. "Really, Ace, unless you're interested in me, it's none of your business, is it?" Turning to look at him over her shoulder, she raised a brow. "Or have you decided to make it your business?"

The need to know what had been done to her clawed at him like sharp talons in his stomach. Seeing the others approach, he kept his voice low, clenching his hands into fists to keep from grabbing her again. "I'll pick you up at seven. You and I are going to have a little talk, and you're going to tell me everything." He walked away as the others began to file out, no longer in the mood for their camaraderie.

He jumped into his truck and made the short trip back to the building that housed the sheriff's office, lifting a hand in acknowledgement to several people who greeted him. He didn't stop to talk to anyone as he pulled into his parking space and got out, slamming the door behind him. He strode straight back to the office, covering the ground quickly in his need to be alone. Once there, he closed and locked the door behind him and dropped into the chair behind his desk, wincing as his cock protested the movement.

Something had to be done. And soon.

He wanted answers and somehow had to keep his hands off of her in the process. He'd tried to tell her many times that it would never work between them, but Hope was the kind of woman who charged into things without thinking them through.

If she knew what he'd demand from his woman, she'd look at him in disgust.

Worse than that, though, she would avoid him like the plague.

Perhaps it would be best that way. It sure as hell would be a lot easier to avoid her if she did her best to stay the hell out of his way.

It would hurt. That look of revulsion on her face when she faced the truth about him would hurt like hell, but he couldn't see any way around it.

Fuck.

Once he scared her, that would be the end of it.

Damn it. Why the hell did that have to hurt so much?

Chapter Two

Standing naked in her bedroom, Hope couldn't stay still. She didn't remember being this excited since the night she lost her virginity in the backseat of Todd Rigg's car just a few weeks after graduation.

Ace had given Todd an ass-kicking for it, and Todd had left Desire to work in Tulsa soon afterward.

To this day she didn't know how Ace found out about it.

None of the men she'd ever dated could hold a candle to Ace, and the two dominant men she'd slept with during her senior year in college educated her and even thrilled her, but she'd been fantasizing about Ace the entire time. She could never find the connection she needed, and both times she'd walked away frustrated. Even though her body had been satisfied, her hunger could never been appeased.

It appeared that the only man in the world who made her weak in the knees was a six-and-a-half-foot, hard-headed sheriff with a body packed with thick muscle and an ice-cold wall around him she couldn't resist butting up against.

Go figure.

He had that dominant, hard-as-nails quality that a lot of men played at but could never quite pull off combined with a heart of gold he tried so hard to deny. She shook her head, smiling to herself. Men like that could be found in abundance just by walking down any street of Desire, but in the outside world, they'd been a little harder to find.

She'd grown up in a house in which she had three fathers, all of whom ruled their house with an iron fist wrapped in velvet. Even though they'd always been in charge on the surface, her mother's happiness meant everything to them, and they absolutely adored her. In return, her mother had always been madly in love with her husbands and did everything she could to please them.

Even their fights were filled with love. Hope chuckled to herself as she thought about some of the fights her parents had over the years. Even when arguing, their respect and devotion to each other showed through. She'd taken it for granted just how happy relationships could be.

She wanted a marriage like that.

Going away to school made her realize just how hard it would be to find a man like the men she'd grown up around. Alpha male qualities combined with loving tenderness were an irresistible combination.

The sheriff of Desire, Oklahoma, had both in spades.

And she wanted him badly.

He'd moved to Desire as a teenager with his father and his stepmother when his half-brothers, Law and Zach, had been in grade school a few years ahead of her. His father had been elected town sheriff, and when he quit to move to Dallas several years ago, the town elected Ace as his successor.

His father had since divorced and remarried, *again*, and travelled extensively with his new wife after turning over his oil company to his three sons. He'd inherited it and was smart enough to know that he didn't know the first thing about running it, so a board ran it until his sons could take over. Law and Zach loved the business, but Ace wanted nothing to do with it and cared only about being a good sheriff.

Nobody could fill out a sheriff's uniform like Ace. Damned if he didn't look like an erotic fantasy in that tan shirt and black pants. The boots he wore with it made him look even taller. With those cool shades, tan hat, and a holster on his hip, he looked hard, rugged, and absolutely irresistible.

Knowing he wouldn't be wearing it tonight, she inwardly shrugged. He looked damned good in anything he wore, and if she played her cards right, she'd have him naked one day soon anyway. She couldn't wait to see the body that uniform hid. Imagining it kept her awake at night.

Glancing at the clock, she cursed and ran to her closet. Cleaning up after Rachel's baby shower took longer than she'd expected, even with all the help they had. She ended up talking way too much as the women watched the men load up all the gifts, and the time had gotten away from her.

Wondering if she could earn herself a spanking from Ace by being late, she decided not to chance it. He already considered her immature because of her speeding, but she'd only done it because she'd become desperate. She didn't mean to play games, but she'd tried everything else she could think of.

How had he known she only did it to get his attention?

It backfired on her anyway. She had to pay the damned tickets, her insurance rates went up, and she got a stern lecture from her fathers. She'd just about given up hope of ever getting Ace to notice her until this afternoon.

Not quite knowing where they would be going caused a little bit of a dilemma until she remembered a casual dress hanging in her closet which would be perfect for just about any occasion. The cool night forbade wearing it alone, but she had a shawl her mother and fathers had given her for Christmas that would be perfect with it.

She loved bright colors, and this dress was no exception. Fire-engine red, it clung to her slight curves beautifully and made her feel sexy as hell. She laid the dress on the bed and went to her underwear drawer and paused.

She would be out with Ace. What the hell did she need a bra or panties for? Having small breasts made it easy to go without a bra, but it also made her a little insecure. Hoping he wouldn't be too disappointed in her less than ample breasts, she shoved the bra and panties back into the drawer, her eyes lingering on her garter belts.

Grinning, she pulled out a sexy black one she'd found at Erin and Rachel's lingerie shop. She'd been thinking of Ace when she bought it, vowing not to wear it for anyone but him.

Slipping it on now with the black silk stockings she'd purchased to go with it, she shook with excitement. A moan escaped as she slipped the dress over her breasts. The feel of the soft material sliding over her pebbled nipples made her shiver, her stomach tightening just thinking about having Ace's hands on them.

Instead of having a zipper in the back, the dress had about a dozen decorative buttons in the front, which made it easier for her to get dressed and undressed when she had no one around to zip her. As she buttoned it, she imagined Ace slowly unbuttoning each one to expose her breasts to his gaze, sliding his hand over her skin and bending to take a nipple into his warm mouth.

Would he be disappointed in her? Could she really handle the needs of a man like him? She wanted him so badly that she couldn't even imagine something going wrong. She compared every man she met to him and found them all lacking.

Ace was the man of her dreams, and she couldn't just sit back and let him find someone else. He belonged to her.

Seeing a flash of movement out of the corner of her eye, she turned to smile at her sister, who walked slowly into the room as she read from her never-ending supply of books and nibbled on a carrot.

"Well, Charity, what do you think?"

Charity looked up from her book and blinked, swallowing before answering. "You look great, Hope. You always do. Ace won't know what hit him." Draping herself over the foot of Hope's bed, she carefully bookmarked the page and laid her book aside. "I knew you'd wear him down eventually. Everyone knows he's crazy about you."

Hope grimaced and went back into her closet for her highest heels. "I haven't exactly worn him down yet." Finding the shoes she wanted, she grabbed the matching purse and went back into the bedroom. "I told him about experimenting and that I'd been with dominant men and—"

"Ace Tyler, being the kind of man he is and caring about you even though he tries to deny it, wants to know everything." Charity took the last bite of carrot, chewing thoughtfully.

Grinning, Hope transferred a few things into her bag. "Got it in one. He wants to talk about it, which means he plans to grill me. He's probably mad at himself because he *has* to know but at the same time doesn't *want* to know. I'll bet he regretted asking me out as soon as he did it."

Propping her chin on her hands, Charity bent her knees, swinging her legs back and forth as she watched Hope. "So, the extremely large and cold-as-ice sheriff is going to be angry with himself—and with you—and you're excited about going out with him because?"

Hope shrugged. "Unlike *some* people, I'm willing to go after what I want. He's everything I always wanted in a man, Charity, and I'd never forgive myself if I didn't give it everything I have before somebody else takes him."

She loved her sister dearly but sometimes wanted to shake her. It broke her heart to see Charity so resigned to being alone, turning away a man who was crazy about her.

Grabbing her book, Charity crawled off of the bed and stood, looking more like a teenager in her ripped jeans and oversized T-shirt than a college graduate and business owner. "Don't nag me for not going after Beau. He's only interested in fun and games, not in a serious relationship. He's a walking heart-breaker, something I sure as hell don't need in my life. Have fun with Ace. I just came in to tell you that Mom sent dinner, but I'll put yours away."

Hope blew out a breath and plopped on the edge of her bed, watching sadly as Charity left the room. She wished Beau Parrish would see through her sister's brusqueness and realize just how much Charity cared about him.

It scared Hope to think he knew it and just didn't feel the same.

Beau owned, of all things, the only adult toy store in Desire and would be the perfect man to lighten Charity up and teach her how to play. Charming and too damned good looking for his own good, he eyed her sister like a hungry dog eyed a bone.

Charity had dismissed all of his attempts so far, and Hope wished her sister would just give Beau a chance before he moved on to someone else, if he hadn't already.

Maybe she should do something to get the two of them together...

A knock at the apartment door interrupted her musing and had her scrambling to her feet. Nerves and excitement battled for supremacy as she hurried out of her room, through the small living room, and to the front door.

Taking a deep breath that did nothing at all to calm her, she wiped her damp palms on her dress before reaching for the knob and swinging the door open. As always, her heart leapt at the sight of Desire's sheriff.

He wore black khakis and a light blue button-down shirt that stretched across his massive chest as he stood there with his hands on his hips. His already hard features, hardened even more as he looked down at her. His dark brown eyes narrowed as his gaze moved over her, from the top of her head to her toes, before moving back to her breasts. Meeting her eyes, he lifted a brow, letting her know without words that he knew she wore no bra.

Not bothering to cover herself and very aware that her nipples poked at the front of her dress, she smiled, hoping her nerves didn't show. "Hi, Ace. I hope you're taking me somewhere to eat. I'm starving."

Ace's lips twitched, his expression softening slightly. "You're always starving. I don't know where you put it. You must use it up bouncing around the way you do. Get a sweater or something and let Charity know you're leaving."

Hope lifted a brow. "Bossy as always."

Ace surprised the hell out of her by closing the distance between them and taking her shoulders. Bending, he got right in her face. "Always. Remember it." When she still hesitated, he straightened, folding his arms over his chest and raising a brow in that arrogant way that turned her on despite her best intentions. "I know you don't like obeying orders. I give orders a lot and have no intention of changing. Orders that I expect to have obeyed. That's why I said we should stay away from each other. Change your mind about tonight?"

Hope wouldn't abandon her plans tonight for anything. "I would love to see what you'd do if I kicked you in the shin."

Ace bent again, his eyes twinkling. "Try it."

"I'd rather touch you." Running a hand down his chest, she toyed with a button. "I can't wait for you to kiss me." Elated at the surprise that flashed in his eyes, she turned. "Excuse me. I'll just get my wrap and tell Charity we're leaving." Good, she'd surprised him. She'd have to keep the sheriff on his toes until she made it clear that she was the only woman for him.

Turning to look over her shoulder, she grinned when she saw the hungry way that he looked at her ass. What she lacked in breasts she sure made up for in that area, something Ace seemed to appreciate.

He looked up, his eyes narrowing when he saw that she caught him.

Yes, the sheriff definitely liked what he saw. She winked at him and went to find Charity.

* * * *

Hope stood aside as Ace opened the door of his huge pick-up truck, a sharp jolt of need sizzling through her when he put his hands on her waist and lifted her onto the leather seat. Without a word, he fastened her seat belt, letting his hands linger on her hips a few seconds longer than necessary, staring at her lips the entire time. At Hope's slow smile, he seemed to come to his senses. Scowling at her, he whipped his hands back and straightened, closing her door with more force than necessary and leaving her feeling bereft. Placing her hands over where his had been, she shivered with nerves and need. Watching him walk around the front of the truck, she licked her lips, which still tingled from his stare. If her lips tingled from a stare, what would it be like when he actually touched them with his?

The power and authority in every purposeful step sent her pulse racing as she watched him come around the truck. He opened his door and slid into the seat next to her, sliding a glance her way before starting the powerful engine.

"Steak okay?"

Her stomach was so tied up in knots, she knew she'd never be able to eat a thing anyway. Nodding, she tore her gaze away to look out the front window.

"Of course. I love steak, but I thought you would take me to the hotel." Reaching over and trailing a finger down his arm, she smiled her most seductive smile while inside she trembled like a virgin. "I was kinda hoping you'd reserved one of those private booths." The thought of it had driven her crazy all day.

She'd heard all kinds of stories about what went on inside those booths and wanted to experience it for herself with Ace. The booths had heavy curtains all around them and were reserved weeks, sometimes months, in advance. No one could enter the booth while it was closed. Even the waiter had to wait for a signal from the people inside before entering.

Narrowing his eyes, he looked pointedly at her hand on his arm. "This isn't that kind of a date, and you know it. You and I are going to have a little talk. You're going to tell me what I want to know, and I'm going to explain to you once and for all why it would never work between us."

Resigned, she pulled her hand back and folded her arms across her chest. "Tell me now."

"No."

Taken aback at his sharp answer, she frowned. "Why not?"

"Because I want to see your face when we talk, and I want my questions answered first."

Hope had trouble looking away from him as he drove. He showed the same confidence and easy control with driving as he did with everything else. She could only imagine what kind of lover he'd be. A confident, controlled lover who had a penchant for dominating his lovers…it aroused her every time she thought about it.

Hating the lengthening silence, she curled her hands together to keep from tapping her thigh and attempted conversation. "I heard your siren today. Did something happen, or did you catch a speeder?"

Ace's expression hardened. "The last person I caught speeding was you. Today some idiot turfed the field behind the men's club. When some of the men ran out to stop him, he took off, but not before doing a hell of a lot of damage."

"I didn't hear anything about it. Did you catch him?"

A muscle worked in Ace's jaw. "No. He was gone before I got there, and nobody could get a good look at his license plate."

Still frowning, Hope turned to him. "I don't know why I didn't hear about it."

"You were probably soaking in a tub full of vanilla bubbles when it happened, which is just how it should be." Ace pulled into the parking lot of a steakhouse in a nearby town. Coming around for her, he lifted her down from the seat, dropping his hands as soon as her feet touched the ground. "It's better to talk in a place like this. If we're seen eating together in Desire, everyone's going to get the wrong impression, and I don't want our discussion to be interrupted or overheard."

Money exchanged hands to make sure they were seated far enough from the other diners to afford them privacy. Ace seated her in the booth and took the seat across from her, his back to the wall as he faced the room. He waved the menu away and ordered steak dinners and iced tea for both of them, leaning forward as the waitress walked away.

"What did you mean this afternoon when you said you've been with dominant men before? Don't turn away from me. No one can hear us. I want an answer. You'd better not have done something stupid."

A shiver went through her at his cool command, and she immediately turned back to face him, trying not to show how much that low, steely tone of his turned her on. She took a sip of her water and quickly set it back down so he couldn't see how badly her hand shook. Wrinkling her nose at him, she leaned back.

"I'm a big girl, in case you haven't noticed, and I told you not to treat me like a child."

"And I told you I want an answer. If you can't handle a conversation with me, what makes you think you could handle being in my bed?"

God, she couldn't wait. Just hearing him say it sent a shiver through her and had her rubbing her thighs together as her juices coated them. Not about to back down and risk losing him, she leaned forward, too. Her happiness depended on doing this right.

"I'll be happy to tell you what you want to know, but you could ask nicely. I'm not a suspect you're grilling."

To her surprise, Ace reached out to take her hands in his, running his thumbs over the tops of her fingers, sending alarming sizzles of hot pleasure racing up her arms and straight to her breasts. His brown eyes darkened and sharpened, an intensity glittering in them that called to every feminine instinct in her. He held firm when she tried to back away, the gentle strength in his grip straight out of her fantasies.

"Hope, I'm not nice. That's what I've been trying to tell you. You need a nice man who will give you all the softness you need. Now, tell me what I want to know. Right now. Or we go."

Hope leaned toward him, keeping her voice at a whisper. "What would I get out of telling you? If I don't tell you anything, you'll walk away from me. Once I tell you what you want to know, you'll want to leave. I'd have to have an incentive to tell you. How about a chance to show you? To prove that I'm right about us."

Ace's eyes glittered like chips of ice, his hands tightening on hers. He didn't speak for so long, she wondered if she'd pushed too far. Finally, to her immense relief, he nodded once, his jaw clenched.

"One chance. Talk."

Not wanting to make a scene or appear immature by struggling, she forced herself to relax in his hold. Elated, she looked into his eyes, trying not to show her excitement at her small victory, even as flutters went through her pussy and clit, and her breasts ached badly for his touch. Fighting to keep her voice from trembling, she took a deep breath and blew it out slowly before speaking.

"I grew up in Desire, remember? I know all about different kinds of relationships. I used to fantasize about submitting to a man in bed, but the women in Desire are watched too closely and generally considered off-limits. After what you did to Todd Riggs, no one would come near me so there was no one I could experiment with, especially when the one I wanted was you, and you wouldn't even look at me. Blade, Royce, and King wouldn't let me come anywhere near the club. I had several run-ins with their butler, Sebastian." Smiling, she leaned closer. "When I went away to college, I decided to satisfy my curiosity."

Keeping her hands in his, he idly ran his fingers over her knuckles, sending more of those sizzles of heat up her arm and making her nipples even more sensitive against the material of her dress.

Although he kept his touch gentle, his jaw clenched. "So you found someone to experiment with. What did you learn?"

Her pulse leapt at the flare of heat in his eyes. "I learned that I like it. I like erotic pain. I love submitting. I wanted to be sure I would before…" Shrugging, she looked away, cursing the fact that her face burned. How could he make her feel so shy and insecure with him when she was anything but with other men, even the ones who'd dominated her?

"Before you came back and decided that you wanted that with me?"

Needing honesty between them, Hope looked directly into his eyes. "I knew I wanted you before I left. I knew then what you'd need from a woman, from *me*, and the more I imagined it, the more I started to need it, too. The men I met could never have me completely because I thought of you the entire time. *I'm* what you need, Ace, and you're the man I need. No one else could ever wipe you from my mind."

The waitress came with their food, preventing him from answering. Judging by the look on his face, it was probably a good thing. Releasing her hands, he sat back, eyeing her thoughtfully, his jaw clenched until the waitress left again. He sighed, his expression softening. "You don't know what you're asking, Hope. Desire's a small town where everyone knows everyone else's business. I don't have relationships. I fuck. I'm not what you're looking for."

"Then fuck me." Ignoring his startled look, she leaned closer. "I want you, Ace, and if it doesn't work out with us, I won't hold it against you." The flare in his eyes had her squirming on the seat. His way of looking right through her made her jittery and tongue-tied, something she never experienced with anyone else. She struggled continuously not to show it, but the knowledge of his effect on her glittered in his eyes.

A muscle worked in his jaw. "I'm the *sheriff,* Hope. I enforce Desire's laws and rules. I believe in them, but I can't see myself letting a woman get away with the things the other men let their women get away with. It's put several of them in danger already."

"But what about sex? Don't tell me you never have sex because I wouldn't believe you."

Tearing a roll in half, he looked up as he buttered it. "I take my pleasure elsewhere."

Hope reached for her iced tea, hiding a smile when Ace put the buttered half on her bread plate. "I know that, and it pisses me off that you won't even consider having sex with me. We would be great together. Don't you think you're capable of a lasting relationship?"

Ace's eyes held a hint of sadness before he looked away to reach for another roll. "You're too young to handle what I'd demand from a woman. You need to accept that."

She knew that if she backed down even the smallest amount, he'd end this now. Pressing her advantage, she shook her head. "No. I won't accept it. You have no idea what it would be like for us if you're not even willing to give it a chance."

Ace sat back and scrubbed a hand over his face. "Hope, I'd hurt you, and you'd end up hating me."

Hope touched his hand, lifting her eyes. "I hurt now."

He sighed in resignation, but his eyes darkened and narrowed. "You won't be happy. I won't change."

Hopeful, the butterflies in her stomach took flight. "I'm not immature, and I'm not stupid." Pulling her hand back, she cut into her steak, glancing up at him. "And you, my darling sheriff, are full of shit. You and I are perfect for each other. I don't want to change you, Ace, not at all." Going for broke, she reached for his hand, covering it with hers. "I notice you're not saying you don't want to see me because you don't care about me."

He cut a piece of his own steak, purposely dislodging her hand. "That doesn't mean we could make it work. I'm very demanding and possessive. It would drive you crazy. You'd rebel. I'd overcome it. You'd resent that I could. I can't change the way I am, even for you, *especially* for you. I'd paddle your ass for speeding or just because I wanted to, and it wouldn't always be an erotic spanking. You'd get pissed off and leave. I've seen it over and over. I won't put up with that shit."

Setting her fork aside, she leaned forward, all appetite for food gone. Her appetite for him, however, continued to grow stronger. "I've known you for a long time, Sheriff, and I know inside that you're loving and tender. You might spank me, but it would be because you love me. I won't play games, well, sometimes I will, but I think that's something about me that you'll get addicted to. I won't play games, though, with my feelings or yours. I won't get mad and leave. I'd fight it out with you." Frustrated at his chuckle, she glared at him. "Damn it, Ace. I thought you were taking this seriously."

Sitting back, he sighed. "Hope, you say that now, but when that temper flares, it would be another story. Trust me on this."

"All men of Desire drive their women batty. Why should I be any different? Don't they all fight?"

Raising a brow again, he smiled a cold smile that sent a chill down her spine. "Let's talk about what we came here for. How many of these dominant men have you been with and how long ago?"

She took a sip of water before answering. She vowed to tell him the truth and she would. She wanted no secrets between them. "Two. I met them at a club that I knew was safe. It's been almost two years since I had sex."

"How did you know it was safe?"

Hope sighed, hoping he wouldn't ask, but of course the inquisitive sheriff would latch on to every detail. "I went to school with Brett Madison. You know the Madisons. They work with Boone and Chase."

"I know the Madisons. Keep going."

"Brett's a few years older than me, and we met in a business class. We became friends, so of course we talked about family. When I told him about my family and that I have three fathers, he was surprised and then told me that he and his brothers had shared women in the past, but only for sex, and wished there was a way they could all live with one woman." Taking another sip of tea, she smiled. "His brothers wanted to meet me, to ask me questions about my family. I told them all about Desire, and they were stunned to learn that there was a place where people actually lived the way they wanted to."

A muscle worked in Ace's jaw. "Did they want *you* to be that woman?"

Smiling at the jealousy he hadn't been able to hide, Hope shook her head. "No. We're just friends. They felt like freaks because of what they wanted and couldn't stop asking me questions about Desire. They also started watching out for Charity and me. They used to spend a lot of time at a club, one like Club Desire. When I told them what I was looking for, they helped me find the right men. They went along with me and stayed downstairs in case I found myself in over my head." She smiled up at him, determined to get him to understand. "They took care of me, Ace, like a sister. They looked out for me. Even though Brett finished school, they didn't move here until Charity and I did because they wanted to watch out for us." Laughing, she sat back and picked up her fork again. "I told them that they would fit right in here. They're happy here and getting adjusted to the town."

Ace studied her for several long seconds, making her squirm in her seat. "Why haven't you had sex in two years?"

Meeting his eyes again, she licked her dry lips. "Because I also learned that I couldn't let go the way I need to because neither one of the men I let dominate me was you." Remembering their frustration, she smiled. "Besides, they weren't very happy with their restrictions, and Sloane and Cole Madison were *very* clear about what would be allowed and what wouldn't."

Ace raised a brow at that and took a sip of his own iced tea. "What kind of restrictions?"

She hadn't counted on the intensity of Ace's stare when practicing this conversation in the mirror at home. She had trouble looking away from his hands, imagining how they would feel on her body. Forcing herself to meet his eyes, she could feel her face burn even hotter. "They were never allowed to touch my...bottom." She turned to make sure no one could overhear. "I mean, they spanked me, but they couldn't—I wouldn't let them..." She wasn't a prude by any means, but talking this way with Ace proved to be a hell of a lot harder than she thought it would be.

"You wouldn't let them breach your anus?"

Relieved that he understood, she nodded and looked away. She should have known he'd have no trouble saying it and couldn't believe she did. "Right."

"With anything at all?"

Hope shook her head. "No."

Ace sat back, his eyes hooded. "I wouldn't allow any restrictions. If there was something a woman I was with sincerely didn't like, that would be taken into consideration, but to have something off limits without even exploring the possibilities wouldn't be permitted."

Hope played with her silverware, forcing herself to meet his eyes even though her face burned hotter than ever. "I know that about you. I can accept that." If only he knew.

* * * *

Ace fought the urge to adjust his pants where his cock pressed against his zipper. "I don't think you realize what you're getting into. A Dom-sub relationship is a lot more intense than I think you realize. In a long term relationship, the bonds are stronger than a lot of marriages. That's why I only have one-night stands." He didn't think she needed to know that even those had become practically non-existent because it had become so unsatisfying that it no longer seemed worth the effort.

Hope nodded, the eagerness in her eyes impossible for him to resist. "Don't you think I see what's around me? All the men I know in Desire are too arrogant for their own good, but the love they have for their women is stronger than anything I've ever seen. The women get frustrated as hell with their men, but they're totally devoted to them. Cheating is rare, divorce even rarer. The relationships in Desire are strong because everyone involved gives it their all and lives their lives the way that gives them the most pleasure."

Ace nodded. "True. But everyone goes into it knowing what they want. You're too young to know what you want. We'd both end up getting hurt."

"Damn it, just because you're thirteen years older than I am doesn't mean we're not perfect for each other." Hope reached over to touch him, and automatically he turned his hand to cradle hers. "I can't go on the rest of my life regretting that I hadn't tried. Can you?"

No, he couldn't. God help him. She was his Achilles heel, and he knew he wouldn't be strong enough to watch another man come along and sweep her off her feet.

Besides, he'd already agreed to try, and he hated like hell going back on his word.

Signaling for the check, he leaned back, the hopeful excitement in her eyes deciding his fate. Staring at her for several long minutes, he wondered what the hell it was about her that got to him so much. If he had a taste of her, maybe he could rid himself of this unrelenting need, and prove to her that he would always be far too demanding and possessive for her. In everything. Nodding, he grimaced at her excited grin and quickly added, "*I* set the pace. Not you. Red."

"Red?"

"It's your safeword. As soon as you use it, this is over."

"I don't want a safeword."

"Too bad. My rules, remember?"

"I won't use it."

"We'll see. Let's get out of here."

"Are we going to have sex?"

"No. I'm taking you home."

"Damn it, Ace."

"I'm in charge, remember. Your first lesson is in patience."

Chapter Three

He was trying to kill her.

No, he was trying to make her insane.

Either way, he teased her with his dark looks, filling her thoughts with erotic images of what he would do to her, and she couldn't stand to wait much longer.

Hope paced her office at the club, wishing she had something to do to take her mind off the town sheriff, but she'd caught up with her phone calls and had even gone through a cleaning frenzy but still couldn't get rid of this restless energy. Thank God Charity took care of most of the paperwork because Hope couldn't concentrate worth a damn. She hadn't slept much at all, spending most of the night tossing and turning and dreaming of Ace.

After dinner the other night, he'd driven her home in relative silence, his expression thoughtful as they made their way back to town. He'd walked her to her door and kissed her on the forehead, looking a little preoccupied.

"I'll be in touch. Be good."

She'd long ago come to grips with becoming aroused at an order to be a "good girl." Although she didn't let herself be ordered about and had never been a doormat, hearing such a command in a sexual connotation never failed to excite her.

With him, it made her practically orgasmic.

She'd known it would be different with Ace, *special*, but she hadn't counted on just how strongly she'd react to even the most casual touch. Thinking about how it would feel when he finally touched her intimately kept her on edge, so needy and frustrated she snapped at the people around her.

She just didn't know how much longer she could wait until he did something. Not even masturbating could ease her torment. It only made it worse.

She absolutely ached for him.

"Since there's nothing else here that needs to be done, I'm going to the bookstore. Do you want to come with me?"

Hope turned at her sister's voice and shook her head. She and Charity devoured erotic romances like they were candy, but she just couldn't read any right now. It would only make the ache worse. "No. Go ahead. I'm going to leave in a few minutes anyway. Maybe I'll go down to Indulgences and see Jesse and Kelly. I know Kelly's been upset."

"Yeah. But Blade won't let her dwell on it. The doctor said because of all the scar tissue, it might be difficult for her to get pregnant, but not impossible. If I know Blade, he'll do everything humanly possible to get Kelly pregnant."

Hope dropped in her chair. "The doctor told her to give it a little more time. They haven't been trying for very long. The dads went to the club to play cards and said Blade's quieter than normal and that he's doing his best to keep Kelly's mind off of it."

Charity smiled. "Knowing Blade, that ought to be interesting. Speaking of handsome, dominant men, have you heard from the sheriff?"

"No, but when I do, I'm going to kick him in the balls."

"Brave words."

Hope gasped and looked up, stunned to see Ace moving into the doorway behind her sister. "I didn't know you were there."

Ace's lips twitched. "Obviously. Hello, Charity."

Charity smiled back, winking at Hope. "Hello, Sheriff. I guess I'll be going. I was trying to convince Hope to come to the store with me, but she's too busy sulking."

Hope glared at her sister. "I never sulk."

Charity laughed, earning an indulgent smile from Ace. "Sure, you do. It's part of your charm. See you later. I'll lock the front door on my way out." Waving her fingers, she walked past Ace, leaving the two of them alone.

As soon as the front door closed, Ace lowered his big body into the seat in front of her desk. He sat there watching her thoughtfully, his eyes hooded, for what seemed like forever, tapping his finger on his chin. "Come here."

Taken aback at a tone she'd never heard from him before, she hesitated.

He leaned back, his arms on the armrests stretching his uniform tighter over his hard chest as he waited her out. After several seconds, one arrogant brow went up, but still he said nothing.

Excitement made her heart beat faster as she waited for him to make his move. She couldn't wait to have his hands on her.

Still silent, he stood and turned toward the door.

Where the hell was he going? Panicked, she jumped out of her chair. "Wait!"

Ace stopped and turned, but still said nothing.

Taking a deep breath, she slowly approached him, looking up to meet his eyes. "I thought you would touch me."

He inclined his head, a small, cold smile playing at his lips. "That was my intention."

When he turned again to leave, she ran up to him and grabbed his shirtsleeve. "But you didn't come after me."

"I don't tolerate topping from the bottom."

"What?"

"When I tell you to come to me, you're supposed to come to me. You want to be dominated but balk at the simplest instruction. Don't waste my time, Hope, pretending to be something you're not." He smiled sadly, running a finger lightly down her cheek. "Don't sell yourself short. I'm not the right man for you, and trying to be what you think I need will only end up making both of us miserable."

Terrified, Hope gripped his arm. "No, Ace. Please. You don't understand."

"Hope, stop it. You need a man who's capable of a hell of a lot more tenderness than I am. If that's what you're looking for, you won't find it with me. If you were mine, you'd have no say in what I do to you and would be expected to obey my commands without hesitation. I told you that this won't work. I don't think you know what you want."

Hope ran to block him from leaving, knowing how easily he could brush her aside. "No, damn you. I'm trying. I want this, and I'm willing to fight for it." Why couldn't he understand her need for him to just grab her and take what he wanted? Damn it. She wanted to tell him but didn't quite know how. What would he think if he knew she had desires even darker than his?

He stared at her for so long, fear knotted her stomach. If he ended this now, she didn't know what she would do. Finally, he sighed and reluctantly nodded. "Think about what you really want, Hope, before we do this again. I'll be in touch. Be good."

A large lump lodged in her throat when he turned and started to walk away. "Ace, it's not over, is it?"

He paused, not turning around. "I don't think you're up to this, Hope, and I think you're going to be severely disappointed."

Hope closed her eyes as a wave of need washed over her, her eyes snapping open when Ace continued.

"You have to think about that. Is that something you want to do?"

The lump got larger, threatening to choke her. She couldn't let him walk away now when she'd finally convinced him to see her. Damn her stubbornness. If it got in the way of getting what she wanted, she'd never forgive herself. "Please. Don't give up on me. One more chance. I know what I'm doing." She wanted desperately for him to come back and give her what her body and her heart craved.

The second hand of the clock in her office ticked loudly as she waited breathlessly for his answer. She swallowed, trying to get rid of the lump in her throat as her stomach turned to ice. Tears pricked at her eyes, and she hurriedly blinked them away, not wanting to miss the slightest nuance of his expression.

Finally, he turned to her, the look on his face so cold and forbidding it weakened her knees.

In all the years she'd known him, she'd never seen him like this.

He nodded once. "One more chance. That's it. You either do what I say or you'll have to admit that this will never work."

Letting out the breath she'd been holding, she smiled tremulously, only to have her smile fall when he turned and walked away.

Listening to the sound of the front door opening and closing again, she moved back to her desk and dropped into her chair.

"Patience, he says. Okay. I can do patient." Dropping her head in her hands, she cursed herself. If she'd done as he demanded right away, she'd probably have relief from the torment raging inside her. She needed to feel close to him and knew that with a man like Ace, a physical connection would be of utmost importance.

Looking up, she stared toward the front door. "Patience is not one of my strong points, Sheriff, but I'll be damned if I let you get away."

Sighing, she gathered her purse, resigned to spending another night alone.

This was definitely not working out the way she'd planned it.

* * * *

Dressed in comfortable sweats and thick socks, Hope reclined on the sofa, flipping channels. She occasionally glanced at Charity, who sat curled in a nearby chair reading one of the books she bought this afternoon. "There's nothing good on television."

Charity never looked up as she waved a hand toward the impressive stack of erotic romances on the coffee table. "Read one of those."

Still flipping channels, Hope shifted, seeking out a more comfortable position. "No, thanks."

Reading one of those right now, while she still thought about Ace, would drive her nuts. After several more minutes of searching unsuccessfully for something to take her mind off of him, she stabbed the off button in frustration and tossed the remote onto the coffee table. Sitting up, she reached for the book on top.

"Hell with it. How much worse can it get?"

A half-hour later, Hope had already become engrossed in the story.

When a knock sounded at the door, she frowned at the interruption and looked up at her sister. "Did Mom and Dads say they were coming over tonight?" Since the apartment she and Charity lived in was right above the diner their parents owned, they sometimes stopped in after they closed for the night.

Charity shook her head, glancing at the clock. "No. They closed an hour ago. It's probably Ace." She started reading again, leaving Hope to answer the door.

Hope had already had that thought and just as quickly dismissed it. "No. Ace won't be here tonight. He's a little upset with me."

Charity lifted her head and blinked. "I'm not surprised. You could drive anyone batty. So, are you going to answer the door or not?"

Hope grinned and shook her head as her sister's nose disappeared into her book again. Standing, she flipped the book she'd been reading face-down on the coffee table.

"Damn it, Hope. Use a friggin' bookmark."

On the way to the door, Hope looked over her shoulder and stuck out her tongue. "You should have answered the door." Laughing softly, she swung the door open, her laughter dying when she saw Ace standing outside. "Ace?" Glancing at her sister, she kept her voice low. "I thought after this afternoon—"

He stepped forward, forcing her to step back into the apartment. "Do you always open the door without checking to see who's standing outside?"

Hope rolled her eyes. "I live in Desire, Oklahoma, Ace. There are no strangers here—" She turned to walk away, yelping when Ace grabbed her arm and pulled her up short. "Hey!"

He shook her once, glaring at both her and Charity, who looked up in surprise. "Haven't you heard about the women being hurt around here? We haven't taken care of them the way we should have. All that's changed. If I catch either one of you opening that door without checking, I'll tan your backsides. Are we clear?" He closed and locked the door behind him before ushering her into the room.

Hope rubbed her arm when he released it, not because it hurt but because of the delicious tingling where he'd touched her. A quick mental flash of him turning her over his lap made her involuntarily clench the cheeks of her ass. "Ace, we'll check, but you really don't have to get all caveman on us."

Ace's smile sent a chill through her as turned her and lifted her to her toes. "You live in Desire, Oklahoma, remember? You've lived here your entire life. You and your sister know the rules of this town," releasing her shoulders, he gripped her chin, "and by God, you'll abide by them."

Charity stood with her book and smoothed a hand down her robe. "It's nice seeing you again, Sheriff. I'm going to my room and leave the two of you to fight this out."

Ace's eyes narrowed. "I'm serious. You'll be over my knee if you don't look before opening the door. Unless Beau wants to do it."

Charity's eyes flashed as she opened her mouth to say something, only to snap it closed again. Smiling serenely, she lifted her chin and turned. "Good night."

Hope waited for Charity go into her bedroom and close the door behind her before turning to Ace and gripping his arm. "How did you know about Beau? Did he say something? Is he interested in claiming Charity?" She smiled as music came from Charity's room, secure in the knowledge that she and Ace wouldn't be disturbed. "Come on, tell me. She won't hear you."

Ace chuckled. "I try to know everything that goes on in my town. Whether he said something or not is none of your business. Stay out of it." Moving to the sofa, he reached out and picked up the book she left on the table. "Hmm."

Damn it. She reached out to snatch the book out of his hand, but he deftly avoided her, blocking her attempt without even looking up.

"You make sweet tea like your mother, don't you? I'll take a glass of that."

Cursing under her breath, she turned away to go into the kitchen to get his tea, knowing she'd only embarrass herself with a useless struggle for the book. Pouring his drink, she looked toward the living room to see him reading the book where she'd left it open. Remembering the part she'd been engrossed in, she shook, spilling tea on the countertop. "Damn." The heroine had been in the process of getting a sound spanking for arguing with her lover. Hope had a sneaky suspicion the hero would be taking the heroine's ass very soon.

Ace looked over his shoulder toward the kitchen. "Something wrong?"

Averting her eyes to wipe up the mess, she shook her head. Nervous as hell, she had to clear her throat before speaking. "No. Just clumsy." She carried the tea back to him, wondering what he thought of her reading material. "Why did you come by tonight? After this afternoon I didn't expect to see you." The low arousal she'd endured for days flared to life as soon as she opened the door and just kept growing stronger, but she was nervous as hell, hoping he hadn't changed his mind. He'd come over, at least that was something.

Accepting the tea, Ace took a sip and murmured his approval before setting it on a coaster on the coffee table. He still had the book in his hand open as he patted his thigh. "Come here." He kept reading, not even looking at her.

Her pulse leapt. Not about to give him an excuse to walk away again, she hurriedly sat on his lap, thrilling at the shift of hard muscle beneath her thighs. Trembling at being held by him for the first time, she gripped his shoulders, only to have him take her hands in one of his and put them in her lap.

"Do you and your sister read these often?"

"All the time. I should tell Beau the kind of books Charity reads. Maybe it'll give him some ideas."

"Hmm." Ace set the book aside and reached for the remote control.

"There's nothing worth watching."

"I didn't come here to watch television. I don't know yet how much noise you make when you're aroused, and I don't want Charity to think I'm killing you." He turned on the television, adjusted the volume, and tossed the remote aside.

Jeez, he had to know how saying something like that would affect her. Hope shook in earnest now, her excitement growing by the second. Although her body had become overheated, she shivered when he reached for the hem of her sweatshirt and lifted it over her head, never taking his eyes from her breasts as he tossed it into the nearby chair. She was glad that she hadn't worn a bra underneath, but worried that he might be disappointed with her less than full breasts. Damn it, she'd never cared what anyone ever thought before, but with Ace she wanted to be perfect.

He took her hands in one of his and lifted them over her head as he laid her back against the arm of the sofa next to him. With his other hand, he began to lightly run his fingers over her stomach.

"Beautiful."

She felt beautiful in his arms, her need growing at the flash of heat in his eyes as he ran his fingers between her breasts and over her chest and shoulders. "I'm small." She hadn't meant to blurt that out and regretted it the moment the words left her lips. Damn it, she couldn't remember ever being this nervous.

Ace's huge hand covered a small mound and massaged gently. "Delicate." His expression softened, a sign that he understood that her trembling came from more than arousal. A smile curved his lips when she gasped. "And very sensitive. We'll have to be careful."

Testing his hold, she writhed with excitement to discover she couldn't break his grip. "Not too careful, I hope."

Still holding her wrists firmly, he reached for the iced tea on the table and took a sip before touching the bottom of the cold glass to her erect nipple.

Fisting her hands, she closed her eyes on a moan as he moved the cold glass back and forth over first one nipple and then the other, taking his time, his gaze going from her breasts to her face and back again. Despite the cold, fire raced from her nipples to her pussy, and she dug her heels into the sofa, rocking her hips to try to relieve the pressure. Doing that also moved her ass back and forth over his cock, which seemed to grow larger with each pass.

Ace groaned harshly and slid from under her, lying down against the back of the sofa and, still holding her hands in his, covered her thighs with one of his thickly muscled ones. "You keep teasing me with that ass, you're going to find yourself in a lot of trouble." Leaning over her, he put the glass back on the table and watched her with gleaming eyes as his fingers traced over her cold nipples, running them up the underside of her arm to her wrists which he held firmly in his other hand, and back down again.

"Ace, the light."

Restricting her struggles, he strummed his fingers over a nipple. "I want it on." The steel in his low tone as he caressed her was better than any fantasy she'd ever had and reignited some of her trepidation. Suddenly she couldn't breathe, couldn't draw enough air in her lungs. The sophistication she'd tried to adopt fell away under his caress, until she became nothing more than a trembling mass of need, a woman vulnerable in her man's arms.

Keeping her eyes tightly closed against not only the light, but against Ace seeing too much, she squeezed her thighs together, overwhelmed by the exquisite throbbing of her pussy and clit. She hadn't worn panties either and wanted so badly for him to strip off her sweatpants and fuck her. Oh, God. For the first time in her life, she wondered if she could handle what he wanted from her. Already she burned uncontrollably.

He ran his fingers over each of her breasts. "Would you like these to belong to me?"

Hope shuddered, the low huskiness in his tone drawing her deeper into his web of seduction. "Yes. I belong to you. Please, Ace."

"Please what?"

"Please take me. Fuck me. Do something. Anything. I can't stand it."

His soft chuckle made her shiver. "You're shaking, and I've only just begun to explore you. I've already told you that you're going to have to learn patience. Is this body mine or not?"

"Yes, oh God, yes."

"If it belongs to me, I can do what I want with it. If I can't, I don't want it. I'm a first class bastard, Hope, and I'm not about to make any excuses for it. What's it going to be? Are you ready to admit I'm not what you want?" He pinched each of her nipples a little harder than before, sending shards of white-hot pleasure to her slit.

"No. You're exactly what I want. I'm yours. I'm yours. Please, Ace, I can't stand it."

"You're trying to convince me that you're capable of submitting to me and yet you're undisciplined and demanding. If you want to belong to me, you're going to need extensive training, especially with patience. I've barely touched you and already you're crying for release."

Her eyes popped open to search his, desperate to get through to him, but she had trouble organizing her thoughts. "I don't know how. Teach me, Ace. I'll do whatever you want, be whatever you want, just don't stop. Make me yours."

He dropped his hand, leaving her bereft, and bent over her to lightly nip her bottom lip, his eyes hard and cold but holding a fierce possessiveness that called to something deep inside her. "I can arouse you this way and leave you if I choose. I can tie you up and bring you to the verge of release and leave you there, only to come back and do it again. And again. As many times as I want to. *Never* demand from me and *never* think to tell me what you can stand and what you can't. You have a safe word you can use when you can no longer take it."

"But if I use it, we're through."

"We are."

Hope bit her lip and arched toward him. The strength of her arousal alarmed her "Ace, I have no experience with need like this. Please be patient with me. I burn everywhere."

Ace nuzzled her jaw. "I know, baby. You're amazingly responsive."

His softly spoken endearment melted her heart and eased her fears just enough to allow her to catch her breath. Letting everything she felt for him show in her eyes, she smiled, whimpering when he touched his tongue to the tip of her breast.

"Only for you."

Ace lightly scraped his teeth over a nipple, drawing a gasp from her. "For now. I want to see the rest of what now belongs to me. Stand up." He rolled his weight off of her and pulled a paper out of the pocket of his shirt and handed it to her. "This is my doctor's report. I'm safe."

It took a moment for his words to penetrate. "What? You want me to stand up?"

Ace smiled slowly. "I want to explore all of you, and I want you standing for this part. Are you going to obey me, or am I leaving?"

Slightly dazed, she took the paper from him and impatiently tossed it aside. "I'm safe, too. I have one ready for you." She didn't want to interrupt what they'd been doing, but some things had to be addressed. She shakily got up from the sofa with the intention of getting it, shuddering as he traced the line of her back with a warm finger and tugged at her waistband.

He sat up, watching her with hooded eyes. "Take those pants off first. I want to see you walk naked."

Blinking at him in surprise, she opened her mouth to ask why, snapping it closed again when his brow went up. Nodding, she hooked her thumbs into the waistband of her sweatpants, lowered them slowly to the floor, and kicked them off. Her body burned hotter, tingling everywhere his gaze touched as he looked her over from head to toe.

"No panties? Good. Go get the paper for me. Slowly."

She couldn't have walked fast if her life depended on it. Her limbs shook so badly it took every ounce of concentration just to put one foot in front of the other, more aware of her body than she'd ever been. She probably looked ridiculous walking naked except for thick socks, but she didn't dare say anything. She didn't bother to try to hide herself, knowing he wouldn't allow it anyway, and she wanted desperately to please him. She crossed the room to her purse, reached into the side pocket, and pulled out the envelope.

"I meant to give this to you earlier, but you left."

Ace wagged his fingers. "Come back here and give it to me now."

Hope crossed back to him at the same measured pace and handed him the envelope.

Without taking his eyes from her body, he folded it and stuck it in his shirt pocket. Leaning back, he rested his arms on the back of the sofa and waved a hand toward her body. "All of this belongs to me?"

The two dominant men she'd been with before paled in comparison to the man sitting before her. "Yes." She'd never been so aroused, never so conscious of her body than at that moment. This is what she needed, what she'd craved for years.

Ace.

The tenting of his jeans told her that he was just as turned on by this as she was, which sent her own arousal soaring.

He put out his hand, which she readily took, and pulled her closer to stand in front of him. "Spread your legs." He sat back again, his eyes holding hers steadily as he waited.

Hope swallowed heavily and took a deep, shaky breath before spreading her feet about a foot apart. Knowing he could see her juices coating her inner thighs, she automatically brought her hands up to cover her mound.

"No. Hands at your sides. Spread those thighs a little more."

Taking a deep breath, Hope nodded hesitantly, fisting her hands at her sides. She shuddered as his eyes raked her body and spread her legs another few inches wider.

Leaning forward, he ran a finger lightly over her bare folds.

"Why are you waxed?"

Hope sucked in a breath at his touch. "I did it before I went to the club. I thought a submissive should be bare there."

"Why do you keep it that way? I thought you said you haven't had sex in two years."

Hope smiled tremulously. "I like the way it feels."

Ace nodded. "I want you to keep yourself waxed for me. I want nothing to block my view. Open yourself to me. I own all of you tonight, and I want to see everything that belongs to me."

Hope closed her eyes on a groan, his words and actions fulfilling every fantasy. Even though he kept his voice low and with the background noise of the television and music, the steely undertone in his voice carried loud and clear. Reaching down, she parted her folds, biting back a moan when her fingers slid over her clit.

Ace sat close enough that she could feel his breath on the swollen nub. "Quiet."

Not until then did she realize she whimpered. Her clit felt huge, the bundle of nerves throbbing with the need for his touch. When it came, she cried out, her knees buckling at the intense wave of pleasure.

Ace caught her. "Stand up. I'm not through examining my property. Lock your knees."

His sharp demand intensified her dark needs, her lust so strong she couldn't stop shaking. His features hardened, making her determined not to disappoint him. She'd never give him an excuse to walk out on her again.

"I'm sorry." Standing again, she locked her knees and once again opened herself to him, concentrating on trying to remain motionless. She'd do anything at that point—even beg—for his touch.

Once again he touched a rough finger to her clit, lightly moving it in circles. "Don't you dare come. If you do, I'll leave."

With one rough and callused finger, he controlled every fiber of her being.

Her chest heaved as she fought to get enough air into her lungs. Her arms and legs shook with the effort it took to fight her orgasm. "I can't. Please. I can't hold it off."

Ace withdrew his hand and sat back, his eyes raking over her body before lifting to hold hers. "I don't know who those other Doms were, but your training is definitely lacking."

Hope gulped air. "I only saw each of them once. I want to be trained by only you. I want to be yours, Ace, to be trained and possessed by only you."

Ace's eyes flared hotly. "We'll see if you can be trained. Keep your legs spread. I want to explore more of you. Do. Not. Come. Bend your knees."

Hope stared at him in disbelief. She shook so badly she had trouble standing. "I'll fall."

"I'll make it easier this time. Hold on to my shoulders." Ace lifted her with no apparent effort, placing her over his spread knees and leaving her slit wide open.

Hope looked into his eyes as she held on to his massive shoulders. "Thank you. I'll get better at this, I promise."

Ace's lips curved, warming her inside until he spoke. "There'll be penalties for this kind of thing in the future." His smile fell as he sobered once again. "Although I doubt that we'll get that far before you realize what I'll do to you."

Her entire body trembled as he slid a hand around to the small of her back to hold her in place while the other slid between her widely splayed thighs. Fisting his shirt in her hands, she waited breathlessly for his finger to enter her. She shuddered, moaning as he circled her opening, her eyes fluttering closed.

"Open your eyes and keep them on me."

Hope snapped them open, a tremor of fear racing through her at his tone. His firm coolness and iron control excited her, but they also filled her with apprehension, making her worry that she didn't have the experience or ability to hold back enough to please him.

Keeping her eyes on his, she moaned when his finger entered her pussy, her slick juices easing his way.

"Is this mine?"

"Yes. Forever."

"I can do whatever I want to it, whenever I want?"

"Yes."

His eyes narrowed. "You belong to me for as long as this lasts?"

Hope leaned forward and touched her lips to his, just now realizing that they'd never kissed. "Yes. Everything I am is yours."

Brushing his lips over hers, he slowly withdrew his thick finger, only to slide deep again. His strokes came faster as he curled his finger inside her and rubbed at a spot that stole her breath, every stroke driving her closer and closer to the edge.

Hope held on to him, her breath coming out in pants as she tried to hold it off, nearly crying when his lips lifted from hers. "Oh, God. I'm going to come. Ace, I can't stop it."

Ace withdrew and slapped her sharply on the ass, his eyes fierce. "I said no."

Hope jumped, the sharp sting stunning her. The heat from it spread, making her ass and slit warm, the nerve endings brought alive and becoming more sensitive than before. His dominance thrilled her, his cool, commanding presence even better than her wildest fantasies. Wrapping her arms around his neck, she buried her face beneath his chin, his scent somehow simultaneously centering her and taking her arousal higher. She wiggled on his lap, trying to rub her clit against him, which earned her another slap. Gripping his shoulders tighter, she rubbed her cheek against his jaw, raw need clawing at her as he positioned her so that nothing touched her slit as he kept it spread wide.

"Ace, I have to come. I can't stop it."

"Demands again? Drape yourself over my lap."

She sat up with a gasp. "You're going to spank me?" The thought of being naked over his lap filled her with equal parts of anxiety and anticipation.

Ace's eyes narrowed and turned to ice. "You're questioning me? It doesn't matter what I'm going to do. I gave you a command, and I want it obeyed. Now, Hope, or I'm walking out that door right now and never coming back."

Her own dark need and her fierce love for him gave her no choice. God, she ached everywhere. As gracefully as possible, she got up and draped herself across his lap, her breaths coming faster as she waited for the touch of his hand. Five sharp slaps landed in rapid succession, hard slaps that startled the hell out of her and set the cheeks of her ass on fire.

"Never again question my commands." He delivered one more slap she didn't expect, startling her into crying out. "And don't clench when I spank you."

Hope buried her face in the cushion as the fire spread, nerve endings in her bottom and slit coming alive with a vengeance. "I'll try not to do it again. Oh, Ace, spank me more." Warning tingles of a fast-approaching orgasm startled her into squirming. From a spanking?

"This ass is virgin?"

"Yes." Oh, God.

"Is it mine?"

"Yes."

"All of it?"

"Yes."

"Show me."

Confused, Hope turned her head to look at him. "Show you? I don't understand."

Ace ran a hand over her flaming bottom, igniting fires all over her body. "Spread the cheeks of your ass and show me what you're giving me. Show me that tight opening I can explore or fill however and whenever I wish." At her startled look, he raised one of those arrogant brows again in the way that always had more of her juices flowing. "You are giving it to me, aren't you?"

Nodding tremulously, Hope gulped, shaking like a leaf with an arousal so intense it scared her. "Y–yes."

"Then show me. Present my gift to me."

Knowing she had no choice other than using her safeword, Hope reached down and gripped the cheeks of her bottom, drawing a deep breath as she worked up her courage before she could spread them. Her hands on her bottom renewed the fire, making her cheeks burn all over again.

"Wider." He slid a hand between her thighs to spread them several inches apart.

Burying her burning face again, she pulled them apart as wide as she could, backing off at the pinch of her bottom hole. It was too intimate, made her feel too vulnerable. Tears pricked her eyes as sensation after sensation bombarded her and filled her to overflowing.

"I said wider."

Did he know what it did to her when he spoke to her that way? "I can't. It hurts."

"It's going to hurt a hell of a lot more if you don't obey me. At least I can see how to get your attention. Whenever you misbehave, I'm going to take a whip to this." He ran his finger lightly over her puckered opening.

Shuddering at being touched where no one had ever touched her before, and alarmed at his threat, Hope hurriedly obeyed him, amazed at the heightened intimacy and erotic tension that now filled the room. Each stroke of his finger over the delicate tissue took more and more of the fight out of her until she buried her face in the pillow again, giving herself over to him.

"This is mine to do with as I wish. It belongs to me and only me?" His voice held an edge now that hadn't been there before.

Trembling, Hope turned her head to lick her lips, her voice barely a whisper. "Yes. It's yours."

"Get up."

Hope released her bottom and swung her head around, blinking. "What?"

"Get up."

Sitting up, Hope grabbed his arm. "I'm sorry."

Ace helped her to her feet and reached into the front pocket of his jeans, frowning down at her. "For what?"

"For whatever I did wrong."

Ace gripped the back of her neck and brushed her lips with his. Straightening slightly, he stared down at her, his eyes gentler than she'd seen them in years. "You did nothing wrong. Nothing at all." He applied pressure, forcing her lips open to slide his tongue inside.

Hope opened to him completely, holding on to his shoulders as she pressed against him, rubbing her nipples against his chest.

Ace stilled, lifting his mouth from hers, his eyes narrowed but shining with amusement. "Did I say you could do that?"

Hope swallowed heavily and blinked again. "Do what?"

Sighing, he sat back down on the sofa, tugging her back onto his lap, and for the first time, she noticed a small tube in his hand. "Did I say you could rub your nipples against me?"

"But I thought—"

Shaking his head, he tugged a nipple. "No, you didn't think. You just do whatever feels good. I have a feeling you're going to have to be tied down quite a bit for your training."

The sharp pull went all the way to her clit, now so swollen and sensitive it threatened to drive her mad. Just the thought of being restrained and at Ace's mercy almost made her come on the spot.

"Tied down? I've never been tied down."

"You will be." Settling her in his lap, he positioned her head on his shoulder, allowing her to watch as he uncapped the tube and applied a liberal amount of the clear lube to his middle finger. He re-capped it and tossed it aside before sliding his right arm beneath her legs.

Shaking, Hope lowered her gaze, unable to tear it away from the sight of his sinewy forearm that kept her legs raised.

"Hope, look at me."

He waited until she met his gaze before speaking "I'm going to explore your tight little ass. I need to see how well you adjust to it and need to know how tight you are. I want your eyes on me the entire time. The fear I see in them now belongs to me. The vulnerability in them when you realize that I've entered a part of you that no one has ever entered before, the most private part of you, is also mine. So is the surprise and helplessness when you realize that, except for using your safeword, there's nothing you can do to stop me from pushing deep, stretching you, or stroking your anus however I want."

Hope's breath hitched, her stomach clenching as the implications of Ace's demand sank in.

He'd told her himself. He wanted it all.

She'd counted on giving him her body. She'd counted on giving him her love. She just hadn't counted on giving him her deepest inner self. She'd kept that part hidden from the other men with no trouble, but it appeared Ace had other ideas.

She licked her dry lips and took a tremulous breath. "Ace, I don't know how to do this."

He smiled tenderly, sliding a hand beneath her hair to cradle her neck, holding her up with one muscular arm. "Just keep your eyes open and on me, baby. I'll take care of the rest."

Hope nodded and swallowed heavily, her pulse racing as Ace bent over her, his face mere inches from hers as he bent her legs higher. At the first touch of the cold lube on her bottom hole, she jolted in his arms. Fisting her hand in the front of his shirt, she struggled to keep her eyes open as his thick finger began to press into her, pinching as it stretched her.

The liberal amount of lube eased his way, as did her position, but her body nevertheless fought his invasion. The relentless press of his finger forced the tight ring of muscle to give way, allowing him to enter her, the level of vulnerability at having her anus breached stealing her breath.

Whimpering in her throat as she fought to adapt to such a foreign sensation, she knew the fear he spoke of had to show plainly on her face. The stark intimacy in such an act surprised her and she tightened on him, involuntarily attempting to deny him entry even as her mind screamed for his possession.

He smiled reassuringly even as his eyes darkened, sharpening as he stared down at her. He continued to press his large finger steadily into her with a firmness that made her more than aware that she couldn't stop him.

He partially withdrew only to slide deeper, and no matter how tightly she clenched, she couldn't slow him down at all.

His words came back to her, and the vulnerability he'd warned her about hit her hard, somehow only adding to her intense arousal and the astounding intimacy of what he did to her. It excited her even more that he'd known what she would be experiencing. Without hesitation, she spread her legs wider in an act of acceptance, an act of submission, biting her lip against the moans she couldn't suppress.

Ace slid his finger deep. "You're so damned tight. So hot. Do you have any idea how hard my cock is just thinking about taking your ass? The next time I have you like this, it'll be somewhere you can scream."

When he touched his thumb to her swollen clit, she jolted, gasping as it moved her on his finger. As soon as he began stroking, all of her inhibitions vanished in a haze of lust. She burned hotter than ever, the feeling of something inside her bottom adding to the sheer eroticism of his possession.

He owned her.

Her mind ceased to function, her body now completely under his control. He controlled the wave that kept building inside her, slowly intensifying its power. Her eyes closed at the intense surge of need, only to snap open again when she remembered that she had to keep them on his.

Ace smiled indulgently. "Good girl. Now you can come. I want to feel your ass clench on my finger."

Hope needed no further urging. Her orgasm washed over her, making every other orgasm she'd ever had pale in comparison. Her clit throbbed under his caress, her entire body swept up in a sizzling wave of intense pleasure. The strength of it forced her to clamp down on the finger pressed deep inside her, increasing the sensation of being stretched there. Her cry was quickly smothered as Ace covered her mouth with his. Oh, God! Nothing had ever felt this good. The strokes on her clit slowed, dragging out her orgasm until she sobbed, the sharp tingles continuing for so long it became painful. When he lifted his head, she begged.

"Please, Ace. No more. Please make it stop. It's too much."

"Demands again?"

Opening her eyes, she didn't realize she'd closed, she gasped for air, shuddering as every inch of her body screamed with ecstasy. "No. I'm sorry.

It's just—I can't—Oh, my God. It won't stop. Help me. I don't know what to do."

Ace took pity on her and stopped stroking her clit and waited, watching with hooded eyes until she settled. His lips curved before he kissed her lightly, gathering her against his chest. "You know, of course, that if I want to, I can keep caressing your clit until you sob and just keep going. And already you cry for mercy. Training you is going to take the rest of my life." He immediately sat straighter, putting some distance between them, his look hardening again as though he realized what he just said.

Hope smiled weakly, stroking his jaw, needing him to smile at her again. "Promise?" Her smile became a gasp when the finger in her bottom moved.

"Don't be a smartass. I can sit here and play with your ass all night if I want to, remember?"

Hope's face burned, but she didn't look away. "I'd never survive it."

Ace shook his head in amusement as he eased his finger from her anus and rubbed her bottom. "I'm beginning to wonder." His lips twitched as her eyes began to droop. "You're hot as hell, but I wouldn't exactly call you submissive. You still fight it. Get some sleep. You're exhausted."

Hope sat up in alarm, wide awake but lethargic and clumsy. "What about you? Don't you want to have sex?"

Ace helped her to her feet and sighed. "I'm too demanding, too dark for you, Hope. I made you come because I'm selfish and wanted to see what you looked like when you have an orgasm. I wanted to hear the sounds you make when you come. I played a little, that's all. You wouldn't always get to come so quickly, and if the mood suited me, not at all. You said for yourself you couldn't stand anymore." With his arms around her, he rubbed her back, staring deeply into her eyes. "Let it go, Hope. Please. Before one of us gets hurt."

Hope panicked. "Ace, no! What can I do to make you understand that you're exactly what I want? Do you know how good this felt to me tonight? Don't you see how much I care for you?"

Ace's lips firmed, his hands on his hips as he glared down at her. "I think you care for me, just as I care for you, but I don't think you know what you're getting into. Tonight was just a little sample. I need you to promise me that you'll think about this."

Hope cuddled against him. "There's nothing to think about."

Looking away, he appeared to be deep in thought, the length of his silence scaring Hope to death. Finally, he looked down at her, his gaze raking over her still-naked form.

"Lock up behind me and go to bed. I'll be in touch."

Chapter Four

The chilly night air did nothing to cool Ace's ardor. At this point, he doubted that anything short of sinking his cock into Hope could.

Sitting on the front porch of the house he shared with his brothers, he ran his thumb up and down the cold glass of iced tea he held, trying to block out the image of Hope's face when he ran the glass over her nipples. He'd been sitting here for over an hour now and his cock still pressed painfully at his zipper.

She was perfect.

After all, what would be the point in earning the surrender of a woman who didn't have some fight in her?

Damn it, he knew this would happen. He knew better and still let her get to him. Her daring attitude made him forget sometimes just how sweet and damned *fragile* she was.

If he didn't love her, his life would be a hell of a lot easier. She was a weakness he just couldn't afford.

He turned his head at the familiar sound of his brother's truck coming up the dirt road. Good. Hopefully they'd be able to help get his mind off of her.

When Law and Zach came home they always visited the club, a place Ace carefully avoided. As sheriff, he felt it would be inappropriate for him to go there and didn't particularly care to be in the club fucking another woman when Hope's fathers came in to play cards.

He looked at his watch as Zach got out of the passenger side and climbed the steps to the small porch. "Home a little early tonight, aren't you?"

Zach sighed and dropped into the chair next to him. "Just not in the mood tonight. Tired, I guess."

Ace blinked. "Is that a fact?"

Law went into the house, came back out with two beers, and tossed one to Zach. "Royce and King were busy with clients, but we saw Blade."

Something in his tone alerted Ace that his brother had something other than small talk on his mind. Keeping his face bland, he shrugged. "He's one of the owners. He's usually there even though he and Kelly finally moved into their house."

Law took a long pull of his beer and sighed. "Blade sure has changed."

Ace nodded, wondering where this was going. "Yep. Love'll do that to a man."

Zach sat back in his chair, propping his feet on the railing. "Jesse went to see Kelly, so Clay and Rio came by the club."

Ace waited, taking another sip of his tea and saying nothing.

Law paced back and forth, finally leaning against the porch rail. "Some amazing women have been coming to town lately."

Zach looked pointedly at Ace. "And there's some already here."

Ace ignored his brother's look. "It takes a special woman to put up with the men in Desire."

Zach's brow went up. "Including you?"

Ace had to consciously relax his clenched jaw to take another sip of his tea. "Especially me. Women want to be independent now, and a lot of them would never want to abide by the rules of this town."

Zach blinked. "But the laws here protect the women. They're all for their benefit. The laws of this town keep them safe and punish men for abusing them or cheating on them."

Ace shrugged. "A lot of women don't see it that way. It takes a special kind of person to live here, male or female. What works for us won't work for the rest of the world." In an effort to change the subject, he forced a smile. "So you two didn't find anybody you wanted to fuck tonight?"

Law stood, waving his hand in the air dismissively. "Yeah. She was good, too, but…"

Zach took another sip of his beer. "When you see Clay and Rio and the way they talk about Jesse—it's not talk about sex like it used to be. I mean, you can tell just how much they love her. They talk about the things she likes and how nice it is to have a woman at home. How she drives them crazy and the pleasure they get from doing little things for her. It's the same with Blade. Something's going on with him because he's been even quieter than normal, but if you mention Kelly, his eyes light up."

Law sat on the railing, only to come to his feet and start pacing again. "We saw the Prestons and the Jacksons in town. Boone and Chase look nervous as hell and won't get more than a few feet from Rachel. Jared, Duncan, and Reese have these ridiculous grins and look like they found the pot of gold at the end of the rainbow."

Ace started to get a crick in his neck from watching his brother pace back and forth. "You guys had a chance with Rachel when Boone and Chase wouldn't go near her."

Law shrugged. "I like Rachel a lot, but the spark wasn't there. I see it between the others. Hell, I've watched it with you and Hope for years. I want the spark."

Thinking of Hope, Ace averted his gaze. "Sometimes the spark isn't enough, especially if a man wants too much."

Law's lips twitched. "The generosity of women never ceases to amaze me. They seem willing to give it their all as long as they have their man's love."

Zach appeared lost in thought, the silence stretching. Suddenly, he sat forward. "Jesse came to town because of Nat. Kelly came because of Jesse. Erin came because of Rachel. Those men got lucky. They scooped those women right up, and everyone's happy as clams. As far as I know, none of those women ever lived the lifestyle they live now. And those women don't have any more sisters. We've gone years without any new women showing up here, and the ones that have are all taken."

Ace nodded. "And you want to find a woman like that."

Zach shrugged and looked out into the night.

Law opened his mouth to say something, apparently changed his mind, and turned to go back inside, coming back with fresh drinks. Sighing, he leaned against the rail and shared a look with Zach. "We've been in all kinds of clubs in Dallas and seen all kinds of women, but we haven't found what they have."

Surprised, Ace looked up. "I didn't know you were looking."

Law shrugged. "We didn't either. We talked about it a little tonight."

Ace eyed each of them thoughtfully, more than a little surprised at his brothers' sudden desire for a relationship. "None of those men found their wives in a club. They just appeared when they least expected it. Rachel knew what she wanted, but Jesse, Kelly, and Erin weren't looking for a relationship at all and certainly not the kind they found. But their men love them and make sure they know it. They all ended up with more than any of them expected. You just have to find a woman you share that spark you talked about with. If you love them, make sure they know it. And hope like hell they can love you back."

Zach finished his beer and stood. Smiling slightly, he touched Ace's shoulder. "Maybe you ought to take your own advice. Hope's a good woman, and she's already in love with you."

Ace stood and moved to the railing, wondering how the hell this conversation had become about him and Hope. "I'm too domineering, too possessive for someone like her. I can't change, and she's too much of a fireball to live with it." Looking out into the darkness, he sighed. He'd thought it over so many times, especially since she'd come home. It wouldn't be fair to her to promise that he'd change. He couldn't. Wouldn't. "I've tried like hell to convince her we're no good for each other, but she's too damned stubborn. I'm gonna have to find some way to prove it to her."

Law smiled. "Excuse me if I don't wish you luck with that. You two belong together. You need someone as fiery as she is. What the hell would you do with a woman who just rolled over every time you got mad?"

Zach nodded. "It'll take a strong man to keep her in line. She's impulsive and playful and would run headlong into trouble, flipping it the bird."

He had a mental picture of Hope bouncing around her club, her bubbly personality making everyone around her smile. "I'm too dark for her. You know that as well as I do."

"You love her. Maybe you need someone like her. If Hope Sanderson can't get you to lighten up, nobody can."

Ace finished his tea and turned to go back inside, knowing he'd get very little sleep tonight. "Or she could be miserable wondering why she hooked herself up to somebody like me. And regret it."

Chapter Five

Hope couldn't wipe the grin off her face as she and Charity readied the main room for the demonstration scheduled for tonight. What she and Ace had done the night before convinced her more than ever that he was the only man for her. Her body still tingled, but more than that, she felt closer to him than with any other man. She loved him so damned much, and it ripped her heart out to see him so cold and alone.

She lived for those rare smiles of his and vowed to herself that she would do everything in her power to make him happy.

Setting up the stage, she made room for the props the dominatrix would be bringing with her and couldn't help but wonder how many toys Ace had in his arsenal and how often she could get him to play.

Ace's doubts that they could be happy together both frustrated and frightened her. He almost never changed his mind about anything, and if she couldn't get him to change his mind about her...No, she couldn't think about that. She'd waited too long for him to even contemplate losing him before she ever really had him.

What she lacked in patience she more than made up for in determination. She'd just have to chip away at his misgivings until they crumbled at his feet. After that, she would spend the rest of her life making him happy and showing him just how much he meant to her.

"You've had that stupid grin on your face ever since you got up this morning. Can I assume it's due to our late night visitor?"

Hope turned her head at her sister's approach. "Absolutely. Sheriff Tyler came to show me that I could never handle a man like him and that we're absolutely wrong for each other."

Charity busily made notes to herself. "So, how did he do?"

Hope eyed the small stage where the dominatrix would be doing her demonstration, vowing to take lots of notes and use some of those techniques on Ace at the first opportunity. Grinning, she turned back to her sister. "The Sheriff failed. Big time. Jeez, if you knew what that man could do with one hand..."

"Please spare me the details."

Hope wrinkled her nose at her far-too-serious sibling. "Don't be jealous. As soon as Beau convinces you to have some fun, you'll go around grinning all day, too."

Crossing another item off of her checklist, Charity shook her head. "Nope. Not gonna happen. I want a real man, not a little boy who wants to play all the time. I don't want to talk about it." Smiling, she elbowed Hope in the ribs. "So the sheriff is still protecting you from himself, huh?" At Hope's nod, her smile fell. "Hope, you're not just going after him because he's playing hard-to-get, are you? Ace is a very serious man, and he's not going to take kindly to your games."

Surprised that Charity would even think that, she hugged her reassuringly. "You are such a worrywart. I've been in love Ace forever, and you know it. But he's too serious. I understand him just like I understand you. You both need to learn to play a little. Having some fun with the person you're in love with doesn't make your love any less real. I would think both of you would have figured that out by now."

Charity shook her head, her lips twitching. "Sheriff Tyler's not gonna know what hit him, but I think he's going to have a few surprises of his own."

Hope kissed her sister's cheek, nearly jumping out of her skin with excitement to see Ace again. "I'm counting on it."

* * * *

Absently watching the show taking place on the small stage, Hope strolled around the club, making sure everyone enjoyed themselves and that the waitresses kept up with the orders. From across the room, Charity did the same. They'd both taken to the business like ducks to water and both enjoyed it immensely. Charity loved to organize and keep the books, while Hope did more of the planning for events.

Of course, who wouldn't enjoy demonstrations like this? The two naked men on display vied for their mistress's attention, begging her for release to the rapt attention of the audience.

Jesse Erickson leaned toward her sister, Nat, as Hope walked by. "I'm going to try some of this on Clay and Rio. Did you see what she did to keep him from coming? Damn, I can't wait to get home tonight."

Hope smiled as she passed. Most of the women here had voiced variations of the same thing and seemed to enjoy this immensely. The club had quickly become a success, and she and Charity just had to make sure it stayed that way.

Glancing again at the men on the stage, she grinned at their obvious devotion to their mistress. She kept looking at them, as curious as everyone else about the naked men in the room, and couldn't help but compare them to Ace. Sheriff Tyler, though, had a body that would be hard to beat.

Damn it. Where the hell was he?

He hadn't called at all today. Because of the show he knew she had tonight, she figured he'd call or stop by or *something,* if only to nag her or threaten her with a spanking if she touched any of the other men. Or to remind her that only the single women could touch them.

The fact that he didn't depressed her. It only drove home the realization that he hadn't claimed her. Damn it.

Strolling through the club, she worked her way to the window and moved the heavy curtain aside to peek out. She smiled when she recognized the cars filling the well-lit parking lot of Club Desire situated right across the street. The men who married in the past year didn't frequent the club as often now, more than satisfied to stay at home with their new wives. Tonight their wives had come to Lady Desire, curious to learn everything they could about pleasing their men, and, as she expected, their men stayed close. Business at Club Desire was booming.

Such was the town she lived in, and she couldn't help but wish she had a specific someone to watch over her.

Spotting Rio Erickson and Jared Preston looking out the window of the men's club, she chuckled, knowing damned well they reported anything they saw to the others inside.

"What's going on?"

Hope turned at Erin Preston's approach. "The men are watching out the window of Club Desire. As soon as this is over and the door opens, they'll be running across the street to get to all of you. It's funny as hell to watch." She tried to keep the wistfulness out of her voice, suspecting she failed when her newest friend's eyes shone with sympathy.

Erin sipped from her glass of wine, and it pleased Hope that Erin felt comfortable having a drink here. After being drugged a few months ago with spiked drinks, Erin had nothing but bottled water when she went anywhere.

Smiling now, Erin stuck her own head to the window, smiling broadly and waving to Jared, one of her husbands. With a soft laugh at his antics, she shook her head and moved away from the window. Gesturing toward the stage, she smiled as the leather-clad woman finally took pity and used a dildo on one of her submissives and gave him the release he'd been screaming for. "I'm kind of anxious to get back to them, too. Damn, I want to see if I can get Duncan to make those sounds. Tonight's going to be very interesting."

Looking away from the stage, Erin gazed around the club. "I think this club was a great idea. Not just for things like this, although this is more than worth the price of the membership, but for having a place to talk without being overheard. I mean, no one else would ever understand how damned hard it can be to juggle three husbands." Erin put a hand to her head, closing her eyes. "Every time I say that, I find it hard to believe. A woman has to be nuts to live the way I do."

Rachel, Erin's very pregnant sister, joined them, looking a little pale. "Yeah, I can see what a hardship it is for you. Three men eating out of the palm of your hand and all that. You're going through a hell of a lot of skimpy lingerie lately. If we didn't own the lingerie store, you'd be broke."

Erin grinned. "Yeah." Putting an arm around her sister, she frowned in concern. "You look really pale. I'm going to call the men, and we'll get you home."

Rachel grimaced. "Hope, I'm really sorry about this, but I was just coming to get Erin. I'm in labor. I have been for about two hours now, but the contractions are starting to get closer together."

Erin whipped out her cell phone, leading Rachel to a nearby chair. "Why the hell didn't you say something?"

Rachel's lips curved. "Come on, you really didn't expect me to leave before he finished, did you?" Wincing, she put a hand over her abdomen. "But I don't think I can wait any longer. Call Boone and Chase for me."

Erin had already started dialing. "I'm calling Jared. He'll tell Boone and Chase and keep them level-headed and get them right over here."

Hope pulled out her own cell phone. "I'm calling Ace. He can give an escort to the hospital so we can get there faster." Waving Charity over, she smiled at Erin's clipped tones as she waited for Ace to pick up.

"Tyler."

Just the sound of that deep voice sent a shiver through her. "Ace, it's Hope. Rachel's in labor, and the contractions are really close together. Can you ride to the hospital with—"

"I'm on my way."

Hope blinked when he disconnected, staring blankly at the phone. "Well."

Charity raced over with several of the other women hurrying to join them. "Rachel's in labor? Did you call Boone and Chase?"

Hope nodded. "Erin's taking care of that now. Since the show is over, get Mistress Liza and her guys into the back room. The men are going to storm through the door any second."

Charity nodded. "Nothing'll keep them out. I'll take care of it."

Within seconds the men came barreling through the front door, the looks on their faces making the other club members rush to get out of their way. The other women were hurried out the door until only the close-knit group of women who lived in Desire remained.

Boone got to Rachel first, his face like granite, with Chase only steps behind. Kneeling in front of his wife, Boone forced a smile. "Hey, darlin', I let you out of my sight and look what happens. I thought you were going to wait for me."

Rachel held on to him, the panic on her face disappearing when she saw her husbands. "We just wanted to keep you on your toes."

Chase, looking more than a little pale himself, kissed her forehead as Boone stood and lifted her into his arms. "Does it hurt, baby? What a stupid question. Of course it does. Let's go have this baby, and I'll give you the best foot-rub in the world."

Rachel groaned through another contraction as Boone strode for the door. "I'll hold you to that, cowboy."

Hope lifted her gaze as Ace came through the door, the sheriff easily cutting a swath through the crowd. For a split second, their eyes connected. She had no doubt they thought the same thing.

What would it be like to be having a baby together?

The contact broke when Charity rushed back, promising to take care of everything.

Within moments, several trucks and assorted vehicles raced through the night to the hospital behind Ace's work SUV.

Hope turned to look at Boone and Chase's truck right behind them, raising her voice to be heard over the siren. "I want that with you, Ace. I want what they have. I want us to make a family together."

Ace looked formidable at the best of times, but wearing his uniform, he looked even more so. The scowl on his face would have scared the hell out of most people and even managed to intimidate her on occasion. This was one of those occasions. "Rachel's got two men that pamper the hell out of her. If that's what you're looking for, I'm not the right man for you."

Hope grinned to cover her apprehension. "I don't want two men, just one big one. One that knows how to use handcuffs. You're a big softy under all that gruff, and you know it. I have no doubt that you and I can take good care of each other."

If possible, his face hardened even more. "I'm not what you need, Hope, and the sooner you realize that, the better it'll be for both of us."

Chapter Six

Ace stood just inside the doorway of the hospital waiting room, not at all surprised at the number of people who filled it despite the late hour.

He'd moved to Desire with his family while still in his teens, and within weeks learned that, in good times and bad, the residents of Desire stuck together.

He'd never seen anything like it before or since.

Hope, of course, flitted like a beautiful butterfly from person to person, laughing and joking, hugging a teddy bear she'd run down to the gift shop to buy. She sparkled, her dark eyes twinkling, her long, dark hair shining under the florescent lights. Her wide smile flashed often, bright against her olive skin and showing off her dimples. A woman comfortable in her own skin, her familiarity with everyone apparent.

Hell, she'd grown up in this town, and half of the people here probably remembered her in diapers. One of the town's darlings, she was treated as a little sister by most of the men in this room.

Ace could only imagine what they would think of him if they knew some of the things he wanted to do to her, some of the things he'd already done.

Although he carefully avoided looking at her, he always knew her exact location and whom she spoke to. He listened with half an ear when she spoke to her mother on the cell phone. Gracie and her husbands wouldn't be able to leave the diner until after they finished closing, but she would be beside herself waiting for news.

Nat Langley and Erin Preston laughed at something one of the men said, both basking in their men's attention. Next to them sat Jesse Erickson, Nat's sister, and Kelly Royal, speaking in low tones to each other. Blade watched Kelly, his face unreadable as usual, while Clay and Rio talked to the others, their gazes frequently sliding to their wife.

Hope continued to flutter from group to group while her sister, Charity, sat quietly, listening to Jesse and Kelly's conversation and nodding occasionally.

Ace didn't know quite how it happened, but anytime they all gathered like this, the men somehow herded the women to the middle and surrounded them. It was just the kind of thing that the men in Desire did, the customs and rules of this town so ingrained into their personalities that they probably no longer even gave it any thought.

Noticing his own position, he realized, with no small amount of surprise, that he'd done exactly the same thing. Seeing Hope's approach out of the corner of his eye, he involuntarily tensed. Sweeping his gaze over the rest of the room, he sighed at the inevitable stirring of his cock anytime she came close. He kept her in his peripheral vision as she finished the call to her mother and closed her cell phone.

Leaning forward, she enticed him with a whiff of vanilla as she whispered, "Are you giving me the cold shoulder because I said I want to have your baby along with that magnificent body?"

Gritting his teeth, Ace cursed under his breath. Looking up to make sure no one overheard her, he glared at her, fighting the inconvenient and inevitable erection. "I'm not giving you the damned cold shoulder. Last night was just a little selfish play on my part. You're going to keep up with this until someone gets hurt, aren't you?"

Hope toyed with one of the buttons of his shirt. Looking up at him from beneath her lashes, she smiled coyly, making his hand itch to paddle her fine ass. "I thought I showed you last night that I can take whatever you dish out, Sheriff."

Ace smiled coldly. "Last night was just a little exploring. Even then you hesitated. You'd never be able to accept what I would want from you, and you wouldn't be happy with a man you couldn't wrap around your little finger."

Hope's eyes flashed in the way they did when she was up to no good. "Try me. I dare you. Tonight I'll come to your place and sleep over."

Shaking his head, Ace fought the image of her head cradled on his shoulder as she slept. Knowing that kind of intimacy would only make matters worse, he shook his head. "No. I don't do sleepovers."

"Then I'll just come over for sex." Her voice fell to a seductive tone as she ran her fingers over his stomach, making the muscles there clench. "Or whatever game you want to play. You can wrap me around your little finger. Or, better yet, wrap yourself around me."

Furious at the fact that his stomach muscles quivered beneath her fingers, he grabbed her hand to push it away. He had to do something to change her mind about him, soon, before she managed to worm her way even closer. If she knew she already held his heart, there'd be no stopping her.

Having her come over tonight would give him the opportunity he needed.

And it would give him an excuse for just one more taste.

"Fine. Call me when you finish here, and I'll pick you up." He couldn't pass up the opportunity to hear her cries of ecstasy again, the echoes of which kept him awake at night. Grabbing her arm when she smiled in triumph and would have walked away, he found himself both filled with satisfaction at the flash of apprehension in her eyes and remorse that it had to be that way. "Wear one of those sweat suits like you wore last night. It's easy to get you out of and will keep you warm on the way home. No bra or panties."

Hope surprised the hell out of him by turning back to lean into him. "Be careful, tough guy. If you start worrying about me staying warm, it might give me the impression that there's tenderness underneath that hard shell and that you're starting to fall for me."

* * * *

Hope hid a grin at the stunned look in Ace's eyes before he quickly masked it and turned to where Chase raced into the room. Thank God he'd agreed to see her again. Flushed with victory, she turned to smile at Chase's exuberance.

"It's a girl!"

Amidst congratulations and back slapping, Chase grinned with pride, his eyes moist with unshed tears. "Everyone'll be able to see them both in a few minutes. Thanks for sticking around."

Nat came forward and kissed his cheek. "Are you kidding? Nothing short of a bomb would have made us leave. I can't wait to see her. What's her name?"

Chase tugged Erin to his side and kissed her forehead. "Rachel wanted to name her Theresa Rose after her and Erin's mother."

Hope blinked back tears as the always strong and steady Erin inhaled sharply and began sobbing.

Jared, Duncan, and Reese, all wearing similar looks of alarm, rushed to Erin's side. Reese got to her first and pulled her against his chest, wrapping his arms around her to hold her close. Smiling, but with eyes filled with concern, he made room for his brothers to offer comfort. "It seems being a new aunt has overwhelmed her. Excuse us for a minute."

Hope wiped her eyes as the men led Erin to a corner where Reese sat and pulled Erin onto his lap as Jared and Duncan hovered over her. Not wanting to intrude on such a private moment, she turned her head, smiling as Ace congratulated Chase.

Shaking his head, Ace chuckled. "It's only poetic justice that the worst flirt in town now has a daughter."

Chase grinned sheepishly as the others laughed in agreement. "She's got Boone and me to make sure no men ever come sniffing around her."

Nat patted Chase's arm. "Good luck with that, and you have all of us to help you. She was born here, just like Hope and Charity, and we'll all watch out for her the same way we've always watched out for these two." She patted Hope on the shoulder and winked at Charity. "Charity's always been such a good girl, but Hope's been a handful. Chase, I can't stand waiting. When can we see them?"

Isabel Preston came racing through the doorway, holding a huge white teddy bear with a big yellow bow tied around its neck. "Did she have the baby yet? Is everything okay?"

Ben Preston, one of her husbands, came in right behind her, carrying a stuffed giraffe and a large bouquet of flowers with at least a dozen balloons tied around it. "Slow down, Isabel. The baby's not going anywhere."

She turned to give her husband a scathing look. "I'm the honorary grandmother, and if you didn't drive like a turtle, we could have been here a half-hour ago."

"If you didn't feel like you had to buy out the gift shop before we even got up here, we would have been here even sooner."

Hope smiled as everyone laughed, everyone except Ace, who'd separated himself from the others and stood staring at the way Jared, Duncan, and Reese comforted Erin. She waited until he turned to look at her, alarmed at the raw anguish she saw in his eyes. Approaching him, she reached out to touch his arm, trying not to show her hurt when he deftly avoided her.

Inclining his head in their direction, he murmured softly. "What do you think these people would think of me if they knew what kind of things I would do to you?"

Forcing a smile, she reached out to touch him again, encouraged when he let her. "They know I'm a grown woman, and I doubt if there are too many people in town that don't know how I feel about you. You're not a cruel man just because you like to dominate. Don't you think the people who live in Desire would understand that, especially when most of them are the same way?"

A muscle worked in Ace's jaw as he looked over the faces of the people in the room. "Tell Rachel and Boone I'll stop by to see them tomorrow."

Hope rushed forward when he turned to leave. "Don't forget our date." She held her breath when he paused, not releasing it until he nodded curtly.

"I'll pick you up at midnight."

"Good, Sheriff. I want to see how good you are with those handcuffs."

Chapter Seven

Hope hurried from the window as soon as Ace pulled up in front of the diner downstairs. She grabbed her shoes and sat on the sofa to put them on, grinning like a fool at her sister, who came out of the kitchen eating a bowl of cereal.

"He's here. Don't wait up. If I'm lucky, he'll let me stay over."

Charity swallowed a mouthful, waving her spoon. "I thought you said he didn't let anyone sleep over."

Hope finished tying her shoes and jumped up, grabbing a jacket to wear over her sweat suit. "Nope, but for me he'll make an exception."

Charity paused next to Hope, running a hand over her hair. "I think you should slow down, Hope. You always go into everything full steam without worrying about the consequences. I know how you feel about Ace, but *please* be careful. He's a good man, but he's already told you countless times that you two are wrong for each other. I'm afraid you're going to get hurt."

Hugging her sister, Hope laughed softly. "Sometimes I think you should have been the older one." Holding on to Charity's shoulders she smiled. "Relax. I know what I'm doing. I can't be like you, Charity. I can't wait for something to happen. I want Ace, and I'll do whatever I have to in order to get him."

"Hope—"

"Come on, Charity, you've known Ace almost your whole life. He's one of the sweetest men in the world, and you know it." When Ace knocked at the door, a rush of moisture coated her thighs, her anticipation at seeing him again making her giddy. Grabbing her jacket, she raced to answer it. "Wish me luck." She swung the door open, catching the flash of surprise on his face as she launched herself at him. "Hi, Sheriff."

He caught her easily as she'd known he would. His lips twitched when she wrapped her arms and legs around him and held on tight, his small smile filling her with a deep satisfaction.

"That's quite a greeting."

"Yep." Held against Ace's hard body, Hope nibbled at his bottom lip, breathing a sigh of relief when he moved his lips on hers. It took no time at all for the relief to become something much hotter as Ace took her mouth, his kiss even deeper and more possessive than the night before.

He'd kissed her last night, but he'd done it cautiously, not taking much but also careful not to give too much.

She hadn't even realized it until now.

She kissed him eagerly, pouring everything she could into it in an effort to show him in action the words he wouldn't believe. After a few seconds, she forgot she'd been trying to convince him of anything.

One big hand on her bottom held her in place while the other slid under her hair, both gently massaging. Lifting his head, he used the hand at her nape to hold her when she would have followed.

"A hell of a greeting."

Hope grinned, her head spinning from his kiss. "I'm full of surprises."

Ace lowered her to her feet, slapping her bottom lightly before zipping her jacket. "So am I, little girl, as you're about to find out. Did you look out before you answered the door?"

Hope fluttered her lashes at him. "Nope. I've been bad. Whatcha gonna do about it?"

He ran a hand over her bottom. "The options are staggering."

* * * *

Hope could hardly sit still on the way to Ace's house and had trouble keeping her eyes off of him. Dressed in dark jeans and a black T-shirt, his overlong hair curling over his collar, he looked like every woman's erotic fantasy. "If you're taking me to your ranch, can I assume Law and Zach went back to Dallas?"

Ace shot her a glance, his lips curving. "They left this morning."

Turning as much as the seat belt allowed, Hope faced him, wishing she could see him better, but the semi-darkness prevented it. "Most of the brothers in Desire share wives. I guess I never really thought about it, but now that I do, it seems kind of strange that you don't."

Ace finished turning a corner and snapped his head around. "I've already told you I don't share. Ever. I'm too selfish."

"Possessive." She hid a smile at his tone, wondering if he realized that he spoke to women in softer tones. Didn't he know that his deep voice lowered and gentled when he spoke to her, even when he barked out demands or told her what a hard-ass he was?

Shooting her a cool glance, he nodded. "That I am. Why? Have you decided that you want Law and Zach, too?"

Wondering if he heard the insecurity in his own voice, Hope gave him a playful smile, trying to lighten his mood. "Nope. Just you. I'm afraid you've ruined me for anyone else. Now I just have to do the same to you. One day soon, darlin', you'll realize you can't live without me."

Staring straight ahead, Ace mumbled under his breath as he turned onto the dirt road leading to his property. It sounded like "That's what I'm afraid of," but she was afraid to ask. He said nothing else until they stopped in front of his house and he killed the engine. He pushed his seat back and turned to her. "Come here."

Hope scrambled out of her seat belt and onto his lap, cuddling into him as his big arms came around her. She wondered briefly if she'd ever get used to having his strength wrapped around her this way. In his arms, she felt safe and warm in ways which both surprised and delighted her.

Ace's lips brushed her hair. "I need you tonight. The taste I had of you only whetted my appetite for more." With a finger beneath her chin, he lifted her face. His eyes glittered in the faint light coming from the porch, the tenderness gleaming from them an irresistible lure. "Can that be enough for you?"

Hope leaned forward to brush her lips over his strong jaw before biting his chin. "For now, but eventually I want it all. Take me inside. I can't wait any longer."

Ace narrowed his eyes but couldn't hide the amusement in them. "Demands again?"

Rubbing her breasts against his chest, Hope nibbled at his bottom lip, thrilling when his grip on her hips tightened. "I'm a bad girl. I think you should spank me."

Ace shook his head. "I'm in charge here, remember?"

Hope covered his hands with hers and continued to rub against him. "It was only a suggestion, but if you don't want to spank me—"

"Damn it, Hope. I *am* going to paddle your ass if only to teach you to stop clenching and to stop answering the damned door without checking first."

Hope grinned and reached down to open the door. "Good. You need to teach me a lesson. Let's go."

Ace's jaw tightened, his eyes hardening into the look that frightened her just a little. "You think this is some kind of game. It's not. Tonight won't be a picnic for you. I was way too easy on you last night, a mistake I won't repeat. After tonight there'll be no doubt in your mind that there can be nothing between us."

Hope leaned her head against his shoulder as he lifted her and strode for the house. No matter what he said, she trusted him completely. Because of that trust, his words made her apprehensive, but not afraid. The apprehension added a dark element to her arousal, making it more potent, more…erotic. Running her fingers through the hair curling over his collar, she nuzzled his jaw. "There'll always be something between us, Ace, and you know it. Now hurry up. I want that spanking you promised."

* * * *

Ace carried Hope into the house, kicking the door behind him before setting her on her feet. Careful to keep his expression cool, while his desire for her burned hot, he took her jacket before locking the door behind him. Crossing his arms across his chest, he gave her his most intimidating look.

"Strip."

Hope looked around the room, not looking as intimidated as she should have. "You can tell only men live here, but I've gotta tell you, it's a hell of a lot cleaner than I thought it would be."

Ace gritted his teeth, frustrated that she didn't seem to be taking him seriously enough and reluctantly amused at her ploy. "I told you to strip."

Hope toed off her sneakers and stood. "Is it okay for me to keep my socks on? My feet get really cold."

Scrubbing a hand over his face, Ace silently counted to ten. He sat to remove his boots, scowling at her, determined to wipe that smug look off of her face. "You are in so much trouble tonight. Keep your damned socks, but I want the rest of it off right now. When you're through, go into my bedroom, last door on the right." He wagged his fingers impatiently. "Give me those clothes." He'd learned long ago that taking a woman's clothes away and putting them where she couldn't see them increased her sense of vulnerability. With Hope, he'd need every advantage he could get until he learned her body and responses well enough to control her.

It was time to see if Hope could stand a little erotic pain. He couldn't stand much more of being with her and holding himself in check, and if it scared her, they could end this thing tonight.

Every damned time he was with her, she stole another little piece of his heart, and this had to end before she had it completely. If she walked away then, it would kill him.

He had a sneaky suspicion that it was already too late.

* * * *

Hope hurried to follow Ace's demand and raced into his bedroom, where a low light burned, and flung herself onto his bed. Smiling, she turned to the doorway, only to find it empty. Her smile fell. "Ace?"

Hearing his footsteps coming down the hall, she relaxed, positioning herself on her back in the middle of his bed.

When he appeared in the doorway, it alarmed her that his hands were empty. "Stay in that position."

Hope sat up, watching as he pulled a duffel bag from under the bed. "Where are my clothes? What's in there? Aren't you getting undressed? I can't wait to see you naked. Are you going to let me touch you?"

Kneeling beside the bed, Ace stared at her, his jaw clenching. "You're never going to survive tonight." He raised his finger when she started to speak. "Quiet. Not another word. You don't speak again unless I ask you a question. Lie back down and don't move a muscle unless I tell you to. Do you understand?"

"Yes, of course I understand. I'm not stupid."

Hope got back into position, her heightened sense of anticipation making her tremble all over. Her trembling got worse when he gripped her wrists and started to fasten her arms above her head.

"What are you doing? Are you going to tie me up?"

Ace tied her wrists to the headboard with a velvet cord. "Do you want me to gag you?"

Hope blinked, wondering if he could be serious. "Of course not." Pulling experimentally at her bonds, she realized that, although soft enough not to hurt her, the cord held strong.

Leaning over her, he lightly pinched a nipple. "Then be quiet. Not another word."

Hope bit her lip to hold back the moan that threatened to escape. With her arms over her head, her small breasts lifted and had become completely vulnerable to whatever Ace wanted to do to them. She'd never been restrained before and found the added sense of helplessness even more arousing.

"Ace, I've never been tied up."

Ace leaned over her, stroking the nipple he'd just tugged, heightening her awareness that there was nothing she could do to stop him. "Are you using your safeword?"

Hope tried to sit up, momentarily forgetting that she couldn't. "No! I'm just nervous."

Holding her gaze, he bent to take her other nipple between his sharp teeth, biting lightly before letting go. "You're going to be downright scared before I'm done with you. Just say your safeword and it stops. That's why I don't want to gag you, but I will if you keep talking."

Trying her best not to show how much it frightened her to see his teeth close on her nipple, she dug her heels into the mattress as the slight pain had more of her juices leaking from her slit.

She groaned and sucked in a sharp breath. "I'll be quiet."

Ace licked her nipple, smiling when she lifted again. "You don't have to be quiet. I want to hear all the little sounds you make, but no more talking unless I ask you something. Now, we're going to have to do something about your inability to stay still." He lifted her legs to her chest, keeping them close together, effectively lifting her bottom from the bed. "You're going to learn to stop clenching when I spank you. In this position I can spank you, and you can't clench as much. I want you to see how this feels."

Hope cried out when he delivered a sharp slap to her bottom, involuntarily pushing against his hold to straighten her legs, unsurprised to find she couldn't straighten them at all. The slap stung more than the ones had last night and almost immediately started to burn. Biting her lip, she said nothing as the heat spread, enflaming her entire slit. Her juices coated her thighs, more leaking from her as he delivered two more slaps.

Keeping her legs high, he lightly rubbed her bottom, making it hotter and spreading the heat. "If you insist on clenching your bottom, this is the position I'll be forced to spank you in. If I do have to spank you like this, your pussy is also going to get spanked."

Hope shuddered at his tone, the cool look in his eyes telling her he meant it. Not wanting to risk being gagged, she didn't speak. Her clit throbbed steadily and they'd only been here a few minutes. Her pussy clenched frantically with the need to be filled, but something in Ace's expression told her it would be a while before she got any relief. She had no idea what it would feel like to have her pussy spanked and didn't know if she wanted to.

Ace took the decision out of her hands. Lifting her legs even higher, he spanked her again. This time his fingers came in contact with her slit.

Hope gasped at the sensation and struggled furiously against his hold. It stung, especially on her sensitive clit, making it burn and throb worse than before. She couldn't stop pushing against Ace's hold, whimpering in frustration. Her entire slit warmed and tingled, becoming so sensitive that she knew the slightest touch would send her over. Thrashing on the pillow with her eyes squeezed shut, she gulped for air, her whimpers becoming moans as the heat spread and intensified.

"I can do that as many times as I want to. Would you like another? Five more? Ten? I can spank your pussy until you come, screaming my name, the pleasure and pain combining until you don't know which is which."

Hope grabbed on to her restraints, her chest heaving as she arched her back. "Please no. It's too much. Yes, do it."

Ace slid a thick finger into her slick pussy. "If you stay with me, it'll happen. We've only just begun, love. I can do the same thing to your ass. I can spread you and use a whip on your tight little hole and then fuck you there. And I will. Think about that."

Hope clamped down on the finger inside her, amazed that the thought of him doing those things to her aroused her even more. She wanted it. She wanted to experience every one of his dark desires and have him help her explore her own.

The way her body reacted to his erotic threats, convinced her even more that they were a perfect match. "Yes. I want it all with you, but I'm a little afraid. Can we go slowly?"

Ace blinked and began stroking her pussy, his finger pushing deep inside her. "Are you sure you're afraid? You don't look like a woman who's scared."

Unable to stop clamping down on his finger, Hope moaned. "Just a little. Oh, Ace. It feels so good. I'm going to come. I'm sorry. I can't stop it."

Ace stopped his intimate stroking. "Concentrate, love. Listen to my voice and block out everything else. Hold it back. Breathe slowly. If you come, I'm going to spank your pussy again."

Hope whimpered. "I don't know how to stop it. I want you to spank me there, Ace. Please. I need it."

Withdrawing from her, Ace slid his arm out from under her thighs to lean over her, using his thickly muscled thigh to hold her legs in place. Reclining on his elbow beside her, he gathered her against him, running a soothing hand over her stomach. "Deep breaths, baby. Force it back. You can do it. I know you can."

Hope turned her body toward his, readily accepting the strength he offered. This had turned out to be harder than she thought. Being naked while he remained dressed the night before had been hard enough, but having the added disadvantage of also being restrained took her far out of her comfort zone. Being at Ace's mercy also aroused her in ways she'd never experienced, even with the other men she'd been with.

Disappointed in herself, she lifted her eyes to find him watching her, his eyes sharp and, to her amazement, lovingly possessive. "You're not mad?"

Still rubbing her stomach, Ace brushed her lips lightly over hers, gently nibbling. "Of course not. It's up to me to teach you."

Surprised at his soft tone, she blinked. "It is?"

"It is. Now that you've settled some, let's see if you can keep from clenching that tight ass while I spank you."

* * * *

Ace flipped her to her stomach, resisting the urge to pull her over his lap. Having her over his lap would be too intimate and would only increase his possessiveness toward her that had already become way too strong.

Sliding a hand under her hips, he lifted her onto a pillow and adjusted her position. He ran a hand over the luscious globes, barely resisting the urge to bend and take a bite as he moved between them. He'd never seen a finer ass in his life. In this position, he had full access, but most importantly, she couldn't see his face. When he flipped her to her back again, he would blindfold her.

Hope saw way too much of what he desperately fought to keep hidden. If she had the smallest inkling of how much he wanted her, she would never give up on the idea of them being together.

Listening to the soft sounds she made, seeing such a vivacious woman in this submissive position had his cock pressing painfully against his zipper. Running a hand over her bottom again, he smiled at her shiver. Her amazing responsiveness made him want to tie her to his bed for days and thoroughly explore every inch of her.

"Scared?" He glanced at the bowl on the nightstand, partially hidden by the lamp.

"No."

He smiled at the anticipated response and slapped her ass, delighted with the firm fullness under his hand. Vowing to himself to make this a night neither one of them would ever forget, he did it again, his cock jumping at her needy cry and the way she wiggled her ass at him, inviting him to do it again.

"Liar. You're a smart woman, Hope, and a smart woman would be afraid. Don't lie to me again."

Hope twisted to look at him over her shoulder. "But it's you. I'm not afraid of you, Ace."

Ace grinned coldly, fighting his own desire at the absolute trust and need in her eyes. "You will be." Running his hand over her luscious, warm bottom, he smiled again at the moisture coating her thighs. The little brat loved this. Now would be the perfect time to take her farther out of her comfort zone.

"You clenched your ass when I spanked you. You're going to have to learn that I won't allow that." As he expected, she watched as he reached for the bowl on his nightstand and removed the contents.

"What's that?"

Clamping his jaw in an effort to hide his amusement and surge of lust at her apprehension, he held it up, letting her get the full effect.

"Ginger." As he settled back between her spread thighs, he held a hand on her back to keep her from twisting.

Hope might like to submit with her body, but her strong will kept her from submitting completely. What a challenge it would be to see how far he could take her until the needs of her body overrode everything else. It would get harder and harder, the challenge never-ending.

"W–what are you going to do with that?"

Ace's cock came to rapt attention at the tremor in her voice. "I thought you weren't allowed to speak. You'll have to be spanked for that…let's say five slaps. But first I'm going to insert this into your ass. If you clench, it'll release oils that burn."

"What? You're going to put that inside me?"

"Are you using your safe word?"

"Go to hell."

"Let's make it ten slaps. Would you like to add anything else?"

Hope buried her face in the pillow, another reason he would have her on her back soon. "No."

He smiled at her muffled reply. "Good. Then we can take care of this before we go any further."

* * * *

Hope buried her face in the pillow, not believing what Ace was about to do to her. She expected to be spanked, hell, she looked forward to it, but now he wanted to make sure she didn't clench her ass cheeks when he did it.

How was she supposed to do that?

Being spanked in the past required nothing on her part, but Ace wanted her to be an active participant in her own submission. He'd made her open herself to him, and now he expected her to concentrate on not clenching her bottom while he spanked her!

Gripping the soft restraint, she had to turn her face to the side before she suffocated, only to gasp when she saw his big hand holding the ginger root right next to her head.

The outer skin had already been removed to reveal the ginger beneath, the finger-sized, pale flesh glistening with moisture. He'd left the larger base intact, the skin darker and much rougher looking than the rest. "Every time you clench on the ginger, your anus will get warmer until it burns. The more you clench, the hotter it gets."

Hope shivered as he ran a hand down her back and settled himself between her thighs again.

"Oh, God."

Once again burying her face in the pillow, her breath hitched as he slowly slid the piece of ginger past the tight ring of muscle and into her. The coolness surprised her after his warning, and it took a tremendous amount of concentration not to clench on it. She wondered if she'd ever get used to the feel of something invading her anus. Ace always seemed to want to touch her there as though seeming to know that's what made her feel the most helpless. It always felt so naughty, so decadent, and she couldn't believe how much it heightened *all* of her senses.

"Good girl."

Hope trembled helplessly, as she always did when he spoke to her that way and focused on not clenching.

She could only imagine how she looked with her bottom high in the air, her legs spread wide and a piece of ginger protruding from her ass. In this position, he could see everything, do anything he wanted and, other than using her safeword, she would be helpless to stop him.

Her own reaction stunned her and made her glad that she'd saved her bottom for him.

"Hmm, very nice."

Hope involuntarily clenched at his voice, and she immediately stilled, panting as she waited for the burn.

Ace's hands covered her ass cheeks and began to massage gently. "Focus, baby. I want you to count each slap of your spanking. Five on each cheek."

Hope turned her head, gulping in air. She nodded, not speaking for fear of earning herself an even longer spanking. The ginger in her bottom no longer felt cool. In fact, it had started to warm and tingle, and she feared clenching on it again. It felt so good, the sensation like nothing in her experience, but she didn't want it to get any hotter. More moisture leaked from her, embarrassing her at how much she enjoyed this.

"Good girl."

Hope clenched involuntarily, her breath catching as the warm tingling got stronger.

Ace ran his lips over the cheeks of her bottom. "You're not focusing, love. I haven't even begun your spanking and you're already clenching."

Hope thrilled at his endearments, wondering if he even knew he used them or how the tone of his voice had changed, becoming deeper and even more intimate. She couldn't think about it right now. It took all of her concentration to keep her pussy and anus from clenching.

The first slap landed, startling her and reigniting the heat. As hard as she tried, she couldn't keep from tightening on the ginger. Breathing deeply, she squeezed her eyes shut, unable to stop rocking her hips and wiggling. The effect of the ginger inside her startled her, the added heat rapidly ridding her of all inhibitions.

"Ace, please hurry. It's tingling."

Ace ran his hands up and down her thighs, apparently in no hurry to finish her spanking. "It'll get hotter. I may not even let you come. You need to learn patience."

Kicking her legs, she wiggled harder, his soft chuckle infuriating her. "Damn it, Ace. I came here to be fucked. You can't do this to me."

Two more sharp slaps landed, one on each cheek. "Until you use your safeword, I can do whatever I want with you. Now, I believe you have ten slaps coming."

"What?" She twisted restlessly, kicking her feet. "Only seven more. You already gave me three."

"You didn't count them, honey, so they don't count."

Never in her life had she been so aware of her ass, but her pussy and clit also demanded attention. In her current position, she couldn't rub against anything, and she desperately needed the relief. The heat at her slit and those amazing tingles made it nearly impossible to think anymore, which made it even harder to focus.

"I'm sorry. One. Two. Three. Please Ace, I need to come."

Five slaps in rapid succession landed on her left ass cheek, making it burn. Ace held his hand over the heat, making it worse as it spread to her already inflamed clit and pussy.

Fisting her hands, she bit the pillow to hold back her cries as she counted.

"I have other uses for ginger, you know. Can you imagine what it'll feel like to have a sliver of it pressed to your clit?"

Hope almost came at the thought of it. "Ace, please. I'm begging. I can't take any more."

Rubbing a hand over the cheeks of her ass, he growled. "Use your safeword."

Hope tried to rock her hips, so close to coming she couldn't stand it. Concentrating on not clenching *and* not coming proved to be nearly impossible. Fearing she wouldn't be successful only frustrated her more. With frustration came anger, which she drew on like a lifeline.

"Kiss my ass."

"With pleasure."

Hope shuddered again as his lips moved over her bottom that stilled burned from his spanking. The ginger shifted in her anus as he pushed a finger into her pussy again.

"I can also put a nice thick piece of ginger in your pussy and just sit back and enjoy the show. You'll writhe on the sheets, crying and begging me to let you come."

Hope looked over her shoulder to glare at him. "I hate you. If you don't fuck me soon, I'm gonna scream."

Ace curled his finger inside her, stroking her pussy and controlling her squirming with a hand on her back. "You're screaming now. You still have five more slaps before I flip you over and put on the blindfold."

"Blindfold? Oh, God. Ace, I'm so close. Please let me come. Damn it, you son of a bitch. I need it."

Ace withdrew his finger from her pussy and slapped her ass again. While she struggled with the heat, he slowly fucked her ass with the ginger root, making the hot tingles even hotter. "No. I told you I may not let you come at all. We'll see if you can be a good girl. Only good girls get to come."

Hope would be as good as he wanted if only he'd give her relief from an arousal so strong it changed the way she thought about sex. She'd never known such incredible pleasure, never knew it could be so all-consuming. The heat in her anus got stronger, but no matter how hard she tried, she couldn't keep from clenching.

Thankfully, Ace chose that moment to administer the other four slaps to her wiggling ass.

Hope quickly counted them, dying to have him fuck her.

"I had mercy on you this time, but I could delay each smack for a half hour if I wanted and keep changing the ginger. Think about that the next time you clench when I spank you." He slid the ginger root from her slowly, moving it in circles as he withdrew it.

Hope tightened on it, fighting to keep it inside. "Please, Ace. I feel empty." The burning made itself known, but to her surprise, it only increased her desire.

Ace didn't speak for several long seconds. Leaning over her to put the ginger back in the bowl, he kissed her shoulder. "You like the ginger, don't you, baby? You like having something in your ass. You like it hot. I've got a lot of fantasies about this beautiful ass."

Hope shuddered as the denim of his jeans brushed over her bottom and the back of her thighs. So sensitive there she couldn't stand it, she bucked against him. "Damn you, Ace. I need to come. Fuck me, damn it." She shrieked when Ace flipped her to her back, repositioning the pillow beneath her bottom.

"I'm not fucking you tonight. We're not ready for that."

A chill went through her at his tone. "Y–you don't want me?"

A muscle worked in Ace's jaw. "Want has nothing to do with it. When this ends—"

"Stop it." Hope fought her bonds. "I don't want to hear about this ending anymore. I want you to take me. I'm willing to give all of myself to you, Ace, and I expect the same from you."

Ace leaned completely over her, his breath warm on her cheek as one hand settled on either side of her head. "You don't have any right to expect any more than what I give you."

Hope arched, rubbing her nipples against his chest. "Why do you think I came here?"

Ace tweaked a nipple. "To submit to me."

Biting back the moan, she rocked her hips and smiled, arching toward him with the need to make this a memorable occasion for both of them. "Then dominate me, Sheriff, if you can."

A brow went up as his hand slid down her body. He brushed his fingers over her stomach and smiled as the muscles quivered under his hand. "Oh, I can, baby. Until you realize the truth and see it my way."

The moan she'd been holding back escaped as his fingers traced over her bare folds. Frustrated that he couldn't see how perfect they would be for each other, she met his gaze. "Or you do."

His eyes flashed with something that disappeared before she could read it. "Brave words. Be good while I go wash the ginger from my hands before I touch you anywhere else." Keeping his hands clear of her body, he worked his way down, lightly kissing each nipple before running his tongue down her belly. Smiling at her attempt to rub her clit against him, he shouldered her thighs apart. "Keep them spread until I get back. I don't want to catch you rubbing your thighs together, or I'll spank your bare pussy. Hard."

Hope watched him pick up the bowl and leave, rocking her hips on the pillow in an effort to fight the unbearable ache. His light kiss on each of her nipples had been like an imaginary string tugging at her clit.

God, she couldn't stand much more of this.

It seemed like forever until Ace came back, but in reality was probably only a few minutes, which had given her just enough time to pull back from the edge.

She'd bet anything that it had been his intention all along.

Sitting on the edge of the bed, he removed his socks and stood facing her as he grabbed the hem of his T-shirt to pull it over his head. "Good girl. I'll bet it was hard to stay that way. I'm proud of you."

Hope gulped as he came toward her, his naked chest gleaming in the low light.

He was magnificent!

His clothes hid a chest wider than any she'd ever seen, every inch of it and his arms loaded with hard-packed muscle. He had almost no chest hair, his skin smooth and so beautiful she couldn't wait to get her hands on it. He had a hell of a six pack, his flat stomach making her mouth water. As he knelt beside the bed, she couldn't take her eyes off of him.

"God, you're beautiful."

He blinked, his surprise apparent. "You're the one who's beautiful, baby. Let's see how good you look all spread out for me to play with." He held her gaze as he reached for something beside the bed and slid a hand under her thigh, pulling it toward him. He secured a dark band just above her bent knee. It attached to a long strap, which apparently went under the mattress and came out the other side.

"I'm going to restrain you with your legs spread wide open." Moving to the other side of the bed, he smiled coolly as he turned on the lamp on the other nightstand, the brighter light making her even a little more uncomfortable. "I have total access to your clit, your pussy, and your ass. Your breasts are free, lifted, and unprotected. I can do whatever I want and there isn't a thing you can do to stop me. Are you sure you want this?"

Hope couldn't keep from rocking her hips as he fastened her other leg in the same way. Experimentally, she pulled inwardly with one leg only to have it pull on the other leg. Lying there with her arms over her head and her legs wide open, she truly was on display and available for whatever he wanted to do to her.

She loved it!

Arching her back, she lifted herself in offering. "Absolutely. I don't want to stop you. Take what you want."

He stood, holding a wide strip of black material. Without saying a word, he lifted her head off of the pillow and blindfolded her, releasing her as soon as he had it in place.

A sharp tug on her nipple took her by surprise, the feeling much stronger since she hadn't been able to anticipate it. Crying out, she jolted, her pussy leaking even more moisture. Her slit had become drenched with her juices, her nipples sensitive and needy. Her clit throbbed, her bottom still warm from her spanking, and her anus still held a slight tingling warmth from the ginger.

The combination sent her senses reeling. Thrashing on the bed as much as she could, she moaned hoarsely, fearing for her sanity.

A hand cradled her jaw as warm lips moved over her cheek. "And now, love, we begin."

Chapter Eight

Being restrained and splayed wide open gave her a sense of freedom she'd never experienced before and hadn't at all expected. She could let go completely and give in to whatever he did to her with abandon. No holding back, no accusations, no looks of disgust.

Just freedom to explore and enjoy the pleasures to be found.

Freedom to let herself go and surrender herself to the man she loved more than anything.

Knowing that he could see everything and touch her in any way he wanted filled Hope with an even stronger sense of vulnerability, but also connected her to Ace in ways she hadn't expected. Glad that she'd been blindfolded, for it allowed her to hide somewhat, she found herself in another place, an altered state in which all of her senses were heightened as she happily put herself completely in his capable hands.

Each brush of his hands over her heated skin seemed magnified, and not being able to see him, she never knew where the next touch would be. The anticipation of waiting for whatever erotic thrill he would deliver next threatened to drive her mad.

"Hmm. And look at what I get to fully explore. I get to see what happens when I stroke you here."

Hope moaned as his fingers brushed lightly over her inner thigh.

"Or pinch here."

Anticipating a pinch to her nipple, she jolted and cried out when he pinched her clit instead.

"Or kiss here."

Not knowing what to expect, Hope arched, her body tightening when he kissed her nipple, taking the time to lick and gently nibble. She froze when his sharp teeth closed over it, only to writhe again when his warm tongue relieved the sting. Unable to keep still, she thrashed under him, a whimper escaping when he lifted his head.

Placing a hot hand on her stomach, he murmured softly to her until she settled once again.

It occurred to her that he spoke more often while making love to her than he ever did, his voice like a lifeline to steady her. His tone had a unique quality to it now that she'd never heard in it before. Dark and intimate, steely but indulgent, it flowed over her like warm honey, and set off a shower of sparks throughout her body.

Already madly in love with him, she found this side of him absolutely irresistible. She wanted to give everything to him, *be* everything to him, greedily wanting his attention and focus to be only on her.

Everywhere he stroked her, from her arms and shoulders, down her chest and to her belly, he left a trail of heat. She arched, silently begging for his attention to her nipples, which he ruthlessly ignored. No longer able to thrash from side to side, she pulled on the bonds at her wrists to lift herself.

"Please, Ace."

"Maybe I should spank your pussy."

Hope shuddered, biting her lip to keep from replying.

Ace chuckled. "You *are* learning. Good girl."

Something touched her cheek, a light brush of something as soft as butterfly wings. "What's that?" Realizing her mistake, she immediately snapped her mouth shut. The object moved to her lips and brushed over them.

Ace tapped her lips with it. "Open."

Not knowing what to expect, Hope parted her lips, her mind whirling as the need inside her leveled out and remained steady.

"Suck it."

Oh, God, what would it be like if he said that to her with his cock touching her lips?

Hope obediently closed her lips over the small, flat object and began sucking, her stomach muscles tightening as she pushed against the bonds at her knees to lift herself in offering. Using her tongue, she explored the flexible piece that felt about the size of a silver dollar and tasted faintly of leather.

"It's a small whip." He drew the end out of her mouth and brought it down sharply on her nipple.

Her cry surprised even her, the desperation in it evident as the sting from her nipple went all the way to her core. Unable to see him, she whimpered, unprepared when the small piece of leather came down between the cheeks of her ass.

"It's also good for a tight little bottom hole."

Hope squirmed, the sting reawakening every nerve ending in her bottom and making her crave his attention there.

"You're a smart girl. I'll bet you can figure out another good place for this to be used."

Her clit throbbed harder just thinking about it. Already kept on the verge of orgasm for so long, she knew she wouldn't be able to take it. "Please no. Ahh! Oh God!"

The sting on her clit was like nothing she could imagine. It hurt even worse than when he'd used his hand, but the erotic tingling that followed was worth it. Her entire body sizzled, the tingles radiating from it hot and sharp. Her body tightened, her screams filling the room as she fought the restraints. Bucking on the sheets, she cried out repeatedly as a series of small orgasms shot through her, one right after the other. Straining against her bonds, she moaned helplessly as he stroked her clit, too lightly to make her go over completely, but that kept those amazing tingles racing through her.

He doled out her orgasm in small spurts when it suited him without giving her the relief she craved.

Hope never would have believed he could have that kind of control over her body. It unsettled her to realize what he'd told her about the bond between a Dom and a sub was true. Every touch of his hand, every sound he made, every nuance of his mood seemed magnified and became the focus of her attention. Everything else faded into the background. She'd never before even imagined such a close connection could exist and knew that, over time, it would grow even stronger.

She wanted that with him and would do anything to get it.

The way his hands moved over her body now had her struggling against her bonds to get closer. "You know of course, that your ass must be stretched. In case you haven't figured it out yet, baby, I'm definitely an ass man, and yours has to be the most luscious I've ever seen. I want to fuck your virgin ass more than I've ever wanted anything in my life."

Hope's bottom tingled with renewed vigor, her imagination on overdrive. "Yes. Take me. Stretch me. Fuck me. I'll give you whatever you want. I'll do anything you want."

The bed shifted as Ace leaned over her, cradling her head in his hands as he kissed her long and deep, his kiss somehow both exploring and possessive. When he lifted his head, she could feel his intense stare as he remained above her. "Yes, baby. I believe you would. For a while."

Something in his tone alerted her to a deeper meaning, but she couldn't concentrate enough to figure it out. Arching as much as she could, she cried out, moaning in desperation as his lips travelled down the center of her body, detouring often enough to bring tears of frustration to her eyes.

The bed dipped as he knelt between her thighs once again. "You like the idea of having your ass stretched, don't you, baby?" When he ran the small whip over her inner thighs, Hope whimpered, her blindfold damp with her tears. "But tonight I'm going to take care of this pussy." He slid a thick finger through her juices and into her and began stroking.

Hope groaned, bucking wildly at the restraints. "Damn you, fuck me."

Ace's chuckle accompanied a sharp tap to her clit with the whip. "You're so impatient, baby. I'm still exploring."

Hope screamed, the sting on her sensitive clit bringing more pleasure than pain. Her clit felt swollen to ten times its normal size and seemed to have a heartbeat of its own. Right on the edge of orgasm, she frantically pulled at the bonds holding her wrists. If she could just get one hand free she could touch herself and end this endless torment. Her cries of desperation filled the room, becoming louder as Ace curled his finger inside her and tapped her clit with the whip again.

Her legs shook. Her toes curled, her entire body stretching like a rubber band on the verge of breaking. The whip touched her clit again, brushing back and forth. She whimpered and rocked against it, needing any kind of touch Ace would give her.

"You are so beautiful, baby. I want to see your eyes." The bed shifted as he leaned over her again to remove the blindfold.

Opening her eyes, she breathed in his scent, rubbing her cheek against his jaw in the need to touch him.

He seemed to understand her need and wrapped his arms around her, his lips moving over her face, before he lifted his head to stare down at her. "You have to be the most naturally submissive woman I've ever met, and by far the most responsive." Bending, he took a nipple into his mouth and sucked. Hard. His lips curved at her reaction, easily holding her when she bucked against him in an effort to get closer. "Hard to believe I can elicit those sounds from such a smart mouth."

The look in his eyes stole her breath.

Hot. Possessive. Indulgent. Loving.

She'd do anything he wanted if only he'd look at her that way again. She'd gladly give him everything. "Ace, I need you."

Searching her face, he leaned to the side and ran a hand down her center to her slit. Carefully avoiding her clit, he separated her folds. After several long seconds, he nodded. "Yes, baby. Tonight I think we need each other."

He stroked her clit, his touch barely a whisper, but all she needed to have her crying out and writhing again. With a smile, he removed his hand and stood, his eyes raking her body as he reached for the fastening of his jeans.

Hope stilled, not wanting to miss anything, her entire body quivering as she teetered on the edge of orgasm. Her eyes widened as he lowered his jeans and tossed them aside. Holy hell. She couldn't believe the length and thickness of his cock as it rose toward his stomach. His thighs, roped with muscle, bunched and flexed as he moved to the nightstand and were a perfect frame for such a masterpiece.

She watched in fascination as he donned a condom, his eyes holding hers as he rolled it on. She couldn't stay still, her hips rocking in anticipation of his possession.

Ace moved to stand at the foot of the bed and picked up the whip, his smile pure evil as he watched her frantic writhing. "But we're not done yet, are we? Didn't you make another demand? With your pussy waxed, your slit is more sensitive. I'd be careful if I were you about how many strikes to your clit you earn."

Hope groaned as more of her juices flowed from her. Her clit tingled in anticipation. Who would have ever thought she'd not only tolerate but would *invite* such a thing?

"Yes! Do it!" She couldn't stop struggling against her bonds, the firm hold of them exciting her even more. When another lash landed, she screamed, struggling harder. Not hard enough to really hurt, the strike to her clit stung just enough to render her senseless. The ensuing heat and sharp tingles teased her into thinking she would orgasm, but only drew her closer and closer to the edge.

To a place where nothing existed for her except Ace.

The heat in his eyes as he watched her struggle, the dark intent in them as they raked over her body caressed her like a hot breath blowing over her. He fisted his cock and stroked once, twice, before crawling gracefully onto the bed, his movements like those of a stalking panther. He settled himself between her thighs again, his hot hands sliding under her bottom as his thumbs separated her folds.

"Wide open and all mine."

Hope shuddered as the head of his cock pressed against her slick opening. "All yours. Forever."

Ace leaned over her, his cock sinking into her, stretching her magnificently, inch by incredible inch. "At least for tonight you are, and I'm taking what's mine."

Struggling to accept him, her inner flesh quivered, milking him as he entered her. It struck her that spread like this, she had no way of slowing his thrusts, a fact that only excited her more. Gripping him with her pussy, she cried out breathlessly, her voice nearly hoarse now as his thick cock caressed her intimately. It suddenly became too much, the tingles combining to become one great wave of pleasure that washed over her, tumbling her into what felt like an electrical storm.

She screamed pitifully, her tortured whimpers blending with Ace's croons of approval. Her vision blurred, her entire body swept away by the enormity of the pleasure that raced through her.

Ace continued to thrust into her, going a little deeper with each thrust until he filled her completely.

Hope came down slowly, registering the fact that his sack touched her bottom. Amazed, she stared up at him. "You're inside me. You're all the way inside me."

Ace chuckled, his voice even deeper and more intimate. "Yes, baby. Snug as a hand in a glove."

Wishing she could wrap her arms and legs around him, she gasped as Ace began stroking again. His firm, deep thrusts left her in no doubt of who was in charge, and to her intense surprise, her desire quickly built again. "Ace, I can't come again. I never do."

Ace smiled and slid a hand between their bodies, pressing a callused finger to her clit. "You will this time."

Hope shook her head, rocking her hips as, to her amazement, her body began to gather again, her clit so sensitive that it almost hurt. "I can't. I—Oh God!"

Ace fucked her faster now as his thumb found its target. Digging at a spot inside her, he slowly caressed her clit, making the hot tingling there nearly unbearable.

Within seconds, *seconds*, she screamed again, her voice now almost gone. Her body tightened, pleasure and pain combining into something so totally foreign it alarmed her. Her body bucked as though trying to throw him off, to escape the almost unbearable bliss.

Ace pumped deeply, his face a hard mask as he sought his own release, her body quivering all around him.

Still trembling from her own release, she stared wide-eyed as he threw his head back, his eyes squeezed closed as he thrust deep and held himself there, his cock pulsing inside her.

Burying his face in her throat, he reached down and unfastened the restraints on her legs, allowing them to close around his hips. Lifting himself slightly from her, he covered her mouth with his own while releasing her wrists from their bonds. He massaged her stiff arms before rolling with her, his cock still buried deep.

Hope lay on his massive chest, purring like a cat as he rubbed her back and shoulders, working his way down to her bottom and thighs.

"I'm going to bathe you. I want to make sure all of the ginger is gone, and I want to massage your sore muscles. You're not used to being tied up."

Hope groaned. "No. I'm not moving. I'm staying here on top of you for the rest of my life." Turning her face, she kissed his gorgeous chest. "I never knew it could be like that. You completely controlled everything. All I could do was lie there and take whatever you did to me." When he stiffened, she hurriedly looked up. "I loved it. If you would have told me that I could become so aroused by getting my pussy whipped, I would have thought you were crazy."

Ace's lips curved as he ran a hand over her hair. "It's not always like that. Some people like the whip harder, so hard it cuts."

Hope winced. "Ouch." She looked up at him through her lashes. "Is that something you want to do to me?"

Shaking his head, Ace reached under her, repositioning her so he could stroke a nipple and smiling when she moaned. "No. I have no desire to see you bleed. I wanted to show you tonight that sometimes pain can bring more pleasure than you could imagine." He tugged her nipple. "I also wanted to experiment with you a little. Your reaction last night intrigued me. I didn't think you'd take being tied up so well, nor did I think you'd like the whip on your clit. But I was curious." Sighing, he dropped his head to the pillow. "I really thought it would be too much for you."

"What would you have done if I didn't like it? Wait!" She pushed against his chest to sit up. "You wanted me to use my safeword so you'd have an excuse to end this."

Pinching her nipple, Ace sat up and kissed her forehead. "A lot of good that did me." He ignored her grumbling as he carried her into the bathroom. Once there, he set her on her feet and began filling the tub, surprising her by adding bath salts he had sitting in a jar on the edge.

Recognizing them as being from Indulgences, she tried to tamp down her jealousy.

Ace removed the condom and cleaned up, apparently at ease with her. "I can read that look. It's vanilla. I got it from Kelly this afternoon. *For you.* Get in the tub."

By the time Ace bathed her and dried her thoroughly, Hope trembled with need again but had become so lethargic she could hardly stand. Her bones felt like jelly, and she couldn't stop trembling as he soaped, rinsed, and toweled every inch of her between long, drugging kisses and playful and not-so-playful caresses, all while holding her securely and adjusting her body as he wished.

"What have you done to me? I think I melted." Slumped against him, she wrapped her arms around his waist, snuggling into the towel he wrapped around her and, rubbing her belly against his cock. Her head dropped onto his shoulder when he lifted her against his chest, too heavy for her to pick up again.

Ace bent his head to kiss her forehead, his smile indulgent as he carried her back into his bedroom. "You're melting all over me."

Hope pouted, loving the fact that he seemed more relaxed than she'd ever seen him. "I didn't make you melt, though."

Ace chuckled. "I melt enough around you. Besides, you'd walk all over me if I showed any sign of weakness."

Snuggling against him, Hope yawned. "I want to take care of you, too."

His chuckle made her smile. "You took care of my needs tonight just fine." He laid her gently on the bed and pulled the quilt over her before turning away and heading back toward the bathroom.

Lying in his bed, she forced her eyes open, not about to miss the sight of Ace's naked butt.

It proved to be well worth the effort.

Tight and muscular, it had to be the finest ass she'd ever seen. Propping her head on her hand, she watched as he walked out of the room, vowing to herself to take a bite of it the first chance she got.

When he came back, he tossed her clothes on the bed, blowing a kiss at her before heading for the bathroom.

"Sheriff, nice ass."

Ace turned his head and winked, his steps never faltering. "You, too, brat. Stay warm. I'll help you dress when I get back. We'll get something to eat before I take you home."

She smiled even as her stomach knotted with misery. "I'm not really hungry. I think I'd rather just go home and go to bed. I've got some plans for tomorrow morning." Hope kept her smile in place, not letting it fall until Ace closed the bathroom door behind him. Tonight she'd felt closer to him than ever before, but apparently he didn't feel the same. She'd hoped he'd changed his mind and wanted her to spend the night in his bed.

He'd already warned her that he never let anyone stay over, but she hadn't believed him.

Sheriff Tyler appeared to be a man of his word.

Throwing back the covers, she got out of bed and got dressed, not about to wait for him to throw her out. She waited for the shower to start before getting dressed, pulling the warm sweat suit on to cover her rapidly cooling body. Listening to the sound of the shower running, she tried not to imagine how Ace's body looked wet and soapy as she walked into the living room and sat down on the sofa to put on her shoes. She wished she had the right to go in there and join him and see for herself.

With a heavy heart, she went to the window and pushed the curtain aside. The only light came from the front porch. The moon, a mere sliver in the night sky, hid behind clouds, only appearing briefly before disappearing again. It reminded her of how Charity hid her own light from the rest of the world.

And how Ace hid his own desires. Even someone with as little experience as she had could see that he held back.

Hearing the shower stop, Hope turned away from the window, a slow smile spreading over her face as she planned her next move.

If she had her way, it wouldn't be long before she satisfied every single one of the sheriff's dark desires.

Chapter Nine

The little brat was doing her very best to drive him out of his mind.

She'd acted differently since the other night, the night he'd taken her to his house.

Subtle differences that drove him crazy.

Expecting to find her waiting in his bed, he'd come out of the bathroom and been startled to find his bed empty. He'd walked out to the living room, calling her name, surprised and more than a little put out to find her there, already dressed and ready to leave. Biting back a curse, he'd turned to go back into the bedroom to dress.

She hadn't followed him.

Hope obviously respected his decision and made it easy for him by getting ready to leave without any of the arguments he'd been expecting.

And why the hell had she made plans for the next morning instead of wanting to fall asleep in his bed?

He'd been pissed off ever since.

What infuriated him even more was that she'd done nothing except follow his rules and he couldn't say or do a damned thing about it without looking like a fool.

Since then, she'd been as outgoing and bubbly as usual, fluttering around like a butterfly, even more than usual. She never sought him out now and made it harder and harder for him to accidentally run into her.

Damn it, he missed her.

He checked in with the widow he'd only recently hired to work as both a dispatcher and secretary, to learn that Beau Parrish wanted to see him. Nodding, he walked out the front door of the small building that housed the sheriff's department, pausing on the front steps to slip on his sunglasses. He'd have to stop at Beau's store before he could accomplish one of the more pleasant tasks of being sheriff.

Since folks watched out for each other here, crime in this town had become practically non-existent. Except for stunts kids pulled, like the idiot who damaged the field behind the men's club or an occasional problem with Club Desire, it got pretty boring.

He wanted to keep it that way.

The fact that three of the town's women and newest residents had been attacked on his watch still plagued him. Because of it, he and his deputies watched strangers more closely. The men of Desire also tugged the invisible leashes around their women's necks, keeping them all a little bit closer.

He clenched his jaw as the thought of him having the responsibility of holding an invisible leash around Hope's neck made his cock stir. He'd keep a strong hold on that leash to keep her out of trouble and would spend the rest of his life trying to tame a woman who'd never be tamed. Christ, he got hard just thinking about it.

Pushing the barrage of erotic thoughts back for now, he smiled, lifting a hand in greeting as Boone's SUV came to a stop behind his.

Chase opened the window as he approached. "Hey, Sheriff, you're gonna have to change the sign again."

Ace laughed softly as he approached the rear passenger window, peering in to see the newest addition to their family sleeping peacefully in her car seat. "Yeah, I'm on my way out to do it now. I seem to be changing it a lot lately." He smiled at Rachel, who looked tired but radiant. "All these new people keep coming to town and deciding to stay. The last time I changed it, it was for Erin."

Rachel adjusted the light blanket over little Theresa. "What are you guys talking about?"

From the front seat, Chase stretched out a hand to caress her knee. "It's the sheriff's job to keep track of how many people live here. It's been that way from the beginning. Did you ever notice the sign as you drive in to town? It's Ace's job to keep it updated." Gesturing toward the baby, he grinned. "Now he has to add one."

Ace nodded. "It's one of the happier aspects of being sheriff. It's depressing when someone dies and I have to subtract one. I wanted to be out there changing it when you rode by, but I got delayed. I'm going out there in a bit." He moved aside, a little surprised when Beau Parrish came up beside him.

"Well, if she doesn't just look like a little angel." Grinning, he winked at Rachel. "And so does her mother. Hello, darlin'."

Rachel beamed. "Hi, Beau. Isn't she beautiful?"

Beau inclined his head. "Absolutely. She's gonna be breaking hearts all over town before you know it." He grinned and congratulated Boone and Chase. "It's gotta be some sort of irony when the town flirt has a baby girl."

Boone turned to his brother. "I told him his flirting would get him in trouble one day."

After a few more minutes of small talk, Ace waved them off, hiding his curiosity until the Jacksons drove away. Once they left, he turned to Beau. "Talia said you wanted to see me. I was just on my way over to your store. What is it?"

Walking with Ace back to the sidewalk, Beau's expression hardened, something Ace rarely saw. "You'd better do something with your woman. She came to my store earlier asking all kinds of questions about some of the merchandise."

Ace blinked, stunned. "Hope was there? Damn it, she's not my woman. What the hell did she ask? What was she looking at?"

Beau's face relaxed, his smile reappearing. "If she's not your woman, how the hell did you know who I was talking about, and why are you so interested?"

Ace clenched his jaw. Hope would be the death of him. "Spill it."

Beau shrugged. "You know I keep an eye on her and Charity. Hope's like a little sister to me. It made me as uncomfortable as hell when she came into the store and asked about butt plugs."

"What?"

"You heard me. Now, Ace, you know I'm not the least bit shy and I think everyone should have toys to play with, but damn it, I don't want to discuss the wide variety of butt plugs and the pros and cons of each one with a woman who one day may very well be my sister-in-law! You've got to do something."

Leaning against his truck, Ace crossed his arms over his chest. He'd known of Beau's interest in Hope's younger sister for some time and had been waiting for Beau to claim her since she came home from college. Knowing damned well he didn't have the right to ask, he did anyway.

"Are you claiming Charity?"

Beau grimaced. "Not yet. She's convinced herself that all I want to do is play and don't take life seriously. For someone so young, she's entirely too serious. Funny, isn't it?"

"What's funny?"

Beau shook his head. "You're too serious and you fall for the sister who likes to play. I like to play and fall for the serious one."

Ace straightened. "Don't get any ideas about Hope."

Beau laughed. "We'd drive each other nuts. Like I said, she's like a little sister to me. A pain-in-the-ass little sister, but a little sister all the same." Sobering, he lowered his voice. "So you'd better do something about her. She can't come in and ask me which butt plugs are the best and if I can recommend a vibrator for her. She's your woman. Keep her the hell out of my store unless you come with her."

Ace sighed and started to get into his truck. "She's not my woman, and she can shop there just like anybody else." He got into the truck and started it, quickly lowering his window as Beau started to move away. "Did she buy anything?"

Beau turned, his pretty boy grin almost making Ace give in to the urge to smash it in. "If she's not your woman, that's strictly confidential, Sheriff."

Ace put the window back up, cursing a blue streak as Beau turned and strode away. He didn't run out of curses until he'd gotten to the edge of town. Watching for traffic, he did a quick U-turn and stopped in front of the sign. Getting out, he jingled the keys in his hand as he stared at it.

Desire, Oklahoma
Population 397

The first time he'd seen the sign, the number hadn't been much lower.

Because of the lifestyles people in the town embraced, outsiders were under close scrutiny, and when they said or did anything to insult someone, they quickly became outcasts and were run out of town.

He'd been intrigued by the rules of Desire from the first day. They'd moved here when his father remarried after inheriting the property and oil company from a grandfather he'd never met. Through his father, who got himself elected sheriff, he'd learned even more of the intricacies of the regulations and customs of the town and had become even more intrigued.

But as strange as the laws of Desire appeared to be, no one could argue with the results.

Just as they did over a hundred years ago, men guarded and fiercely protected the women who lived here. The resulting arguments were a source of amusement, but no one could deny how well their system worked. As much as their methods sometimes angered the women, he'd never in his life seen a happier group of females.

Getting his mind back on the task at hand, he unlocked the plastic plate that covered the population number and smiled as he thought about little Theresa all bundled in her pink blanket as he changed the seven to an eight. He'd just relocked the case and started back to his truck when a little red car shot past him.

Grinding his teeth, he jumped into his vehicle and took off, kicking up a hail of dirt and stones. Flipping on his siren, he tightened his hands on the steering wheel to relieve the itch in them to turn Hope over his knee and paddle her ass.

The little brat would kill herself on this road one day.

When he saw the stricken look on her face as she looked in the rear view mirror, he couldn't prevent the cold smile from spreading on his own face. It appeared she'd finally realized she'd gone too far.

Relieved when she slowed down, he pulled in behind her as she came to a stop at the side of the road and jumped out of her car to race toward him.

He scrambled from the truck to get to her before another car coming by could hit her. Getting a grip on her flailing arms didn't prove to be easy, but he managed it, practically dragging her to the side of the road as she spoke non-stop.

"Ace, I'm sorry. I swear I wasn't trying to get your attention. I didn't even see you until I passed you. I got caught up shopping and left town late this morning and then I spent too much time looking at baby clothes—you know Rachel's coming home today—and I lost track of time. I have a woman meeting me at the club, and I'm going to be late for my appointment, and Charity can't go because she's at the dentist. It's the same woman who was at the club the other night when Rachel went into labor and the women want her to come back. We have a lot of questions for her and—"

Ace lifted his hand. "Enough! Jesus, you're wound up today. I don't give a damn how much of a hurry you're in. I'm putting my foot down about this damned speeding. I'm tired of you risking your life by speeding up and down this road whenever it suits you, and I'm not going to tolerate it anymore."

* * * *

It figured. The one time she hadn't wanted to get his attention, she somehow managed it. Hope had told him the truth. She'd been in a hurry because she'd had such a good time picking out the perfect gift for baby Theresa, and she really did have an appointment, but she could always take the time to speak to the good sheriff.

Especially when he looked so damned good in his uniform and had decided to put his foot down.

But she didn't want a damned ticket.

Now she had a dilemma, but she just might be able to turn it to her advantage. Taking a step closer, she ran a finger down his chest. "But Sheriff, you and your deputies have already given me a bunch of tickets. I'll lose my license if I get another one. Besides, my insurance rates have already gone up."

Ace narrowed his eyes suspiciously and grabbed the hand moving lightly over his chest. His lips curved into a smile that could only be described as evil. "You should have thought about that before you came speeding into my town."

Everywhere their bodies touched, heat sizzled and memories of what he'd done to her the other night weakened her knees. Batting her lashes, she pouted as she brushed her body against his, thrilling when his cock pressed against her stomach. "There must be some other way you could teach me a lesson. I really need my driver's license."

"It appears to me you were late because you had to stop at Beau's store this morning. What did you buy?"

Hope shrugged negligently, lowering her eyes so he wouldn't see the triumph in them. Growing up here, no one knew better than she did how the men all stuck together. She'd known Beau would go running to Ace as soon as she left his store, which was the only reason she'd stopped by in the first place.

"Just some things. Ace, about that ticket—"

"What. Did. You. Buy?"

Touching his sleeve, she looked up at him pleadingly, barely able to contain her laughter. "Ace, please. Isn't there anything else you could do to punish me besides a ticket? I can stop at the store and pick up some more ginger." Pretending to consider it, she nodded. "I know. You can spank me. Right here." Tugging her arm free, she hid a smile at his look of amazement as she draped herself over the trunk of her car. Staring over her shoulder at him, she wiggled her ass. "I'm ready. You can spank me and then I can keep my license. Can you hurry up, though? I'm going to be late for my appointment." She knew trying to order him around would be a sure fire way of upping her punishment.

Jeez, he was so damned hot, especially in that uniform. If he knew just how many fantasies she had that featured him in that tan uniform and his handcuffs…

The icy heat in Ace's eyes made her nipples pebble. He lifted a brow, staring at her ass as he fingered the handcuffs, the curve of his lips telling her she'd gotten herself in deep.

Her stomach clenched at the cool assessment in his eyes, and she realized she just might have bitten off more than she could chew.

He moved fast for such a large man, and before she knew it, he had her wrists pulled behind her back and handcuffed together. He slid an arm under her belly and helped her straighten before leading her to the side of his marked sheriff's SUV and away from the road. With a hand on her shoulder, he held her against the side of the truck where no passing motorist could see her and lifted her T-shirt almost to her shoulders. With a flick of his fingers he unfastened her bra, exposing her breasts. "What did you buy in Beau's store?"

Need, sharp and hot, went through her like lightning as Ace's gaze moved over her breasts. God, she wanted him to touch her so badly, but remembering her vow to make it a little harder for him, she smirked, knowing from experience what that would do to a man from Desire.

"A little kinky, huh, Sheriff? I have to admit, though, these handcuffs used to be a big part of my fantasies."

Ace's eyes narrowed. "What do you mean 'used to be'?"

Hope shrugged, trying to hide the fact that she was living one of her fantasies right now. "I haven't seen you. I figured you got tired of me already." Smiling, she leaned back against the truck. "Unless you want a quickie right now?"

The look on his face would have had her doubled over in laughter if he hadn't chosen that moment to tweak her nipples. "You like playing with fire, don't you, baby?"

Hope wondered if he noticed that he used endearments with her whenever he became aroused. Batting her eyelashes, she whispered huskily, "So do you."

Gathering her against him, he tangled a hand in her hair to pull her head back. "You're going to be late for your appointment. Tell me what you bought in Beau's store, and I'll give you a spanking instead of a ticket."

Hope pouted, hoping the excitement didn't show in her eyes. "That's blackmail."

Ace traced a finger lightly over her nipple, making her gasp. "That's an ugly word. I'm only trying to help you, but if you want the ticket *and* the spanking…"

Clamping her thighs closed against the rush of need that centered there, Hope moaned. "No. I can't have another ticket. Oh, Ace, do something."

Bending, he sucked her nipple into his mouth, using his tongue to stroke it. He had to hold her up when her knees gave out. Lifting his head, he cupped her breast again, letting the cool air touch her moist nipple. "Tell me what you bought at Beau's store, and I'll make you come and give you that spanking tonight instead of a ticket now."

Hope's head fell back, desire flooding her system when he took the other nipple into his mouth and released it to the cool, crisp air. "Oh, Ace. It feels so good." Although she knew they were well hidden from anyone passing by, being exposed outside this way excited her in ways she'd never thought of. Being handcuffed by the big, burly sheriff and fondled by him while he promised to spank her nearly made her come on the spot.

He bent, brushing his lips over hers, their breath mingling. "Tell me."

Another tug on her nipple made her cry out. "A butt plug and a vibrator. Oh, Ace, please."

"Have you used either one of them?"

Arching against him, Hope trembled. "No. I just got them. They're in my car." She nearly melted when Ace unfastened her pants and slid a hand down inside them and into her damp panties. "I'll use the plug on you tonight for your spanking. Are you going to accept your punishment like a good girl, or am I going to have to give you that ticket?"

Hope forced her eyes open to meet the heat in his. The fact that he not only played along with her game but upped the stakes convinced her more than ever that he was the right man for her. "I can't get a ticket, Sheriff. I'll do whatever you want me to as long as you don't give me a ticket."

His fingers moved lightly, too lightly over her clit. "And no more speeding?"

Hope tried to arch to make better contact, but of course he denied her. Jeez, nobody did foreplay or fantasy better than Ace. "No more speeding. I promise."

Tightening his grip on her hair, he forced her head up. "If I catch you speeding again, I'll tie you to my bed and tease you all night…but I won't let you come. You be a good girl and obey the speed limit, and I'll take good care of you."

Hope whimpered as his finger moved in circles over her clit, not hard or fast enough to allow her to come. "I'll be good, I promise."

Ace leaned close, his breath warm on her ear. He stroked her clit a little harder. "Good girl. Come for me."

Hope's legs gave out completely under his unrelenting strokes as she came apart in his arms. The sharp waves of release washed over her one after the other as he held in her place for his intimate caress. Just when she thought she couldn't stand any more, he eased his strokes, finally allowing her to come down.

Gathering her against him, he unlocked her handcuffs and righted her clothing, all the while holding her upright.

Hope wrapped her arms around his neck, burying her face in his throat as he carried her back to her car. Weak and trembling, she pressed her lips to his jaw. "How about that quickie? I know you're wearing a pistol, but that's not what was pressing against my belly."

Ace set her on her feet. "Are you okay to drive?"

"Yes, but—"

"I'll follow you back." He tapped her nose, running a hand down her hip as she got into her car. "I don't want a quickie, but tonight after your spanking, I'm sinking my cock into that smart mouth of yours. Give me the stuff you bought at Beau's."

Hope reluctantly handed the bag over. "I could have used that vibrator before I came over tonight to take the edge off."

Ace closed her door and waited until she opened the window. "No. Now drive carefully to your meeting."

"My meeting! Damn it, Ace. I forgot all about her. Kiss me."

Obligingly, Ace bent to brush her lips with his. "Drive carefully. I'll be right behind you. I'll pick you up at seven tonight. Dress warm."

Hope watched as he walked back to his truck and waited until he got in it before she drove away. Pleased at the progress she'd made with Ace, she grinned at herself in the rearview mirror, nearly bubbling over with anticipation for the night ahead.

Chapter Ten

Ace hung up the phone, a little stunned. He couldn't believe his brothers actually bought another property and planned to move out. It wasn't far, just across town, but still.

They must be giving a lot of consideration to marrying. It had to be someone from out of town because he didn't know of a single woman in Desire they'd expressed any interest in.

Slightly disconcerted at the news, he went back into his bedroom to finish the preparations for Hope's arrival. She'd been playing with him this afternoon, the kind of play that made him hard as a rock, the kind of teasing he'd never really taken the time to explore.

Damn, she was a natural at playing, but he didn't know quite how far he could take this. He'd have to up the ante, part of him hoping it would scare her away, the other part of him dreading the look on her face when he did.

It had taken a tremendous amount of willpower not to do what he'd wanted to do to her this afternoon. He'd have loved nothing more than to keep those cuffs on her and strip her out of her clothes, not something he could have done on the side of the road.

He wondered what she would think of him if she'd known what dark thoughts went through his mind as he cuffed her and bared her breasts. He'd wanted to rip her shirt and bra from her, not lift them carefully out of the way. He'd wanted to bare her ass and take her from behind as she lay draped over the trunk of her car, again not something the sheriff could be caught doing on the side of the road.

But damn, he'd wanted to.

He'd been careful until now not to let her see much of his dark hungers, but if she wanted to play games the way she had this afternoon, she needed to know what lay in store for her. He'd already washed the items she'd bought at Beau's and added them to his own recent purchases.

Stroking his fingers over the items he'd lined up in his nightstand, he thought about the day he'd become sheriff. That day he'd tossed each and every one of his own toys into the trash, thinking he could change.

He'd known better, of course, but he thought that since he was now the sheriff at least he should try. It hadn't worked at all, and with Hope the need to dominate had become stronger than ever.

She had him so tied up in knots that the smartest thing he could do would be to walk away from her. An image of the way she'd looked this afternoon as she practically dared him to spank her still burned in his mind. Who the hell was he kidding? He couldn't walk away, only pick up the pieces of his heart when she did. In the meantime, however, if the little brat wanted to play games, he sure as hell could oblige her.

Part of him worried that she would like what he did to her tonight.

Part of him worried she wouldn't.

But excitement to see her again raced through his veins, and he'd just have to deal with whatever happened. With his cock already stirring, he slipped into his sheepskin jacket and grabbed his keys in a hurry to get to her.

* * * *

Hope dressed much like she had the last time and kept her make-up to a minimum. Smiling as she fluffed her hair, she looked at the clock for the tenth time in as many minutes.

Laughing at herself, she slipped on her shoes and went to the window just in time to see Ace pull up. She slipped on her jacket as she ran to Charity's room to tell her goodbye.

She found her sister sitting cross-legged on her bed in sweat pants and a huge T-shirt, her dark hair pulled back into a ponytail and her glasses perched on her nose. Surrounded by the ledger from the club and various papers, Charity looked up when Hope opened her door.

"Is the sheriff here?"

Leaning against the doorway, Hope grinned at the picture her sister made. "You know we can do that in the office. It's Friday night. You should be out having some fun instead of being cooped up in here doing bookwork."

Charity shook her head, waving her away. "You have enough fun for both of us. What did Beau think of you coming in to buy toys when he knows you're seeing the sheriff?"

Hope bit the inside of her mouth to keep from laughing at Charity's nonchalant tone. She knew damned well her sister had been thinking about it ever since she'd told her she'd shopped there. "He was a little puzzled at first, but then when I told him they were for you, he flashed that grin of his and was real helpful." She'd done no such thing, of course, but she had mentioned to Beau just how much her sister needed to play.

Charity's face turned white and then bright red, her eyes huge as she stared at Hope in horror. "You didn't!" Jumping from the bed, she sent papers scattering as she raced after her sister. "I'll kill you! You'd better be lying."

Hope ran away, laughing, dodging furniture on her way to the door just as Ace knocked. Flinging the door open, she threw herself at him, secure in the knowledge that he would catch her. Giggling, she snuggled into him. "There's a wild woman in there who says she's gonna kill me."

Ace caught her easily and stepped into the apartment, catching a pillow in mid-air. His eyes widened when he saw Charity approaching, whipping her glasses off to glare at her sister. "What did she do now?"

Rubbing herself against Ace, Hope cursed the fact that their coats kept her from feeling more of his hard body. "Why do you always think it's my fault?" Dropping her head on his shoulder, she stuck her tongue out at her outraged sibling.

Ace stroked her bottom warningly. "Because it always is. What did you do?"

Charity turned red again, shaking her head. "Nothing. Mom and the dads should have spanked her as a child." Suddenly her lips curved into one of her rare up-to-no-good smiles. "Sheriff, I'd really appreciate it if you could help me with her and take her in hand. She gets worse every day. She's been making trouble around town for me and telling lies. She drives like a maniac. It's hard enough trying to keep her away from the subs that come into the club…"

Ace gripped Hope's jaw, forcing her to look at him. "You're touching the subs in the club, too?"

Hope hadn't touched a single one of them, and Charity knew it. As owner of the club, she wouldn't lay a hand on any of the men who came with their mistresses. Also, she no longer considered herself single, no matter what Ace said. But none of that would keep her from having a little fun. Blinking innocently, Hope smiled sweetly. "There's nothing wrong with that. Nobody's claimed me yet, and the men are awfully cute when they beg."

Ace nodded at Charity. "I'll take care of her. Lock up behind me." Turning, he carried Hope down the steps and around to his truck. "You've been causing trouble again? We'll see how cute you look when your ass is on fire and you're begging to come."

Hope buried her face in his neck, loving his warm scent. "Am I in trouble, Sheriff?" She worked her way inside his coat to rub her breasts against his chest.

Ace opened the passenger door, pausing with her in his arms. "Don't you think you should be?"

A little put out that he didn't sound jealous, Hope leaned back to look up at him. "You're not mad?"

He bundled her inside, fastening her seatbelt. "I wouldn't be able to punish you if I got mad, now would I?"

Hope opened her mouth, immediately snapping it shut when he pushed the door closed and walked around the front to get in on the other side. She couldn't believe how much it hurt to think he didn't care if she touched another man or not. Did he think she didn't care enough about him?

"Ace, you know I would never touch another man, don't you?"

"Hmm."

Annoyed and a little alarmed at his non-committal reply, Hope stared at him, just now getting a whiff of something else that smelled delicious.

"What that's smell?"

"Food."

"Oh." Staring at him, she wished she could see him better, but the only light came from the streetlights they passed and the low light from the dashboard. Unsure of his mood, she started to get nervous. He hadn't left her at the apartment so he couldn't be really mad at her, could he? The tense silence stretched, making her more and more uncomfortable. Taking a deep breath, she smiled. "Did you bring your handcuffs?" Reaching out to touch his forearm, she batted her lashes at him. "When I was away at school, I used to fantasize all the time about being handcuffed by Desire's sheriff."

Ace glanced at her and raised a brow before turning to watch the road again. "Did you?"

Hope shivered at the ice in his tone. "Ace, what's wrong?"

Ace turned onto the road leading to his house. "Nothing that won't be taken care of in the next few hours." He pulled up in front of the house and turned off the engine.

Hope barely had time to undo her seatbelt before Ace grabbed her arms, turning her toward him as he forced them behind her back. She lifted her face as his hand went to the nape of her neck, watching with a mixture of relief, fascination, and indescribable need as his head lowered.

Still holding both of her hands in one of his, he parted her lips with his own and plundered deep, pulling her against his chest. Not until she heard the click did she realize he'd handcuffed her.

Hope melted into him. She needed this feeling of closeness with him, this wonderful connection. Every time he touched her she went up in flames, but his icy distance added an element of danger and created an alertness that made it even hotter.

She became more aware of every minor shift in his body against hers, every breath. The scent of him intoxicated her. The lightest stroke of his tongue on hers created an answering pull to her nipples and clit.

Ace lifted his head, staring down at her for several long seconds, his eyes glittering with raw possession. He sat her back onto her seat and got out to come around for her.

When he opened the door, she started to get out, squealing when he lifted her effortlessly and tossed her over his shoulder. He closed the door, retrieved the food from the back, and strode into the house with her, the sound of the lock clicking unusually loud in the tense silence. With her still draped over his shoulder, he unpacked the bag, putting the food in the oven to keep warm, never speaking a word.

Hope blinked in disbelief as he calmly completed his task, never once losing his grip on her. "Ace, put me down. I'll go wait for you in the bedroom."

He ignored her as though she hadn't spoken and started toward the bedroom with her, turning off lights along the way.

Hope twisted, trying to see as the low light from the bedroom illuminated his path, but Ace merely tightened his hold on her as he went inside and closed the door behind him. Hope struggled to lift herself as he calmly removed her shoes and tossed them aside. Moaning as his hand caressed her bottom, she arched.

"Ace, I want to touch you."

His continued silence unsettled her, adding to the erotic atmosphere.

Squeezing her thighs together to relieve the ache that settled there, she gasped when he adjusted his grip and sat on the edge of the bed, tossing her over his lap. With her hands cuffed behind her back, she couldn't balance herself and had to trust his hold to keep her steady. Excited at the thought of the spanking she knew she'd be getting, Hope squirmed.

"Are you going to spank me for touching those other men?"

Ace reached for the hem of her sweatpants and yanked them down to her knees and then off. "No. Your spanking is for lying about it and for speeding." He ran a hand over the lacy red thong she'd bought just for tonight. "And for wearing panties. Didn't I tell you not to wear them when you would be with me?"

She didn't even get the chance to speak before his hand came down on her bottom, several times in rapid succession. Shrieking, she struggled against his hold to no avail. "Ace, that hurts!" Her bottom felt as though it were on fire, made worse when he held his hand on her hot buttocks, holding the heat in. "How did you know I was lying? Wait! Do you mean I'll get spanked for lying but not for touching those men? What kind of crap is that?"

He uncuffed her, keeping her over his lap as he quickly stripped her and had her hands cuffed again before she knew it.

Unprepared, she yelped as several sharp landed on her bottom yet again.

Ace flipped her up and onto the bed and turned her onto her belly, holding her down with a firm hand on her lower back when she began to struggle. "I'm doing whatever I want to do with you. Isn't that what you wanted, baby?"

Hope couldn't deny that every touch, every word he spoke, aroused her.

Knowing that he could do whatever he wanted to her, however he wanted to do it, made her toss all her inhibitions aside in an eagerness to please him. She wanted him to take whatever he wanted from her, desperate to give him whatever he needed from her.

It…fulfilled her somehow.

But she couldn't just make it easy.

It excited her to struggle, especially when she knew she could never escape, no matter how hard she tried. "My butt hurts. I'm going to make you pay for that."

Ace bent to brush his lips across her cheek as he ran his fingers over her bottom. "You're in big trouble tonight, little girl."

Hope's pussy clenched, moisture coating her thighs as she shivered, unable to believe how easily he aroused her.

She only needed one other thing to make this night complete and wondered how he'd take it. "Ace, I need something from you."

His hand moved over her warm bottom to her center where he slid his fingers through the slickness he found there. "I'm going to take care of every one of your needs, but after your lying, you're going to have to wait."

Hope twisted restlessly, trying to get his fingers where she needed them. "That's not what I mean. Ace…please don't let me use my safeword." Groaning when his fingers stilled, she turned to hide her face in the pillow, immediately turning it back. Not used to being so nervous about anything, she had a difficult time facing him while consumed with such need, but she wouldn't hide. Couldn't. He needed to know.

"Knowing I can stop what you do to me with a word…" Shit. She didn't quite know how to finish.

Ace rubbed her bottom again. "It keeps you from letting go all the way, doesn't it? Do you really want me to take what I want and you'll have no say in anything I do?" Bending, he kissed her shoulder, his voice low and soft. "Are you sure this is what you want? You'll be totally helpless."

Hope needed to make sure. "Even if I begged for you to stop?"

Smiling coldly, Ace reached into the nightstand and pulled out the blindfold. "Not even if you scream for me to stop. Make absolutely sure. Right now."

The sharp edge to her arousal would have decided it for her, but the look on Ace's face made her absolutely sure. She'd never seen quite that look before, somehow hot and cold at the same time, but the need that flared in his eyes turned her to putty.

His gaze sharpened and narrowed. "There will be absolutely no mercy and no turning back."

Smiling tremulously, she squirmed, moaning at the friction of the sheet on her nipples. She'd never before voiced her wildest fantasy, and the need to do so now had the words tumbling from her lips. "Don't think badly of me. I need this, Ace. I need to be taken. I...need to fight you. I want to be forced. Oh, God, you're going to think I'm some kind of pervert, aren't you?"

His eyes flashed with surprise and then glittered with a heat that scorched her as his lips curved into the most beautiful smile she'd ever seen. "Not when your needs match mine." He ran a hand over the cheeks of her ass. "Mine."

Hope's stomach muscles tightened when he retrieved the key from the pocket of his jeans and unlocked the handcuffs again, his eyes fierce with intent. "Ace, what are you doing? You're not letting me go, are you?" Relief made her giddy as Ace lifted her hands over her head.

Tossing the handcuffs aside, he brought out the velvet cord he'd used the other night. "I can't have you hurting yourself by pulling against the metal cuffs, and tonight you are going to pull. With these you can tug all you want and not hurt yourself." He deftly restrained and blindfolded her before running a finger lightly down her back and making her tremble. His soft tone had an underlying layer of ice that sent a shiver through her. "You're not going anywhere for quite a while, little girl. You have a few things to be punished for, remember?"

Unable to see, Hope's senses heightened. She gasped when Ace slid his hands beneath her and flipped her to her back, his denim-clad thighs holding hers wide. She automatically struggled to close them, even knowing she couldn't. The sense of vulnerability at her inability to do so added to her arousal, as did being naked while he remained fully dressed. Her trepidation at not knowing what he would do to her had her twisting restlessly. God, he seemed to understand her so well.

"Be still."

The bed shifted, and she heard Ace moving beside it, the sound of the nightstand drawer opening and closing again making her pulse leap. Waiting for him to touch her became torture, her body trembling with the effort to remain still.

Suddenly, it became silent, except for the rip of foil.

Hope's breath came out in short pants as she waited, her mind swirling with possibilities. She had no idea where he stood now but could only imagine the picture she made, spread wide and bound, helpless against whatever he decided to do to her.

Oh, God. Her pussy burned, desperate for his attention. She needed to close her thighs to relieve the ache and began to move slowly, hoping he wouldn't notice.

"You close those legs one more inch and I'm whipping your clit."

Hope froze, her clit throbbing in answer to his threat. Her legs shook as she fought to keep them parted. Several more long seconds passed in complete silence, stretching her nerves to the breaking point. Trying to regulate her breathing proved impossible, her breath hitching at every soft sound.

She jolted when something touched her nipple, the lightest of touches, but remarkably effective in getting her attention, the slight contact enough to push her to the edge again. Digging her heels into the mattress, she lifted herself, rocking her hips in frustration.

"Ace!"

"Quiet. Not a word or I'll gag you."

Not sure if she was supposed to answer him or not, she bit her lip.

She thought she felt another light brush on her nipple, but because it had been so light, she wondered if she'd just imagined it. Unable to stop her body from arching to get better contact, she wasn't prepared for the hard slap to her inner thigh. Twisting restlessly against the erotic heat, she whimpered in her throat.

"Please do something."

Ace lifted her bottom onto a pillow, adjusting her to his satisfaction, his hands hot and firm as they moved over her at will. "Quiet. The more you talk, the longer you'll have to wait."

Hope moaned, wondering if he could read her mind. She didn't want to be able to resist. She wanted him to use her, tease her mercilessly and take his pleasure. Still, the need to struggle was strong, but her desperate hope that he would overcome her resistance was even stronger.

"No. Don't. Untie me."

Ace tapped her clit none too gently and slid his fingers through her drenched slit. "You had your chance to stay still and you didn't. You gave up your safeword."

With the amount of moisture coating her thighs, Ace had to know how much all of this excited her. "What are you going to do to me?"

Chuckling, Ace tapped her clit sharply with the whip again, laughing softly when she whimpered. "Whatever I want to do to you."

She twisted restlessly as his hands moved over her thighs, needing him to touch her more intimately. Her broken moans filled the room as he pushed her knees back, spreading her even wider.

"Now I've got you right where I want you." After repositioning her on the pillow, he ran his fingers over the inside of her thighs. "Beautiful."

Clenching her hands on the velvet cord, Hope shuddered as the low sizzles from his touch traveled straight to her slit. Everything was now available to him, her breasts, her clit, her pussy and bottom, all on display for him and vulnerable to whatever he wanted to do to them. The bed shifted, and she heard the unmistakable sounds of him getting undressed.

When the bed dipped again and she felt Ace's body move next to her, she automatically turned toward him, thrilled at the brush of his naked flesh on hers. The hairs from his thighs tickled hers, the highly charged atmosphere making the sensation much stronger. She gasped in surprise and white-hot lust as strong fingers closed over her nipples and pinched, rolling them between thumbs and forefingers.

He released them just as suddenly, but the sensation lingered. "I'm going to clamp your nipples, not hard, just enough to get your attention." He pinched them again, making her gasp. "You respond well to a small amount of pain."

That almost clinical tone drove her crazy. "Small amount? That hurt. Don't clamp them. Please, Ace, don't put clamps on them. I swear I'll be good." The words slipped out before she could stop them, and she bit her lip, hoping like hell he would realize she really didn't want him to stop. She had no idea why it excited her so much to beg like this, but it did. She'd had clamps used on her before, though, and they'd hurt badly.

It made her a little nervous, but she trusted him to know her limits.

Closing her thighs, she rubbed them together to ease the ache, stilling when she realized her mistake almost immediately.

Ace's arm went beneath her thighs, swiftly lifting them and spanking her bottom several times, one sharp slap after the other. He pressed them back against her chest, leaning on them slightly to keep them in place, his tone incredulous. "So you think you're going to get away with closing your legs when I tell you to keep them apart? And making demands again?"

Hope couldn't straighten her legs at all, no matter how hard she pushed against his arm. The other men she'd had sex with hadn't been as hard as Ace, neither in strength nor temperament, something that became abundantly clear. Gasping as something touched her bottom hole, she struggled furiously.

"What's that? What are you doing?"

He nipped her calf, the sharp sting startling her. "I don't have to tell you, but I will since it'll let you know what's in store for you. It's a plunger filled with lube."

Gasping as he inserted something narrow into her bottom and forced the cold lube into her, Hope froze. Surprised at how stimulating she found anal play, she couldn't help but be alarmed, wondering what Ace had planned.

He'd already warned her that it was something he loved, and she had a strong suspicion that if she spent as much time with Ace as she wanted to, her ass would be getting quite a workout. His cool tone started to worry her, compelling her to remind him that she had no experience in that area. He removed the plunger, still holding her legs high.

"Ace, you know that I've never had anything—"

"In your ass. Except my finger and the ginger. You forget, baby, that this ass is mine now. *Only* mine. My cock is hard as hell thinking about fucking this tight ass, and the fact that you're a virgin there is the only thing that's stopping me from taking it. You're not ready, so don't push me. I'll take your ass soon enough."

If Hope ever heard anything so erotic before, she didn't remember it. Her anus and pussy clenched at the thought of him taking her there. She both feared and anticipated it, unable to even imagine what it would feel like to have Ace's large cock being worked into her ass.

"But first you need to be stretched, don't you, baby?"

God. When he used endearments in that cool, knowing tone, it drove her wild. His threat of stretching her vulnerable bottom made her even wilder.

Damn, he was good at this.

Chuckling, he poised something at her bottom hole again. "You're soaked, so don't even try to tell me you don't want me taking your ass. The last time I watched your face. This time I'm going to watch your ass while I open you up with this butt plug you bought from Beau. You were smart to get a small one."

Hope couldn't keep her bottom from grasping desperately at the plug as it pressed insistently, the lube easing the way for it to breach her opening. A chill went through her as he continued to press it into her, stretching her bottom hole with the cone-shaped plug. Her nipples still tingled from his ministrations, and her clit felt heavy and swollen. Thrashing her head from side to side, she couldn't get over how sharp her senses had become.

Her anus burned as it stretched, the overwhelming intimacy of having her ass invaded making her tremble. Hot little sizzles of pleasure swept over her, gathering strength as they centered at her slit.

"You really like your ass filled, don't you, baby? That's good because I'm going to enjoy this ass every chance I get. That's it. Just a little more. I know you want to come, but you can't yet. You've been bad, remember?"

Shaking, she tried to buck against him as her body gathered. "I can't stop it. Oh. I'm coming!" Reaching for it, she screamed in frustration when he backed off, withdrawing the plug from her just as her orgasm began. The relief she anticipated became anguish, her orgasm cut short just enough to leave her suspended in a tortuous state of need. "Damn you, Ace. I hate you. Leave me alone. Help me. Fuck me, you bastard."

Ace clicked his tongue and pressed at the plug again. "No. You'll have to learn, honey, that I can make you come, even against your will, or I can pull you back. Your orgasm is in my hands now, darlin'. Soon you'll see you have no choice but to surrender to get what you want." He tapped her ultra-sensitive clit none too gently, chuckling at her whimpered cries of need.

Hope shook harder now, unable to escape the pleasure and at the realization that relief wouldn't be coming any time soon. The cone-shaped plug continued to press into her until it narrowed sharply and the base fit snugly against her. Panting, she struggled to adapt to the full, stretched feeling, reaching for an orgasm Ace continued to deny her.

"That's my girl. You should see how beautiful you look with your ass plugged." Ace lowered her legs, keeping them spread wide by moving to sit between them. "It's a nice small one. As soon as you become accustomed to that, I'll use the larger one that I bought for you."

The plug felt much larger than it looked in the package and seemed to grow every time it shifted inside her. Hope arched toward him, groaning when it moved the plug inside her again. Her body was so sensitive now that she could even feel the heat from his body as he leaned over her. Whimpering as his hands closed over her breasts, she rocked her hips, crying out when her clit brushed against his cock.

Ace took a nipple into his mouth, closing his teeth over it to suck gently. She moaned in frustration when he released it, only to scream when he attached a smooth clip to it, not a jagged one like she'd been expecting. Relieved, she absorbed the pain of the strong pinch, holding her breath as she struggled to adjust to it.

"Breathe, baby. It's gonna feel so good in just a few seconds. That's my good girl."

She focused on his voice as he crooned softly to her, and unbelievably, the sharp pain eased. The erotic pressure combined with his low, deep voice lulled her deeper into another place. Another world.

God, it felt amazing.

She'd been paying so much attention to the clip on her nipple that it startled her when Ace attached a clip to the other. The pain took over again, and she immediately began breathing the way he'd instructed.

Ace lightly rubbed her stomach. "Good girl. You deserve a reward." He slid down her body, nibbling and kissing his way down to her center and lifted her thighs over his shoulders.

Although it took tremendous effort, Hope remained motionless. "Please Ace, I have to come. Please. Do it." She jolted at the sharp nip on her inner thigh.

"You just couldn't wait, could you, baby? I was going to give you the release your poor body's craving for taking the clips so beautifully. As soon as I praise you, you're bad again. Now, you're just going to have to suffer a little more."

Holding her thighs firmly, he lifted her, pressing against the plug with his thumbs to shift it again. His silky hair brushed the inside of her thighs as he lowered his head to run his tongue over her bare folds.

Hope pushed against his hold, trying to get him to touch her clit, but he deftly avoided it, chuckling against her slit as he ran his tongue over her folds again before sliding it into her pussy.

His murmur of approval at her taste vibrated against her sensitive flesh, driving her need even higher. His tongue swept through the juices that continued to flow from her as though starving for her taste.

She kicked at him, digging her heels into his back, overwhelmed by all the sensations. Thrashing helplessly caused a tug on her nipples from the weight of the clamps. Her bottom burned from clenching on the plug, and her clit was on fire. Having Ace's strong hands on her body provided even more delicious tremors.

He took his time, holding her still as he devoured her. Lifting his head, he pressed harder at the plug in her ass, tightening his grip when she squirmed. "Be still. I'm not through yet. This is about what I want, remember. You're just going to have to be a good girl and stay still while I take what I want."

Hope shuddered, her orgasm building with each passing second. Knowing that he did this for himself, that he would continue to eat at her for as long as it suited him, made her feel more desired, more a sexual being than ever before. She existed only to please him and had no choice but to let him take whatever he wanted from her, his entire demeanor that of a man uncaring of what she needed.

She knew better.

Ace Tyler knew exactly what she needed and cared very much. It was in his hold, in his voice.

He lifted his head slightly, his breath warm on her slit. "Come. I want more of this sweet juice."

Hope's body went tight, bowing as he sucked her clit, coming just as he demanded.

As if she had any choice.

Sparks shot behind her eyes as the incredible wave of release washed over her, her body shaking uncontrollably as it went on and on. The wave crested and crashed, the powerful flow seeming to go on forever, but through it, Ace's attention never faltered.

His tongue moved from her clit to her pussy and back again, until the pleasure became so intense it bordered on pain. Reaching up, he removed the clips from her nipples, the blood rushing back into them sending her crashing again.

Her cries for him to stop went unanswered as he continued to feast on her. Spent, she slumped weakly, whimpering softly. Her body trembled at the collapse of her defenses all around her.

He must have tasted her surrender because only then did he lift his head to kiss her inner thighs. "That's my girl." He worked his way up her body, kissing and nipping along the way, and she never knew which it would be. Or where.

His kisses warmed her, his affection for her apparent with every brush of his lips. No matter what he said, the big sheriff loved her. With his arms around her, she felt safe and secure, as though nothing in the world could intrude into the world he'd created just for the two of them.

His sharp nips excited her, each a reminder of who was in charge, and each building her need for him all over again.

Her skin tingled wherever he touched, each kiss causing a languorous heat, each nip sharpening her senses.

Running his hands up her arms to her wrists, he tangled his fingers with hers and slowly began to press his cock into her.

Hope automatically wrapped her legs around him, gasping as the plug in her bottom shifted.

Ace cupped her jaw before sliding his hand up to push the blindfold out of the way. "I want to see you eyes when I take you."

Tears of happiness, of surrender trickled into her hair. Caring and desire combined, making her pliant and needy in his capable hands. Her need for him nearly overwhelmed her—not just the physical closeness, but the emotional bond.

Ace gave her both, a combination so potent it filled the lonely parts of her that had been empty for too long and that only he could fill. As he entered her body, his slow, smooth strokes filling her and shifting the plug in her bottom, she automatically reached for him, surprised to find her hands free. She wrapped them around his neck, tangling her fingers into his silky hair, and with a whimper, breathed him in.

He slid his fingers beneath her neck, his thumb lightly tracing her jaw. His face looked as if it had been carved from granite as he slowly, steadily thrust his thick cock inside her. On a groan, he sank to the hilt. Sliding his other hand around her, he lifted her buttocks, his fingers pressing against the plug. His eyes flared and darkened, holding hers as he once again began to move.

Hope had never felt so taken. The sensation of being totally possessed had more tears falling. *This* is what she'd always needed. *This* is what she'd always known she could find only with Ace.

Paradise.

The rest of the world disappeared until nothing mattered but him. Them.

The overwhelming fullness stole her breath, her pussy and anus stretched unbelievably to accommodate both Ace's cock and the plug.

Her grip tightened on him as he took her, holding on to his strong neck and shoulders to keep herself grounded. "So full. Ace, it's too good. Don't let it end."

He kept her neck arched, watching her eyes as he made love to her, his hand gently massaging with fingers threaded through her hair. His hooded eyes shone with possessiveness, deeper and darker than ever. Slowly, his lips curved into the naughtiest grin she'd ever seen, spiking her lust. "All mine. You're milking my cock, and I'll bet you're milking the plug in your ass, too. When I finally fuck that ass, you'll know what full is, baby."

Wrapped in his tight hold, her movements became restricted, the inability to move making her burn even hotter. Digging her heels into his taut buttocks, she gave herself over to him, more than willing to let him do as he wished with her. Her pussy and ass burned, the tingles growing hotter with each delicious stroke. The friction on her nipples, still incredibly sensitive from the clips, sent white-hot lightning to her center.

Her body grew tighter, shaking uncontrollably as the warning tingles grew, but she knew it would be up to him if she went over or not. The not knowing added another layer to her submission. "Please, Ace. I'm begging."

"Yes, baby. Come for me."

It only took those whispered words in her ear to snap the bands of restraint he held, and she screamed as her orgasm exploded. Bursts of sparkling heat shot out from her pussy and anus to encompass her entire being. Wave after wave of it went through her, forcing her body to clamp down on both Ace's cock and the plug in her bottom. The shock of it, of the sensation of feeling even fuller, triggered another orgasm to join the first until she couldn't tell where one began and the other ended.

As her screams grew hoarse, she began kicking her legs, her body overloaded with sensation. It got worse when Ace bent to take a nipple into his mouth and suck gently. She gasped at his deep thrust, thrilled when his big body trembled under her hands. She never knew she could even endure such pleasure, incapable of anything more than a hoarse scream when he held himself deep while pressing the plug in her ass, so full she couldn't think.

Her vision blurred, her voice nearly gone until she no longer even had the strength to hold on to him anymore and dropped her arms to her sides. When she finally began to come down, she buried her face in his neck, breathing in his wonderful scent as she tried to catch her breath.

He murmured softly against her forehead. "You were wonderful, baby. That's my girl. Nice, deep breaths. Easy, honey."

His kiss brought tears to her eyes once again, making her wonder if she'd ever stopped crying at all. She'd just had the most erotic, the most beautiful and fulfilling experience of her life, and she found herself saddened that it had come to an end.

Her body, however, probably couldn't have taken any more.

Slumping in his arms, Hope lifted her face to kiss his jaw, thrilled when he bent his head to take her lips with his own. Opening to him completely, she sighed as his lips moved over hers possessively, but with a gentleness that melted her heart.

Lifting his head, his eyes were tender and indulgent as they moved over her face. "Let me take care of you, baby, and then you can sleep."

Hope kissed his shoulder, reveling in the heat and strength surrounding her. "You already did take care of me. You turned me into a pile of wet noodles."

Ace chuckled and bent to kiss each of her nipples as he slowly withdrew from her. "That's not what I meant. Stay put and I'll get a warm cloth." He rolled her limp body to her stomach before Hope knew his intention. He put a hand at her back to keep her in place when she would have rolled back over, sliding it down over her bottom. "Stay put or I'll redden your ass again."

Hope froze, stunned when he gently, but firmly, parted her legs and separated the cheeks of her bottom. Struggling to her elbows, she looked back over her shoulder in alarm. "Ace, what are you doing?" She panted, her hands fisting on the pillow as he gently worked the plug out of her ass.

Ace ran a hand over her bottom again and bent to lightly kiss her shoulder. "Taking care of you. Don't move. I'll be right back."

Wide awake now, Hope squeezed her legs closed, moaning softly at the tenderness between them. Dropping back to the mattress again, she lay there hugging the pillow and listening to water run in the adjoining bathroom. When the water went off, she turned, looking over her shoulder to watch Ace's return.

He came to sit on the edge of the bed beside her and flipped her to her back. A warm cloth placed over her breasts immediately began to ease the ache in her nipples. Spreading her thighs, he used another cloth to clean her gently, his hand between her thighs keeping them open until he finished wiping her juices and the lube from her.

Uncomfortable, Hope held on to the cloth covering her breasts. "Ace, I'd rather do that myself."

Ace lifted his head as he finished, looking at her expressionlessly. "I take care of what belongs to me. It's part of the package that you said you wanted so badly. Have you changed your mind?"

Hope stretched, smiling as his eyes flared again. "I thought you said you weren't tender. That seemed awfully tender to me. None of the men I've had sex with ever—"

Ace took the cloth from her breasts and stood, all traces of tenderness gone. "I don't want to hear about any of the other men who've fucked you. I'm not tender at all. I'm possessive. I told you already that I take care of my possessions." He threw a light blanket over her and strode from the room without a backward glance, probably with the intent to show her what an unfeeling bastard he was.

But she'd seen his eyes.

Smiling to herself, Hope snuggled under the covers, confident that he loved her. Not sure why he tried so hard to deny it, she knew she had a lot of work to do and would have to be patient, definitely not her strong suit.

She would do whatever she had to do, though, in order to have Ace.

A delicious awareness of being thoroughly taken pervaded her slit and breasts and made her limbs heavy. Hearing the shower start, Hope turned to her side and huddled into the covers. She would just rest a little before she had to get up and get dressed for Ace to take her home.

Chapter Eleven

When the sound of the howling wind penetrated her consciousness, Hope automatically snuggled into the warmth surrounding her. Remembering that she didn't have to be at the club until later in the afternoon, she kept her eyes closed and dozed again.

"Get out."

Hope jolted at what sounded like a door closing, and started to sit up, only to have hard bands tighten around her. Blinking her eyes open, she lifted her head, shocked to find herself staring down into Ace's face. Frowning, she blinked and looked around in confusion to see that morning had come. The last thing she remembered was closing her eyes for a minute while she waited for Ace to get out of the shower.

"This is your bed." Remembering, she frowned. "Did you just tell me to get out?"

The faint morning light that crept into the room allowed her to see everything clearly, but was dim enough to create an intimacy reserved for lovers. Somehow she'd ended up on top of Ace, her legs on either side of his hips, her face still warm from being pillowed by his chest. Naked, she shivered slightly as she sat up, straddling him, the cool morning air causing her nipples to pebble.

Tousled and sexy, Ace smiled tenderly, running his hands from her thighs and up to her waist before continuing upward to cover her breasts. "This is definitely my bed. And since you're in it, you're at my mercy. I definitely did not tell you to get out." His eyes sharpened, already alert.

Leaning forward, she held on to his shoulders, moaning in lethargic pleasure as he massaged her breasts. The friction of his palm moving slowly over her tender nipples slowly built a heaviness low in her abdomen. Rubbing her slit against his flat abs, she moaned again, smiling when his hard cock touched her bottom. She went willingly as he lowered her to his chest, snuggling into him as his hands came around her to massage the cheeks of her ass. Smiling innocently, she wiggled.

"Since I'm at your mercy, what are you going to do to me, Sheriff?"

Sliding his hands slowly up her back, he pulled her higher. "I'm going to sink into that tight pussy again and listen to your whimpers." He pulled her down for a kiss, his lips warm and firm beneath hers. His hands moved back down her body, pausing to investigate sensitive spots along the way that had her writhing against him.

She threaded her hands into his thick hair, moaning into his mouth as his fingers grazed her slit. When one thick finger circled her damp opening, she shuddered and tightened her hold.

"I love those soft little whimpers you make when you're aroused. You're wet already." Ace wrapped his arms around her and sat up, bending his legs and positioning her to lean back against them. Keeping one hand on her stomach, he reached out to retrieve a condom from the nightstand drawer.

Hope couldn't take her eyes from the sight of his erect cock, which seemed to grow right before her eyes. Sitting up, she wrapped her hands around it, thrilled when it jumped. A drop of moisture appeared at the tip, making her mouth water to taste it. She ran her hands up and down the thick heat in her hands, captivated by its velvety texture.

Ace handed her the condom. "Put it on me."

She accepted it with a grin, shifting restlessly when his hands went to her hips, caressing gently. "I'm on top now, big guy."

Ace sat up and lifted her by the waist until they were at eye level. "No matter where I put you, I'm bigger. I'm also meaner." He nipped her bottom lip, making it sting. "Put it on so I can sink into that tight pussy. If you give me any lip, I'll bend you over and fuck your ass." He lowered his legs to set her back down on his thighs, his eyes hooded as he reclined back against the pillows.

Smiling mischievously, she leaned forward to kiss him, teasing him by running her tongue over his lips before she began to work her way down his body, kissing and licking a trail to his naval and beyond, making a space for herself between his thighs. "I want to lick you first." Opening her mouth wide, she took the head of his cock inside and swirled her tongue around it. Reveling in his taste, she took more, keeping her eyes on his the entire time.

Reclining on the pillows, Ace watched her, looking every inch the dominant male. He reached out a hand to caress her hair. "Did I say you could do that?"

Hope shook her head and began to suck him gently, needing to make him feel good, needing to submit to him, but at the same time struck by just how powerful it made her feel when his thigh muscles quivered beneath her hands.

"Enough." Bending, he helped her sit up and took his cock in his hand. Even though his eyes twinkled, the threat in them was unmistakable. "Be careful. You're trying my patience this morning."

Her hands shook, causing her to fumble as she rolled on the condom. Her nipples craved his attention, tingling under his watchful gaze as she completed her task. "You can't get very far threatening me with something I already want." She held on to his forearms as he lifted her again and guided her, lowering her onto his cock. Hope shuddered as he filled her, still slightly tender from the night before.

"Do you really want Law and Zach to hear you scream when I open that tight ass?"

Hope's eyes flew open, and she whipped her head around, relieved to see the door to his bedroom closed. Keeping her voice at a whisper, she gripped his forearms tighter. "They're here? How do you know they're here? Oh, hell. I woke up when I thought I heard you tell someone to get out. It was them, wasn't it? Did they see me naked?"

Ace ran his hands up her sides to stroke her nipples with his thumbs. "I heard them pull up about an hour ago." He lifted her and lowered her again, smiling at her moan. "I made sure you were completely covered before Law poked his head in. Now be quiet so my brothers don't hear the sounds you make when you come."

She had no idea how she could be on top and still be dominated, but Ace's hold left her in no doubt as to who was in charge. When his hands went to her hips and he caught her clit between his thumbs, Hope cried out, unable to hold it back.

Ace chuckled softly. "You're going to need a lot of training. How are you going to handle being in the hotel restaurant in one of the privacy booths if you can't keep from making all that noise?"

Biting her lip as his cock stroked over a particularly sensitive spot inside her, she held back another moan. Leaning forward, she flattened her hands on his chest. "Will you take me there?" She clenched on his cock as he continued thrust into her, throwing her head back in abandon. The pressure on her clit nearly undid her several times, but each time Ace seemed to know it and eased his grip. Remembering in time to keep her voice low, Hope groaned. "Ace, please." Rocking on him, she had no choice but to let him control her movements.

He sat up, swinging his legs over the side of the bed, one hand at her back easily holding her in place while the other covered her abdomen, using his thumb to separate her folds and stroke her clit. "Please what, baby? Please fuck your ass? Please take you to a privacy booth? Or please make you come?" His cool, almost disinterested tone sent a shiver through her and might have fooled her if not for the tortured look on his face and the glitter in his eyes.

He used one arm to support her weight until she lay suspended on his thighs and impaled by his cock. She had nothing to hold onto as she couldn't reach his shoulders. "Yes. All of it."

Ace's eyes narrowed. "Still making demands?" He circled her clit repeatedly with his callused thumb, stopping each time she started shaking.

Restlessly shifting her legs, Hope felt like a feast laid out before him. Whimpering as he started moving her on his cock again, she clenched at him in desperation, his attention to her clit and his forceful thrusts keeping her on the edge. Shaking her head, she reached for him. "Begging. Please, Ace. Let me come. Please." Her voice sounded small and needy to her own ears. She didn't care. She needed to come and would do anything to get Ace to let her.

He rewarded her by applying more pressure to her clit. "I like how you beg, baby. I think I'll have to make you beg a lot in the future."

Hope's stomach muscles quivered, her abdomen tightening as he took her higher and higher. She didn't comment on his reference to the future, ecstatic that he'd even thought about it. "When I—Oh! When I get used to this, it's not going to be so easy to make me beg. Oh! I'm gonna come, Ace."

"I know, baby. Come for me."

Her body tightened as she came, the pleasure not as sharp as the night before, but the slow warm swell was just as satisfying. While still in the throes of orgasm, she watched Ace's face, thrilled when he thrust himself deep and threw his head back, closing his eyes on a deep groan. Knowing she could bring such pleasure to him gave her as much satisfaction as her own orgasm did.

Still deep inside her, he gathered her close, rubbing her nipples with his chest as he bent her head back and covered her mouth with his.

Finally having the chance to touch him, she wrapped her arms around him and pulled him close. When he lifted his head, she buried her face in his neck, closing her eyes as he ran his hands up and down her back. "I could stay like this forever." Just then her stomach growled, and she grimaced at Ace's chuckle.

Hugging her, he brushed her hair aside to kiss her jaw. "I don't think so. I'd better feed you before you waste away to nothing."

Hope nipped his shoulder playfully. "Is that another reference to my stature?"

Ace stood, and with her legs still wrapped around him, carried her with him into the bathroom. "I've got to get my entertainment where I can find it."

Wiggling on his cock, Hope laughed. "I know how to keep you plenty entertained, Sheriff."

Ace withdrew and slowly set her on her feet. "Yes, I believe you do." Sobering, he gestured toward the shower. "Baby, you mean a lot to me, but I don't want you to get hurt. You're not the type to put up with me for long."

Stepping into the shower, Hope smiled. "That's what you think. Come and join me. I'll wash you."

Ace got rid of the condom and shook his head. "No. I'll shower in the other bathroom. Take your time. I'll meet you in the kitchen."

Hope nodded sadly and watched him go, already feeling the distance. Every time they seemed to be getting closer, Ace put this wall between them, and she couldn't help but wonder why he thought she would get tired of his possessiveness.

She adjusted the spray and began washing. If she hurried, she could talk to Law and Zach before Ace finished his shower. Maybe they could give her some of the answers she needed.

* * * *

She hadn't taken the time to dry her hair, not even knowing if Ace owned a blow dryer, and ran out to the kitchen. She smiled when Zach met her at the doorway with a steaming cup of coffee. "Ah, a man after my own heart."

Zach grinned and gestured toward the table where he and Law had a big breakfast waiting. "Don't let Ace hear you say that. He'd start pounding on me, and I'd hate to have to hurt him."

Law turned from the stove, carrying a large pan filled with scrambled eggs. "Good morning, honey. I'm waiting for him to come out and pound on *me* for poking my head in this morning. I'm sorry, Hope. I didn't know you were here."

Zach pulled out a chair for her and started to pile eggs on her plate. "Ace never brings women home. None of us do. I think we'd better get that house built fast. It looks like you may be living here soon."

Hope looked from one to the other. "What house?"

Zach grinned. "We bought half of the old Sheldon property. There's still a house there, but we helped get the land subdivided, so we're taking the half that's vacant."

"Mr. Sheldon used to have the ice cream shop, didn't he? He's the one who asked my mother how she could go to church when she lived in sin with three men. Fucking asshole."

Zach nodded, his face grim. "Yeah, he wasn't the nicest of people. I felt sorry for his wife and kids, though. When we ran him out of business, they suffered, too. His wife was a nice woman, a little timid, and we always wondered if he beat her. She denied it every time one of us asked. Ace talked to her a lot, but she wouldn't stay behind when her husband was forced out of town."

Hope had been too young to remember much about that but could well remember her mother crying and her fathers' outrage. "What about the house? They didn't want to sell that?"

Law brought over a plate piled with toast. "The attorney said that wasn't for sale yet, at least until they figure out what they want to do with it. Old man Sheldon would never come back to Desire, so we're gonna keep pressuring until they sell us the whole thing."

Zach buttered a piece of toast and handed it to her. "In the meantime, we've got an architect drawing up some plans. We're going to have Boone, Chase, and the Madisons build it for us. We've got to get out of here to give you and Ace some privacy."

Hope sipped her coffee and shook her head. "I don't know. I wish I could believe that. But your brother is the most hard-headed man I know."

Zach sat and filled his own plate. "You've got that right, but you spent the night. That has to mean something."

"Yeah, it means that we both fell asleep." Ace's gruff tone stabbed her heart. He reached across the table for her coffee and downed it. "Don't be filling her head. She's already going to get hurt as it is. That's on me. Don't make it worse. I got a call I have to take. Somebody shot out some windows in town. It looks like they started with the men's club and moved on to yours, Hope." When they all jumped up, horrified, he tossed Hope her jacket. "Come on. Your dads are already at the club cleaning up glass."

Hope nodded and rushed to put on her jacket and shoes. Halfway to the door, she looked over her shoulder to see Law and Zach watching her sadly. "Goodbye. Thanks for breakfast."

Zach lifted a hand. "Next time maybe you'll get the chance to eat it. We'll be there in a few minutes to help you clean up."

Ace hurried her out with a hand at her back. "Let's go."

Chapter Twelve

Furious that he couldn't stay to help her, Ace took pictures and left his deputies, Linc and Rafe, behind to search for slugs while he went across the street to Club Desire to investigate the damage there.

Thankfully, Hope and Charity had plenty of help to clean up the glass. Two of their fathers, Garrett and Drew Sanderson, came to help, leaving Finn at the diner with their mother. Clay and Rio Erickson came over to help, shooing the women out of the way just as Law and Zach came through the door with Beau right behind them.

Sloane, Cole, and Brett Madison took measurements to replace the windows while Boone and Chase did the same across the street at the men's club.

Since both clubs had been closed and, thankfully, empty when it happened, no one had been hurt, but Ace couldn't tamp down his fury that this happened in *his* fucking town and how easily someone *could* have been hurt.

The fact that no one saw anything but that several people heard what sounded like a truck roar by pissed him off even more. The shooting occurred in the early morning hours when most people had still been snug in their beds, and by the time they looked out, the shooter had gone.

It took several hours before he could get back to Hope, long hours that he hated being away from her. Rafe and Linc assured him that the club had been cleaned up and was secure and that they'd sent Hope and Charity back to their apartment.

Thoughts of what could have happened if either woman had been inside the club at the time some asshole shot the windows out ran through his mind all day. He fought a constant battle not to go to Hope, throw her over his shoulder, and hustle her off to his ranch where she'd be safe.

In this mood, he had no business going to her, but he wouldn't settle down until he saw for himself that she was okay.

He'd make it a quick visit and then get the hell away from her. Having this happen while the intimacy of sleeping with her and holding her in his arms all night was still fresh, he didn't trust himself at all. He'd wanted to scare her away, not terrify her with his dark mood and foul temper.

The sun had just started to go down when he pulled up in front of the diner. He turned off the engine and just sat there, forcing himself to calm down before he went up to Hope's apartment.

He hadn't slept much the night before. When he came out of the shower, he'd found her fast asleep and earned nothing more than a grunt when he'd tried to wake her to eat. While she slept peacefully beside him, he'd spent most of the night watching her. When she'd cuddled into him as though trying to get closer, he'd lifted her carefully to lie on top of him, hoping the movement wouldn't wake her, not quite sure how we would explain that he wanted her even closer.

He'd wanted badly to shower with her, had almost insisted on it, but the morning-soft, just-made-love-to look on her face tightened a fist around his heart. The intimacy of having slept with her and making love to her again hung in the air, and he'd desperately needed to get away from her to rebuild the fucking wall she kept knocking down at will.

With her bubbly personality and devil-may-care attitude, she somehow lighted some of the dark places inside him and warmed parts of him that had been cold for longer than he cared to remember.

Fear of what could have happened to her weighed like a jagged block of ice in his stomach. He could have lost her so easily, and she never would have known what she meant to him. His need to overwhelm her, to let her know that she belonged to him, to have her focused solely on him knotted his stomach even as it stirred his groin.

Opening the door, he breathed in the cold night air, trying to force back the erotic images racing through his mind. If he did to her what he wanted to right now, she'd run screaming into the night.

"Hey, Sheriff."

Whipping his head around, Ace stared into Hope's beloved face. Unsettled that he'd been so lost in his thoughts that she'd managed to sneak up on him, he yanked her against him. "What are you doing out here?"

* * * *

Startled by his tone, Hope nevertheless snuggled into him. "I looked out the window and saw you. What are you doing sitting out here? Have you eaten?"

"I grabbed a sandwich. I talked to Cole Madison. He said that they replaced the windows. Are you and Charity all right?"

Hope grinned and tried to crawl into his lap, but the steering wheel prevented it. "Yes, we're fine. It's only glass. But Beau came over to check on Charity." She jumped, startled when Ace grabbed her by the shoulders none too gently and stood, leaning over her threateningly.

"It's not only glass. You could have been hurt, damn it. Don't you take anything seriously? If you'd been inside the club—"

Hope shoved at him. "I wasn't, though, was I? Nobody was. Jeez, I could have been struck by lightning when we had that thunderstorm last week, but I wasn't. Lighten up, for God's sake."

Ace lifted her off of her feet, shook her once and with a curse, put her back down. "You don't fucking get it, do you? This is all some kind of game to you. It's not. You could have been hurt. Or worse, damn it. Do you realize how easily you could have been taken away from—fuck it."

Hope grabbed his arm when he would have turned away. "Taken away from you? Is that what you're afraid of? Is that why you keep me at arm's length and refuse to give in to what you really want? You think I'm going to leave you like your mother left your father, don't you?"

Ace shrugged off her hand. "You don't know what the hell you're talking about. I gave you the kinky sex you wanted, didn't I? Isn't that what you wanted from me, Hope?"

She gasped at the cold blade of pain that sliced into her stomach, but it paled in comparison to the anguish in Ace's eyes. With sudden insight, she realized he was doing his best to push her away. Again.

"You know better than that, Ace."

The big, bad, sheriff had a weak spot. Her.

She'd spoken with Law and Zach while they helped her clean up today, and they'd told her that he didn't let himself get too close to anyone except his father and brothers, keeping all women at a distance.

Fucking them was one thing, but the intimacy of actually spending the night wrapped in each other's arms was something entirely different.

Once she looked back at his actions from that perspective, things made a lot more sense.

The fact that he tried to protect her from his dark desires only reinforced her belief that he loved her. He still didn't believe that she desperately needed him just the way he was, and she knew by the look on his face she didn't have much time left to convince him.

Knowing how much it would piss him off, she kept her tone playful. "You liked playing games, too, didn't you, darlin'? Why don't we go back to your house and play tonight? Law and Zach already told me they have plans for tonight and won't be home until late tomorrow morning."

Ace shook his head grimly. "No. I just came by to check on you. I sent Linc home early to get some sleep because he's going to be working late tonight. I'm going to relieve him at three in the morning, so I'm going home for a bit. I'll be busy with trying to find whoever's doing this. Maybe it's better if we end this now."

If she didn't know him so well, she would have fallen to her knees in agony at his dismissal. Understanding his motive, she nodded. "Sure, Ace. Anytime you want to play, let me know."

The stunned look on his face at her easy acceptance and the flash of pain that followed confirmed what Hope already knew. Clearing his throat, he quickly masked it, his features becoming granite-hard.

"Goodbye, Hope."

Hope didn't move as she watched him drive away. Her heart was heavy as she stood staring at him until he went out of sight. Only then did she run inside to call Law.

* * * *

Almost forty-five minutes later, she shook with nerves as she pulled up to Ace's house just as Law and Zach were pulling away. She got out and closed her door as quietly as possible and ran up to Law, and jumping up on the running board, she leaned in to kiss his cheek. "Thank you."

Law chuckled. "He took a shower and went straight to bed. He should be asleep by now. Hopefully he heard the truck and not your car, but we'd better get out of here before he wakes up or wonders what's taking us so long to pull out."

Zach smiled. "Good luck, honey. We won't be home until noon tomorrow."

Hope waved them off and made her way to the front door, thankful that Law and Zach had left the porch light on. She stepped from the narrow walkway onto the wooden porch, wincing when one of the steps creaked. She froze, barely breathing as she waited to see if Ace would come running out with his gun. When he didn't, she continued, thankful that none of the other boards made any noise.

Lady Luck must have been on her side because the screen door didn't make a sound as she slowly opened it. She didn't have as much luck with the front door, but she hoped the slight sound hadn't been enough to wake him.

She set her purse on the sofa before quietly removing her shoes and jacket. Biting her lip, she decided that it would be better to get undressed out here where she wouldn't wake him.

She wanted him to wake up to find her naked in his bed, her lips on his cock.

The arousal that simmered ever since she talked to Law earlier strengthened as she undressed, and she couldn't wait to surprise the sheriff.

* * * *

Ace heard his brothers leave and turned to his side, knowing that he wouldn't get any sleep tonight. Thoughts of Hope kept his cock hard, his mind racing, and made sleep impossible. He'd made the right decision in not having her come here tonight, though. Seeing those broken windows and the slugs that Rafe found made him want to wrap himself around her to protect her from the rest of the world. His rage at what could have happened made him want to fuck her long and deep, to feel her quiver around him, hear those sweet sounds she made. He needed to feel her wild in his arms, safe and happy and very much alive.

She belonged to him, and he hadn't even been able to stay to help her clean up.

Fuck.

Pounding the pillow, he shifted again, becoming still when he heard a creak. He'd lived in this house for twenty-five years and knew that it came from the second step to the front porch.

Sitting up, he tossed the sheet aside and silently retrieved his gun from the nightstand. The rage inside him turned to ice when he heard the front door open.

They seldom locked doors around here, but they'd started several months ago when trouble came to town. Evidently, Law and Zach had forgotten to lock it when they left and someone had been waiting outside.

He stood, automatically sidestepping the creaky boards in his bedroom and moved silently to the door. Luckily, his eyes had long ago adjusted to the darkness and he knew where every stick of furniture was in his house.

Cracking his door open, he listened intently, pausing when he heard what sounded like the rustle of clothing. He barely managed to stifle a laugh when he heard a thud and softly spoken, but inventive cursing.

Hope.

He'd know that voice anywhere. The extent of his relief nearly brought him to his knees. Clenching his jaw, he turned to open the drawer of his dresser, put the safety back on, and place his gun inside. Holding his breath, he eased the drawer closed again and moved to stand behind it. He should have known she'd given up too easily. If he hadn't been so angry, he might have seen it, but he'd been ready to believe the worst. After all, he'd been expecting it, hadn't he?

His own fierce arousal and the dark mood that plagued him tonight guaranteed a night she would never forget.

He drew in a breath as the bedroom door slowly swung open. He was more than ready for her.

* * * *

Naked and already aroused, Hope tip-toed into Ace's bedroom, holding her breath as she silently approached the bed. She couldn't even see her hand in front of her face and had to feel her way, hoping like hell she didn't run into anything else. Her toe hurt from hitting it on the leg of the sofa, and she didn't want to wake Ace by hitting it again on the bed.

Taking small steps, she reached out a hand in front of her, groping for the bed. She smiled in anticipation as her hand touched the quilt.

A hard band came around her waist, lifting her off her feet, scaring her so badly she screamed for Ace.

"What do we have here?" His deep voice vibrated in her ear, sending a shiver through her.

With her heart pounding nearly out of her chest, she slumped against him in relief, her pulse tripping when the fact that he held her against his hard naked body penetrated. "Damn it, Ace. You scared the hell out of me. I thought someone broke in."

His other hand slid down her body from her breasts to her slit. "Someone did break in. A very naked someone broke into my house in the middle of the night. I'm going to have to deal harshly with her."

She wiggled against him, her thighs already coated with her juices, gasping as he slid a finger into her. "Yes."

"I didn't want to subject you to my mood tonight. You just couldn't leave it alone, could you? This is your last chance to get the hell out of here."

Dropping her head back against his shoulder, she wiggled her bottom against the hard cock pushing against it. She braced her feet against his knees as his finger began to move. "I want all of you, Ace. Not just bits and pieces. I can handle you, Sheriff, in all your moods. I'm not going anywhere."

"We're gonna have to see about that, aren't we. If you stay, you're going to give me every fucking thing I want."

Knowing him well, Hope turned her face to kiss his jaw. "You don't expect me to make it easy for you, do you? If you want my submission, tough guy, you're going to have to earn it. You're going to have to take it."

He withdrew his finger from her slit, running it up the center of her body and leaving a damp trail. "With pleasure."

Shaking with excitement, Hope squealed when he turned and sat at the edge of the bed, tossing her effortlessly over his lap. Without a word, he started spanking her, several sharp slaps in row.

Hope shrieked, kicking her legs. "Why are you spanking me?" It disconcerted her that she couldn't see a thing. She might as well have been blindfolded.

Ace paused to rub the cheeks of her bottom, spreading the heat and making her squirm on his lap. "I don't have to have a reason, now do I, other than I love this tight ass. This belongs to me, doesn't it?"

She reveled in her vulnerable position, but it wasn't enough. Knowing his mood, Hope couldn't even begin to fathom what kinds of things he wanted to do to her, but her absolute trust in him compelled her to push him. For both of them. Their savage needs had to be assuaged, and neither of them would be satisfied until they both let loose completely. She wanted, *needed*, him to take what he wanted from her and make her submit to his every demand.

With her lust for him damned near raging out of control, burning hotter as the heat from his spanking spread to her slit, she did something guaranteed to awaken the dominant beast inside him.

She bit his leg. Hard.

"You brat!" He spanked her harder, several sharp slaps all over her bottom until she let go. "You're really in trouble now. I swear, you would pull a lion's tail." Standing, he lifted her over his shoulder and stormed around the bed, tossing her unceremoniously onto it. With a hand on her belly, he held her in place as he flicked on the small lamp sitting on the nightstand and started rummaging through the drawer. "You're gonna learn not to pull this shit with me."

Hope fought him, her lust spiraling out of control as he made short work of tying her hands above her head. "That's what you think. I'm not scared of you." She struggled to free herself of her bonds, knowing she'd be seriously disappointed if she managed to do it. The entire time, she watched Ace as he went to the closet to retrieve a duffel bag.

He brought it back, dropping it on the floor beside the bed and started taking things from it and placing them near her feet. "Let's see what a smart mouth you have when it's full of cock."

Hope smirked. "Yeah, yeah, yeah. You threatened that before, and I didn't even get a taste. You're full of shit."

The stunned outrage on his face was priceless. His jaw clenched as he reached into the bag again. "I'm fucking every hole you've got tonight. You're gonna be using that smart mouth to beg before long."

"Fuck you."

"No, darlin'. I'm gonna fuck *you*." He overcame her struggles with alarming ease, attaching both of her ankles to a spreader bar, effectively keeping them about three feet apart.

Hope shrieked, thrashing and hitting at him as he untied her wrists. The struggle caused the bunched-up quilt to rub against her slit and made her even wilder. She slapped at Ace's bare chest as he held one of her wrists to attach a cuff to it. Seeing the hook on the cuff, she knew what he planned and fought harder.

"Let go of me, you son of a bitch."

Ace chuckled as he lifted the spreader bar with one hand and attached the cuff to it. "You had your chance and you didn't take it. After tonight, you're not going to be so quick to provoke me."

Her wrist and legs had been attached to the same spreader bar, rendering her nearly immobile. Desperate now, and with her slit leaking more moisture than ever, she punched him in the stomach with her other hand before he could catch it in his.

Ace chuckled again. "You fight like a little girl."

Hope cursed as he managed to attach the cuff to her other wrist and hook it to the spreader bar. "I'm going to get even for this."

Ace yanked the pillow out from under her head and stood, placing it on the edge of the bed. "I'm scared to death. Come here and we'll see if we can't do something about that mouth." He tugged her easily to the side of the bed and placed her head on the pillow. He held the spreader bar high, controlling both her arms and her legs with one hand.

He reached for something at the foot of the bed. "Now you're going to be a good girl and suck my cock until I come. If your teeth touch my cock, your pussy is gonna sting like hell."

Her struggles proved useless, but she froze at his words and looked down to see him holding the small whip he'd used on her the other night. "You're going to whip my clit?"

"And your ass. Until I come. It'll hurt like hell if you use those teeth. Let's see how good you are with that mouth."

Trembling with excitement, Hope still couldn't resist fighting him. He'd already proven to be a more than capable adversary, and she thrilled as the level of erotic tension in the room soared. "I'm not sucking your cock."

Ace lifted a brow and chuckled again, that low, knowing tone driving her wild. "Yes, you are. Now. Open wide so I can fuck that smart mouth of yours."

His cock touched her cheek and she automatically turned to it, remembering at the last second to keep her mouth closed. When the whip came down hard on her clit, she screamed, giving him the opportunity that he needed.

With her head at the edge of the bed and Ace standing over her, Hope closed her lips around the head of his cock as he pushed it into her mouth, moaning as the sharp sting on her clit spread.

"Suck."

Another sharp tap on her clit and she knew she was lost.

He didn't hit it hard, but now that her clit burned, he didn't have to. The slightest tap kept her attention focused there, making it difficult to concentrate on sucking him. Each time she lost her concentration, he tapped her clit again.

Tasting the moisture that leaked from the tip, Hope sucked eagerly as he stroked almost to her throat. She had no choice, anyway, which sent her arousal soaring. Forced to serve him this way, for him to use her mouth for his pleasure, gave her the freedom to let loose, the freedom she found only with him.

Thank God he understood her so well.

When the tingles in her clit started to fade, she stopped sucking and used her tongue. Another sharp tap on her clit had her moaning around his thick heat.

"I said suck. Show me what you can do with that smart mouth. It's nice and quiet now. Maybe you need to have your mouth stuffed with cock more often." He began to move again with slow, shallow thrusts against her tongue.

The need to defy him still urged her to scrape her teeth over him. Smiling around his cock when he hissed, she wasn't prepared when he pushed the bar closer to her chest and brought the end of the whip down on her bottom hole and, startling the hell out of her, following quickly with another to her clit. "If you don't want my teeth on your clit, you'd better not do that again."

Hope groaned, sucking him again, desperate to make him come. Her slit tingled hotly from her clit to her ass, a sensation she'd never before experienced and that threatened her sanity. The need to close her legs, to rub her thighs together had her struggling again, only to gasp when the end of the whip circled her pussy opening.

"You like playing with fire, don't you, baby? Yes, that's it. Suck a little harder. That's a girl." He leaned over her slightly, his strokes becoming deeper. "That's a good girl. Keep those lips closed tight around me. When I come, I want you to swallow every drop."

Hope shuddered as he traced the end of the whip over her clit, teasing her mercilessly as she sucked him deep. Spurred on by his low groans and the tortured hoarseness in his tone, she moaned, thrilling when his cock jumped at the vibration.

His deep groan gave her a split-second warning before his cock jumped again and filled her mouth with his seed.

She swallowed eagerly, sucking him gently as his big body shuddered.

Not at all shy about showing his pleasure, he groaned long and low as he spent himself down her throat. It made her crave her own orgasm even more. When he withdrew from her mouth, she tried to follow, but he held the bar firmly, not permitting it.

He dropped the whip and ran a hand over her breasts. "You're too fucking good at that. Let's see how good you are at staying still."

Arching into his touch, Hope groaned. "I'm not good at it. Make me come." Taking advantage of his momentary lapse in attention, she bent her knees higher and rubbed the spreader bar against her clit. With her clit already hot and tingling, the first touch of the smooth bar felt incredible. Keeping her legs bent, she used her wrists to control the bar and started moving it back and forth over the swollen bundle of nerves. Oh, God. So close.

"Un-fucking-believable!" Ace jerked the spreader bar high again, ignoring her scream of outrage. "You have no fucking patience at all, do you? It's gonna be a long time before you get to come, you brat." With a hand under her bottom and another under her shoulders, he lifted her again, turning her completely around until her bottom lay at the edge of the bed.

Once he settled her in place, he lifted the bar again and picked up the whip. He tapped her tight hole sharply once. "Do you think you're going to get away with rubbing your clit? You don't come until *I* say you can come."

Hope gasped at the sting to her bottom hole, which quickly transformed into sizzling heat. Biting her lip, she waited breathlessly for the tap on her clit. She struggled to hide from him the knowledge that one more tap would send her over. If he knew, he'd never give it. Her eyes widened in shock when he laughed softly and tossed the whip aside.

"You didn't think I was going to let you come so soon, did you? I haven't even played with those sensitive little nipples yet."

Need clawed at her, a force so strong she had no hope of holding it back. Only he could do that. She'd known he would be a dominant lover, but she hadn't counted on him controlling her orgasm so thoroughly. Twisting restlessly, she shuddered to see him reaching into his bag of torture devices.

He straightened, laughing at her look of astonishment when he held up a long feather. "Not what you were expecting?" Holding on to the bar to keep her arms and legs out of his way, he trailed the feather lightly over the inside of her thighs, his eyes flaring at her moans. "Do you know what it does to me to see you this way?" He trailed the feather up her body to flick it back and forth over her nipples. "You'd do anything to be fucked now, wouldn't you? Anything for one little stroke on your clit?"

Hope rocked her hips, her cries desperate now. "Ace, fuck me, damn you."

Ace dropped the feather and delivered three sharp slaps to her slit, one of them hitting her clit, chuckling when she cried out. "You're not in any position to demand anything, brat."

Thrashing harder, Hope panted through the series of little bursts of pleasure that radiated from her clit. Her nipples stood erect, begging for Ace's attention. Her juices flowed from her, her arousal kept on such a sharp edge for so long it hurt. "Ace, no more. I can't take any more." She thrashed from side to side, tears of frustration blurring her vision. Hearing the rip of foil, she shuddered in relief and looked down.

Ace's eyes met hers as he rolled on a condom, and with a start, she realized that he'd released the bar. His eyes narrowed. "Don't you dare move." As soon as he finished, he grabbed the bar again and unhooked her ankles. "Drop your legs and work the kinks out."

Hope obeyed him immediately, frustrated that Ace positioned himself between her thighs, effectively preventing her from rubbing them together. She couldn't stop moaning as he lifted her bottom more fully onto the pillow and bent over her, taking a nipple between his teeth as he lifted the bar over her head and undid her wrists. She heard the bar hit the floor and immediately sank her fingers into his thick hair, gasping when she felt the head of his cock at her pussy entrance.

Lifting his head, he nipped softly at her other breast before easing back to stare down at her and gripping her hips firmly. "Come for me."

Hope shook helplessly now, her eyes held by his hooded gaze as he filled her completely, setting off her orgasm with one deliberate thrust.

She screamed silently as she came hard, the shock of it stealing her breath. Gulping in air, she screamed again, a cry of relief and unimaginable bliss. Her cries continued as Ace touched her clit with light, feathery strokes that made it throb in ecstasy. Wrapping her legs around him, she rocked her hips against his, extending her orgasm until she couldn't take any more. Not until she slumped weakly did it occur to her that Ace hadn't moved.

Turning her head, she blinked her eyes open, her body still trembling in the aftermath. Her pulse leapt at the look of male satisfaction on his face as he held her hips high.

"You are so fucking beautiful."

Hope smiled and arched, moaning as his cock shifted inside her. "So are you. That was magnificent." She stretched, gasping when he pinched a nipple.

His eyes narrowed, his features hardening again. "You didn't think I was done with you yet, did you? There's still the matter of fucking that tight ass of yours. You really didn't think you were going to get away with sneaking in here, did you, baby?" Gripping her hips tighter, he began to move, long, smooth thrusts that had her thrashing again. "I had my gun out. I could have shot you." With incredible precision, he dug at a spot inside her that soon had her on the verge of orgasm again. With each quick thrust, he railed at her. "Don't. Ever. Try. To. Sneak. Up. On. Me. Again."

Unbelievably, Hope's body gathered again, her lust for him seemingly never-ending. Without thinking, she reached down to rub her clit in her need for release, her eyes popping open when he slapped her hand, his thrusts never faltering.

His features hardened even more, his expression as cold as ice, but his eyes flames with challenge. "Who said you could touch yourself? I think it's time you learned who's in charge here." He withdrew from her so suddenly, it left her pussy clenching frantically at the emptiness. He flipped her to her stomach in a move so fast it made her dizzy. He lifted her to her knees, his cock hard against her buttocks as he held her in place.

Hope kicked her feet, pulling at the covers on the bed as she tried to escape to the other side. She both craved and feared what he was about to do, but once again needed him to force her. "No. You're not fucking my ass."

"Oh, yes, baby. I am." Pulling her back, he pushed a thick finger coated with lube into her anus, making her squeal in both surprise and alarm. "You're not going to be able to stop me, but then again, you don't want to, do you? You want me to take you, to force you to submit to me, don't you?"

"No! You're not taking my ass."

Ace froze. "Hope?"

Her ass grasped desperately at his finger as he withdrew it. She needed so badly for him to take her there, to force his cock inside her and make her surrender the most private part of herself to him. She thought he understood her need, but it seemed he had to make sure her protests were just part of her fantasy.

Rising to her knees, she leaned back against him, turning her head to rub her cheek against his chest. She smiled as his arms came around her to caress her breast, lightly stroking her nipple. "I didn't say R-E-D, did I? But if you want my ass, don't expect me to make it easy for you. Fuck it if you can." Pushing away from him, she leapt for the other side of the bed, only to have him catch her by the ankle and pull her back.

He lay on top of her, his weight pressing her into the mattress, easily overcoming her struggles. "You think you're gonna escape from me, brat?" Sitting up slightly, he squeezed more of the lube on his fingertips and used his hard thighs to spread hers wide.

Hope shuddered as he breached her forbidden opening again and shoved in more of the cold lube.

"Two fingers. Yeah, baby. Let's lube you up really good so my cock slides right in. I'm going to open this ass up wide and fuck you until you never forget who you belong to."

Smiling against the smooth sheets, Hope wondered if he realized how often he spoke of their relationship in the future. "Big words, Sheriff. You haven't fucked it yet."

"Big cock going into a virgin ass. This time you're gonna scream my name when you come." He straightened, standing next to the bed again, and pulled her to her knees. With a big hand pressing down on her back, he held her in place to press more of the lube into her. "This tight little ass is gonna burn all around me. You'll be begging me to fuck you hard."

Kicking at him, Hope tried to keep fighting, but the feel of his fingers stroking her so intimately robbed her of reason. When they withdrew, she whimpered, only to cry out when the head of his cock began to press at her tight opening.

Trembling, Hope struggled to accept his invasion as chills went up and down her spine. "No. You're not taking my ass."

Ace chuckled and pressed harder, forcing the tight ring of muscle to give way. "It looks like I already am. Fuck, you're tight. Breathe, baby. No, honey, don't tighten up. I've only got the head inside. Let me get all the way inside you."

Her loud moans sounded desperate and needy to her own ears as she fisted her hands in the bedding and forced her muscles to relax under his relentless invasion. Glad of is firm hold when she tried to pull away, she slipped into the dark world of erotic pleasure. She held her breath, shivers racing up and down her spine as his cock invaded her ass one thick inch at a time.

She'd never felt so taken before. The hard heat that pressed into her made her feel more vulnerable and helpless than ever, the sheer dominance of what Ace did to her more than she could ever have imagined. It burned as he filled her, the feeling of being taken never as extreme as it was right now.

"That's a good girl. This tight little ass is all mine now. I can take it whenever I want to, and there's nothing you can do to stop me." His hand came around to cover her abdomen, his fingers splayed wide as one settled over her clit. "All of this is mine. I can make you come when I want to and deny you whenever I choose."

Hope gulped in air, her whimpers loud and frantic as Ace teased her clit, not touching her enough to make her go over, but keeping her right at the edge. Shivers continued to rack her body, growing stronger by the minute. It felt so foreign, so *invasive*, that she tightened on him, struggling to keep him from going deeper.

"It burns. It's too big."

His voice, sandpaper rough, washed over her. "It's going in, baby. I won't force all of it into you tonight, but I am fucking your ass. You have no choice but to take it, remember? You're in no position to stop me." He began stroking, shallow strokes that took him even deeper. "This ass is mine. I can use it as I see fit. And right now, I want to fuck it. See how the lube lets me slide right in? You can't stop it, baby. It's mine. When I'm ready, I'm going to pinch your clit and make you come really hard. When you do, you're going to milk my cock with those tight muscles, aren't you?"

"No."

Ace bent over her, his hard body hot against hers as he bit her shoulder. "Yes, you will, whether you want to or not. Your body will obey me even if you won't. Yet."

Hope shuddered as his cock went deeper, each slow, smooth thrust taking even more of her.

More of her ass.

More of her heart.

More of her soul.

She latched on to his words like a lifeline, needing the special connection of his voice just as much as she needed his touch. With him wrapped around her, one hand teasing her clit with the other holding a breast and lightly pinching a nipple, she felt him everywhere.

He overpowered her so easily and controlled her responses so completely, she had no choice but to surrender. Nuzzling her neck, his harsh breathing let her know just how much this affected him. "All mine."

Hope arched her neck to give him better access, gasping as his cock pushed deeper. "Yours, to use as you want."

Ace rewarded her with a flick of her clit. "Now this ass is getting thoroughly fucked." He pinched her nipple before he released it and straightened, keeping his finger on her clit as he began to thrust. "Too fucking tight. This ass is gonna get fucked a lot in the future, baby."

Hope swallowed her reply as he began moving faster, the burning in her ass getting hotter as he stretched her and invaded her most private opening with a thoroughness that shook her. Even though he didn't give her all of his cock, the friction and fullness stole her breath, until all she could do was hold on. Nerve endings came alive under his assault as her juices literally soaked her thighs. Taken as never before, she groaned loudly as he began to manipulate her clit.

"Come, baby. Milk my cock."

Overloaded on sensation, Hope couldn't hold back any longer. She screamed Ace's name as her orgasm rolled through her, a strong force that made her body sizzle everywhere. It forced her to clamp down on his cock, and the burning, too-full feeling added another series of smaller orgasms over the first. The relentless strokes on her clit had her ass and pussy clenching desperately while her nipples tingled at the friction of the sheets rubbing against them.

Her head spun dizzily, her entire body caught up in the wave of bliss that washed over her. She cried out weakly as Ace held himself still, his harsh groan filling her with satisfaction that he found the ultimate joy in her body.

Neither one of them moved for several long minutes, their ragged breathing the only sounds in the room.

Hope's body still trembled as Ace withdrew from her and ran a hand over her bottom. She smiled as his lips touched one of the cheeks of her ass but was too tired to lift her head. Hearing him go into the bathroom, she dozed, only to come wide awake when he ran a warm cloth between her legs. She frowned and tried to move away, but he held firm.

"This is mine now. Be still."

Too tired to understand the harshness in his tone, Hope snuggled against the pillow. She'd figure it out tomorrow.

Chapter Thirteen

Hope woke, a little disoriented at first to find herself alone in Ace's bed. A faint glow coming through the window told her it was early morning before she even looked at the clock. Reaching out to run a hand over his side of the bed, she frowned to find the sheet cool to the touch.

Sitting up, she looked around. "Ace?"

Her hand brushed over his pillow and touched a piece of paper. Smiling, she read his bold handwriting.

Went to work. Soak in the tub. Ace.

Shaking her head, she laughed as she crawled out of the bed. No flourishes or sweet declarations of love from him. Bold and to the point as always. She remembered him saying something about having to go to work at three. It was after six now, so he'd been gone for some time.

She missed him already.

Shivering at the cold, she dressed quickly. She'd already discovered that Ace liked to sleep in a cold room, which didn't bother her as long as she had him to snuggle up against. The mornings, though, got downright uncomfortable. The heater kicked on, and she wondered if he'd turned it up for her before he left. It still felt cold without him here.

The house felt too empty, so she made the decision to go home for her bath. Besides, she wanted to put on fresh clothes, not the ones she'd worn here the night before. Wondering what Ace would say if she asked to leave some clothes here, she grimaced. She didn't want to push him at this point. She'd already made remarkable headway into making the hard-headed sheriff see things her way, and she didn't want to ruin it. She'd wait until he suggested it.

She took his note with her when she went out to the kitchen. Finding a pen, she flipped it over and smiled as she wrote her own note on the back of it. She propped it up next to the napkin holder and left, careful to lock the door behind her.

As she drove home, she searched for him on the streets of Desire but didn't see him. Hoping she'd find him at the diner, she raced to get there, grinning when she saw his huge SUV parked out front. She pulled up to the curb and hurriedly undid her seatbelt, smiling when she saw him through the window.

He hadn't seen her yet, and she wanted to get inside and surprise him before he could turn around.

Scrambling from her car, she absently noted the sound of a truck approaching but didn't take her eyes from Ace as he spoke to her mother. She started for the rear of her car to circle it, pleased to see that the diner was full.

Her mother looked up just then, the look of horror on her face startling Hope. She stopped and started to turn to see what scared her mother so badly, alarmed to see a truck driving too close to her. The next instant, the side mirror hit her, and she went flying, her body slamming into her own car before hitting the ground.

Stunned, she lay there, listening as the truck sped away, hardly able to believe what just happened. She heard shouts and the sound of running feet as she tried to sit up, holding her head at the throbbing pain in her temple.

"Don't move! Hope, Oh, God. Talk to me, baby. Where do you hurt? Rafe, go after that fucking truck!"

Ace, looking like she'd never seen him before, bent over her, his hands moving over her body. Her mother knelt at her head while her fathers gathered around, each reaching for her.

"What just happened? Did that truck *hit* me?"

Her mother started crying. "Yes. I saw he was too close. Oh, Hope. How bad are you hurt, honey?"

Her fathers all started talking at once, their voices frantic as they all spoke to her at the same time, and she heard one of them calling the ambulance.

"No. I'm okay. It hit my head." Grabbing Ace's arm with one hand and her mother's with the other, she tried to sit up. "Just help me up and I'll be okay."

The helpless fury on Ace's face as he watched Rafe take off after the truck had her reaching for his arm. "Go ahead. I'm fine."

Ace looked grim. "You're not fine, and I'm not leaving you this time. The ambulance is on its way."

Alarmed at the number of people who stood around staring at her, Hope struggled to sit up again, thwarted by her fathers. "Let me up. The ground's wet, and I don't like feeling like a sideshow."

Hunter Ross looked over Ace's shoulder, his hard expression softening. "We'll get rid of all these people. You okay, honey?"

Hope nodded, gasping at the pain. "Just a headache. Thanks, Hunter."

Ace held her hand as her mother gathered her in her arms. Her fathers knelt with them as they waited for the ambulance to arrive, but Hope couldn't take her eyes from Ace. He looked harder and colder than she'd ever seen him.

She shivered at the misery in his eyes as he looked down at her, and she could actually feel the distance between them growing with each passing second. She didn't understand it at all and tried to smile at him, aching for him to smile back at her. Although he tightened his grip on her hand, he looked away as though unable to meet her eyes.

"The ambulance is here." Bending close, he brushed her jaw with his lips. "I'm sorry, baby."

Although he stood and stayed with her as the paramedics loaded her into the ambulance, he wouldn't meet her eyes again.

* * * *

Hours later, the doctor released Hope, telling her how lucky she was that nothing was broken. Diagnosing her with only a mild concussion, he discharged her. "I talked to Dr. Hansen, and he assured me that you would be better off at home and that there are several people to look out for you."

As her mother started forward, Charity urged her back to her seat and approached the doctor. "I live with her. If you give me the instructions for her care, I'll make sure she's watched."

Hope shared a smiled with her mother as Charity peppered the doctor with questions. "The doctor will be glad to get rid of me by the time she's through. Where are my clothes?"

She'd shooed her fathers out about an hour ago, knowing they needed to get back to the diner, which left her alone with her mother and sister.

Accepting the clothes from her mother, she looked up. "Where's Ace?" Although she tried to keep the hurt from her tone, she didn't quite manage it. "I thought he would be here."

Her mother patted her arm. "If you'd seen the look on Ace's face when we loaded you into the ambulance, you wouldn't have to ask. He feels guilty as hell that another woman got hurt, literally on his watch. It infuriated him even more that it was you. Did you see the way he reached for you right away, but your fathers got in the way. I think he realized that he hadn't claimed you yet and it hit him hard. He'll have to come to grips with that before he sees you again. It wouldn't surprise me at all to find out he beat the hell out of somebody before we get home and that he already spoke to your dads about claiming you."

* * * *

Lying on the sofa, Hope flicked channels, bored out of her mind. Her fathers already had lunch ready when they got back, which she ate with Charity and her mother. After assuring both of them that she was fine, her mother reluctantly went back to the diner. Since then either her mother or one of her fathers came up to check on her every hour.

Since the club was closed today, Charity offered to play cards with her, but Hope's head hurt too much to concentrate, which also meant she couldn't read. Bored, irritable, and feeling sorry for herself because Ace hadn't called or come by, she punched the throw pillow and tried to get into a more comfortable position.

She ached *everywhere*.

She still needed a bath but didn't feel like getting up to take one. Feeling grungy just made her mood even worse.

She didn't blame Charity for leaving to get a few movies to watch. She'd have made an excuse to leave, too, if she had to put up with herself. She hadn't slept much at Ace's place, and it had started to catch up with her. When the image on the television started to blur, she turned it off and closed her eyes, deciding that taking a nap while she waited for Charity. Her headache seemed to be easing and it didn't take long before she started to sink into sleep and dreams of Ace.

"Hope? Come on, honey. Wake up. Let me see those beautiful brown eyes."

Hope blinked, smiling when Ace's face filled her vision, until she remembered. "You son of a bitch. Get out of here."

One of Ace's brows went up. "Is that any way to talk to your future husband?" His hands slid under her, lifting her carefully before he turned and sat on the sofa, cradling her on his lap.

Hope blinked and put a hand to her head. "I must be dreaming. No, I got hit in the head harder than I thought and I'm hallucinating." She reached with one hand to pinch the other arm, but Ace stopped her.

"Stop that. God knows you're going to have enough bruises as it is. You're awake and fine, except for being banged up to all over." Bending, he brushed her lips with his. "Thank God you're hard-headed. I've been thinking about you all day. I called the diner several times to check on you, but I didn't want to call here in case you were sleeping. I had several things to do so I could be here with you tonight. I left Linc and Rafe on their own and came over as soon as I could. How do you feel?"

Still taken aback at his reference to being her husband, Hope frowned up at him. "Like I've been run over by a truck. Did you say something about getting married?"

His eyes narrowed in that arrogant way she loved so much. "I did. We are. Just as soon as you're feeling better."

Hope cuddled into him. If this was a dream, she didn't want to wake up. "You didn't ask."

Ace ran his hand gently down her side. "I'm not taking any chances. I don't know how I lived without you for so long, but now that I've had you, I can't give you up." He surprised the hell out of her by gathering her close and burying his face in her hair. "When I saw the look of horror on your mother's face, I turned just as you screamed my name and went flying through the air. I thought it would be the last thing I heard you say. And then I didn't have the right to pull you away from your fathers and hold you myself. And it was my own fault. I'm so sorry."

Hope wrapped her arms around him, hiding a wince as he hugged her fiercely. "Ace, honey. I'm okay. I love you, you know. You're not getting rid of me that easily." It alarmed her when a shudder went through his big body.

He lifted his head, his lips hovering over hers. "I love you so damned much I can't stand it. I swear, I'm going to do everything in my power to be the kind of husband you need. Damn it, I'm hurting you." He loosened his hold, rubbing a hand up and down her back. "You're so damned little. I'll never hurt you, baby."

Hope grinned and kissed him soundly, a little surprised when he eased back to meet her kiss tenderly. His kiss warmed her, so sweet it brought tears to her eyes. "I know you'll never hurt me, Ace. What a thing to say."

Ace averted his eyes and started playing with her fingers. "How are you feeling? Charity told me you're grouchy and that your head hurts."

She slumped against him, grinning. "Not anymore. You finally see that I was right all along, something you'll have to get used to, and that we belong together. I love you. You love me. We're getting married. Life doesn't get any better."

"Except that you're sore as hell from getting hit by a truck. What the hell were you doing there anyway? I left you in bed with the covers all tucked around you."

Hope snuggled into him, his clean, fresh scent reminding her that she still needed a bath. For the first time she noticed that he'd obviously showered after work and changed. "I got lonely without you, so I decided to come home to take a bath." She wrinkled her nose at him. "I still haven't, but now that you're here I'd better shower."

Ace stood with her still in his arms. "Come on, I'll give you a bath and a rubdown."

Hope rubbed her cheek against him. "I'm definitely looking forward to that rubdown. Hey, by the way, did you catch the guy who hit me?"

A muscle worked in his strong jaw. "Not yet, but it's only a matter of time. Rafe found the truck along the side of the road with the engine running, but the driver was gone. We'll find him, and when we do, he'll pay for what he did to you." Once in the bathroom, he set her on her feet and started drawing a bath.

A little frightened at Ace's tone, Hope started to undress. "Do you think it's the same guy who's been causing all the trouble around here?"

"I have no idea. We didn't get any reports of anything happening last night, but he's already shot out your windows. You and Charity are going to be watched closely until we figure out what the hell's going on."

Ace bathed her, washing her gently, his expression becoming harder with each bruise he saw. When she stood, he helped her out of the tub and gently patted her dry.

"Hope, I'm home." Charity's voice, laced with amusement, came from the living room. "I see you have company."

Hope smiled and yelled back. "I'm in here with my fiancé. We'll be out in a bit."

Ace didn't smile back as she'd expected. Instead, he sat on the edge of the tub and ran his hand gently over the rather impressive assortment of bruises over her hip and bottom. If possible, his face hardened even more. He swallowed heavily and looked up at her.

"Did I cause any of these?"

Nothing he could have said would have shocked her more. Aghast, Hope wrapped her arms around his shoulders and pulled him against her breasts. "No! Ace, I landed on my butt. This is all from this morning. What you did to me last night felt wonderful. None of these are from you, but if you and I bruise each other during sex, Sheriff, I'm a big girl. I can take it."

Charity started beating on the door. "Your fiancé? Ace proposed? Sheriff, my sister's black and blue all over. You'd better not be trying to get lucky."

Staring up at Hope, Ace nodded once, but still looked grim. "I'm already lucky. Talk to your sister. When you're done, come into your bedroom. I'll give you a rubdown and give you your ring." He stood and wrapped a large, dry towel around her before opening the door and stepping back as Charity raced in.

* * * *

Ace left the two of them alone and went out to the living room to retrieve his duffel bag, a little surprised to find Beau Parrish standing near the window. "What are you doing here?"

"Are they in danger?"

Grabbing his bag, he sank into a chair. "I don't know, but I'm not taking any chances. I'll be sleeping here tonight. We should have some answers by tomorrow. We're waiting for results on the prints."

Turning away from the window, Beau came to sit on the sofa, looking toward the bathroom where the women talked excitedly. "You and Hope really getting married?"

Ace nodded and sat back, closing his eyes. Hell, he was tired. He hadn't slept more than an hour or two the night before, and after the adrenaline rush when Hope had been hit, he'd been going non-stop all day. "Yeah, as soon as she feels stronger."

"Congratulations."

Ace opened his eyes. "Thanks. How are you and Charity doing?"

Beau grimaced. "She's still trying to keep distance between us. I've been trying to convince her to let me stay here tonight, but if you're staying…"

Ace shrugged. "I'll watch over them tonight, but I think today was an accident. There's no way anyone could have known she'd be there at that time. She's usually still sound asleep at that hour, and if she goes to the diner for breakfast, she walks down the back stairs and goes right into the kitchen. I think he hit her by accident."

"Why the hell didn't he stop then?"

Ace scrubbed a hand over his face, frustrated and exhausted. "I don't know. It leads me to believe it's the same person, but it's not the same truck. The truck he had today was a rental."

Beau sat forward, glancing over as the women came out of the bathroom. "So if he rented it, can't you find out who it is?"

Ace looked over his shoulder to see Hope approach, wearing a thick, fuzzy robe. Reaching out a hand, he pulled her onto his lap and wrapped both arms around her. "He rented it under an assumed name. We checked the name he used. It's a ninety-year old man in a nursing home, one who was seen eating breakfast at that time by at least two dozen people."

Hope cuddled into him. "I want my ring."

Charity shook her head and sat in the other chair, sitting as far from Beau as possible. "She's always been greedy."

Hope stuck out her tongue at her sister. "I want his ring on my finger before he changes his mind. He thinks I'm too little, and I'm afraid he'll throw me back." Looking up at him, she smiled adoringly. "I want witnesses."

Running his hand lightly over her fuzzy, robe-covered hip, he couldn't help but think about the bruises under his hand. "I'm not letting you get away, baby." He reached into the bag beside the chair and rummaged around until his hand closed over the small box. Handing it to her, he kissed her hair as she opened it, loving the feel of having her safe and warm in his arms.

"I figured a woman with as much fire as you should have a ring to match." A fire that could have easily been extinguished today.

Smiling at her excited squeal, he took the ruby ring out of the box and placed it on her finger, raising her hand to kiss her palm. "Come on and let me give you your rubdown so you can go to sleep. I'm going to have to wake you up several times tonight."

Hope jumped up, trying to hide her wince, but Ace saw it. "Are you kidding? I have to go tell Mom and the dads."

Charity waved her back. "They'll be up later. Go let Ace give you a rubdown. Sheriff, you look beat. I'll wake her tonight. You get some sleep."

Knowing he'd be reliving seeing Hope get hit by that truck every time he closed his eyes, he shook his head. "No. I'll do it. I don't have to be in until late tomorrow. Rafe and Linc are taking care of everything and know where to find me if something comes up. Stop bouncing around before you hurt yourself even more."

Hope leaned over him, giving him an enticing peak at the curves beneath the robe. "I can see that you and I are going to butt heads quite a bit."

Ace fisted his hand in the front of her robe and carefully pulled her back onto his lap. "Your hard head has had about all it can take today." His cell phone rang, interrupting him from saying anything further. Holding Hope still with one hand, he reached beside the chair to where he'd dropped his cell phone on top of the duffel bag.

"Tyler."

"Ace, it's Linc. I just got a phone call here that you might be interested in. A man called and said, 'I didn't mean to hit the girl,' and hung up."

Ace met Hope's eyes. "Is that all he said?"

Linc's anger came through loud and clear. "Yeah. The son of a bitch hung up before I could say anything. We're trying to trace the call now, but on the caller ID it showed up like one of those prepaid phones. He probably ditched it already. There are so many prints in the truck that it's going to take forever to sort them out, so I doubt if it's going to be any help. A copy of the surveillance tape from the rental place is on its way. Let's hope we can get something from that."

"I want this bastard. Let me know the second the tape gets there."

"Will do. How's Hope?"

"Sore and sassy." At her grin, he tightened his hold to pull her closer against his chest, vowing to himself that he would do whatever he had to in order to be the kind of husband she needed. "I must be out of my mind to be marrying someone like her."

"No shit! Congratulations."

When Hope bunched her hand into a fist and hit his chest, he almost retaliated by pinching her bottom until he remembered. Instead, he cuddled her closer. "Thanks. Call me if you hear anything else." He disconnected, absently listening to Hope and Charity talk about wedding plans.

Christ, he loved her. "Come on, honey. Let me give you a massage and then you can talk all you want to."

* * * *

Hope looked pointedly at the duffel bag and leaned close to whisper in his ear. "Are there any surprises for me in there?"

Ace nodded. "As a matter of fact, there is." He reached down to rummage for something and came back with a bottle. "Jesse sent this. She said that Clay and Rio used it to rub her down when she was sore."

Accepting the bottle of vanilla scented massage oil, Hope leaned close to whisper in his ear. "You know this stuff is flavored, too?"

"Is it?"

"Yep. Come on. I want my massage."

Once in her room, Ace closed and locked the door behind them. "Let me get a towel so I don't get this stuff on the sheets."

Hope helped him smooth the towel over the sheet, undid her robe to let it puddle at her feet on the floor, and climbed up onto it, groaning as her muscles protested. "Are you any good at this?"

Ace's lips twitched. "I haven't had any complaints. Lay still."

Stretched out on her belly, Hope closed her eyes, shivering when the oil drizzled over her back. The bed dipped, and she felt the denim of Ace's jeans brush her leg only moments before his hands settled over her back and began to smooth the oil in.

"Would you relax? You're wound up tighter than a drum. I won't hurt you."

Hope frowned and looked over her shoulder at him. "I'm not afraid you'll hurt me. I'm naked, on a bed, and your hands are on me. I'm aroused, idiot, not scared." Waiting for some sort of retaliation for calling him an idiot, Hope stilled when Ace kissed her shoulder.

"My mistake. I'll take care of you, baby. Just lay there and let me do all the work."

Melting under his hands, Hope moaned as he slowly, methodically loosened all of the muscles in her back. "That feels so good." Unsurprised that she slurred her words, she smiled against the pillow, coming alert when he parted her thighs and drizzled more oil onto them.

Ace kept his massage gentle as he slowly worked on the muscles, his slick fingers sliding easily over her skin.

Hope tried to stay still but couldn't. Her juices coated her thighs, blending with the fragrant oil. Her pussy clenched every time Ace's fingers brushed against her slit, heightening her arousal while loosening her muscles so thoroughly she had trouble moving. When he brushed her slit again, Hope moaned.

"Ace."

"Did I hurt you?" His touch gentled immediately.

"No. I need to come. Every time you put your hands on me, you stir me up."

Ace chuckled softly. "I'm trying to make you feel better, not arouse you."

"You're accomplishing both. Don't you even think of stopping until you make me come. You took my vibrator."

"I brought it with me."

Hope turned to look over her shoulder. "You did?"

Ace pressed against her back until she lay flat again. "I did. Now be still so I can finish with this side and turn you over."

"I hit my butt hard."

He bent to kiss her bottom. "I see that, and it's black, blue, purple and some colors I've never seen before. Thank God it's well padded."

Hope tried to turn again, but a hand on her back prevented it. "Are you trying to say I have a big ass?"

Oil drizzled on her bottom. "No. Just a well padded one. It's perfect. Now be quiet so I can finish. You're supposed to go to sleep."

"I will, I promise, just as soon as you make me come."

"You are such a brat."

"Yeah, but you love me this way."

"God help me."

"Think of how bored you'd be with someone who didn't fight back." Hope said it playfully but meant it, worried sometimes that he wouldn't understand her need to be overpowered.

"With you, I don't think boredom is a problem I'll have."

"You bet your great ass it won't. I'm going to keep you on your toes, Sheriff."

"Or talk me to death. Would you please be quiet? I want you to relax."

"Make me."

Ace slid a finger through her juices and circled her pussy opening. "If you're still and quiet, I'll use the vibrator on you when I turn you over and make you come really hard. If you keep fidgeting and talking, you'll get no relief at all."

Hope moaned as her clit throbbed in response to his promise. "I'll be good."

Ace gently massaged the cheeks of her bottom. "You're always good, baby. Except when you're bad."

"I like to be bad."

Ace sighed. "Yes, baby. I know."

His flat reply worried her, but she kept quiet except for her soft moans as he tenderly massaged every inch of her hips and bottom. His firm touch turned her bones to water as he massaged her thighs again before moving on to her calves and feet.

She'd never before thought of her feet as erogenous zones, but in Ace's hands they were.

He stroked his thumbs up her arch, almost, but not quite, tickling her. Instead, his firm touch sent her pulse racing and created an answering pull at her clit.

The sensation of having his fingers working the oil between each toe almost made her come. "Ace, oh, God. How the hell do you do that?"

"Shh." He finished with her feet before moving back up to her calves again. "Time to roll over, honey."

Hope felt as though she floated and was grateful for his strength as he lifted her and carefully turned her over. "I'm horny, but I can't move. You've melted me again." Her heart skipped a beat as she watched him uncap the oil.

His indulgent smile drove her need higher. "If I'm not mistaken, darlin', that's just the way you like it. Now, shush. I've got work to do."

By the time he finished her legs, she trembled uncontrollably. "Aaace...do something."

Moving up between her thighs, he propped them on his own, spreading them, and smiled down at her as he poured a little more of the oil over her belly.

"You are absolutely the most impatient woman I've ever met."

Hope frowned at him. "I don't want to hear about any of your other women." She held up her left hand and tapped her ring with her thumb. "You belong to me now. It's not my fault you're so sexy. You've got me all riled up, and you're not doing anything about it. I thought the men in Desire are supposed to keep their women satisfied."

Ace began to massage her breasts, paying particular attention to her sensitive nipples. "You'll be plenty satisfied, brat. Does that feel good, honey? Do you hurt anywhere?"

Hope gripped his forearms, thrilling at the play of muscle there as his hands moved over her breasts. "It feels wonderful." The oil coating them made it easy for his hands to slide, the gentle caress tugging at her clit. Pushing against him with her thighs, she rocked but couldn't ease the ache there. "My clit throbs. I think it needs a massage. I'm empty inside. Ace, please take me."

"No. The last thing you need is sex. Just relax. I'll take care of you, baby."

Hope groaned in frustration when his hands left her breasts, only to grin with anticipation when she saw the vibrator in his hand. "That belongs to me, Sheriff."

Ace turned it on and smiled as he touched it against a nipple. "I use it better."

Hope closed her eyes on a moan, frustrated because Ace's hand on her belly kept her from moving as he lightly moved the vibrator down her body. When he ran it ever so lightly over her folds, she cried out, squirming.

"Relax, honey. I'll give you what you need."

He turned the vibrator off and tossed it aside, crooning to her when she whimpered. "Shh, I'll take care of you, baby." He slid a slick finger into her, unerringly finding that magical spot inside her. His other hand pressed gently against her mound, the thumb sliding repeatedly over her clit sending her into orbit.

Ace kept her legs parted, her thighs over his as he manipulated her clit, dragging out her orgasm and quickly throwing her into another.

Trembling, she reached for him, breathing a sigh of relief when he took her hand in his. She shuddered when he bent to kiss her folds and worked his way up her body to her lips.

"Ace…"

"Shh." He brushed his lips over hers, gently cradling her against him. "I love you, baby. Go to sleep."

Hope couldn't even lift her arm to stop him when he got up and had to force her eyes open to grumble. "Ace, don't go."

"I'm not going anywhere. I just want to cover you up before you get cold." He pulled the sheet and blanket over her, settling in next to her and turning off the light. "When you go to sleep, I'm going into the other room for a bit. I want to check in with Rafe and Linc. Call out if you need me."

Snuggling against his warmth, Hope nodded drowsily. "Sleep with me tonight."

"I will, baby."

"Ace, don't you want to make love?"

"Not tonight, honey. Once you're not so sore I'll make love to you as much as you want."

"Promise?"

"Promise. Go to sleep."

She needed no further urging.

Chapter Fourteen

Hope woke the next morning, disappointed to find the bed beside her empty. With a sigh, she snuggled into the pillow beside her that still carried a faint trace of Ace's scent.

Since she was in bed alone, she could think of no reason to stay there. She rolled and sat up, groaning when her muscles protested. Coming to her feet, she looked up as her bedroom door opened.

Charity stood in the doorway, her expression full of concern as she looked over Hope's nakedness. "Ouch. You're awfully colorful, honey. You okay?"

Hope straightened and reached for the robe draped at the foot of her bed. "I'm fine. As soon as I take a hot shower, I'm sure I'll be even better. Do you know when Ace left?"

Charity came into the room and started to make Hope's bed. "Early." Seeing the towel and oil-stained sheets, she efficiently stripped it instead. "He looked like hell, Hope. I don't think he slept all that much. You, on the other hand, slept like the dead. I've been looking in on you since Ace left and you hadn't even moved."

Hope pulled a bra and panties from a drawer, holding them away from her body so she didn't get oil on them. "Ace kept waking me up to ask me questions. I think somewhere around dawn I told him that if he woke me up again I'd hit him."

Gathering the sheets. Charity started out of the room. "I'm sure that scared him."

Turning, she smiled at the empty doorway and shouted after her sister. "You know, you're turning into a real smart ass. I must be rubbing off on you!"

"God forbid."

Laughing, Hope hurried into the bathroom, anxious to see Ace again in his uniform.

* * * *

Dressed in jeans and a long-sleeved shirt to hide her bruises, Hope walked into the Sheriff's Department, stopping to introduce herself to Ace's new dispatcher before making her way to his office.

Finding the door open, she went in, coming to a halt at the jolt to her heart. He sat behind his desk doing paperwork, his eyes lifting to hers, the flash of heat and emotion in them like a blast to her senses. When he quickly shuttered them, she smiled, deciding to play this light for the moment. "Sheriff, I'd like to report a missing person."

Ace dropped the pen he'd been using onto his desk, his chair creaking as he sat back. A faint smile tugged at his lips. "You would? Who's missing?"

Hope closed the door, locking it with a deliberate click. "My lover. He was in bed with me last night but when I woke up this morning, he was gone."

Lifting a brow, Ace laced his fingers over his flat stomach. "Maybe he had to go to work."

Moving into the room, she circled his desk, glancing at him often as she idly picked things up and put them back down again. "No, that can't be it. He wouldn't leave me without kissing me goodbye, would he?"

Ace's eyes twinkled, a thrill going through her that he enjoyed her teasing. "Perhaps your lover didn't want to disturb you when you were sleeping so peacefully. Or, maybe he *did* kiss you goodbye and you slept through it."

Hope moved some papers aside to sit on the corner of his desk, her leg brushing against his thigh as she swung it back and forth. "Really? Do you think so? I wonder where he kissed me."

Ace reached out to take her hand in his, his lips twitching. "Probably your shoulder. How do you feel?"

Running her fingers over the backs of his hands, she pouted. "Deserted. I woke up all soft and scented from the oil and there was nobody there to feel it." Shaking her head, she blew out a breath. "A thing like that could give a woman a real inferiority complex." She ran a fingertip over a ring he wore on his right hand, a ring she'd never seen him wear before.

Ace's eyes darkened. "I felt all that softness next to me all night long. I guess I should make it up to you for leaving you alone, though."

Intrigued, Hope grinned and lifted his hands to her breasts. "Really? How?"

Ace turned his wrists to take her hands in his, smiling at her frown as he brushed his lips over her knuckles. "I have a present for you, one that I think you'll like."

Still smiling, she leaned closer, running a hand over his chest. "You look like sin in your uniform, Sheriff. Does my present have anything to do with those handcuffs?"

His eyes flashed, but he quickly averted his gaze. A muscle worked in his jaw as he opened one of his desk drawers and drew out a box. He handed it to her, his face devoid of all expression. "I think you'll like wearing this more than handcuffs."

Hope accepted the box, not at all surprised to see that her hand shook. Something about Ace seemed a little off today, a distance she badly wanted to close. "I don't know. This is gonna have to be really good to compete with being handcuffed by you."

She looked down and opened the box, her breath catching at the beautiful necklace inside. A gold chain held a square-cut ruby pendant, the stone almost exactly matching the ring he'd given her, and the ring he now wore.

"Oh, Ace! It's beautiful. This means I belong to you."

Tears blurred her vision as she reached for him. Elated to be marrying him, this added even more. Every Dom in Desire gave his sub a necklace to match the ring he wore. By giving her this, Ace proclaimed his desire to be her Dom as well as her husband.

Ace looked uncharacteristically uncomfortable. "Yes, you do. But I didn't get you a choker. I thought this suited you better."

Holding it out to him, Hope blinked back tears. "Will you put it on me?"

Nodding, Ace took it from her, staring down at it and running his thumb over the stone. "If you'd like another stone, I can get it changed. I just wanted it to match your ring."

Hope plopped onto his lap, lifting her hair so he fasten the necklace around her neck. "I thought you said you picked a ruby because you liked my fire. Have you changed your mind?"

Ace fastened the necklace and hugged her. "Of course not. Whatever you like is fine with me. How are you today, besides feeling *deserted*?"

Hope wiggled on his lap, wrapping her arms around his neck and lifting her face for a kiss. "A little stiff, but then again, so are you." She giggled, wiggling again, her panties becoming damp as his cock continued to harden beneath her bottom.

Ace obliged her, kissing her deeply, his hands gentle on her waist.

Threading her fingers through his hair, she met his kiss enthusiastically, pouring her need for him into it. She rubbed her breasts against his chest and tangled her tongue with his in an erotic dance that soon had both of them breathing heavily.

His hands tightened briefly when she wiggled again. He broke off his kiss, his smile tender. "I'm always stiff when I'm around you. Why don't you go home and rest today? I can tell by the way you move that you're still sore."

A little seed of dread planted itself in her stomach. Ace kept looking away from her as though uncomfortable meeting her gaze. "Ace, is something wrong?"

His expression hardened. "Other than the fact that women in Desire keep getting hurt on my watch? Or do you mean the fact that I'm the damned sheriff and can't even keep my own woman safe?"

Lifting her from his lap, he stood and stepped away from her. "Why don't you go home and rest? I'm in a shitty mood today."

Reaching out to touch his arm, she closed the distance between them again, at least physically. "Ace, I don't mind your bad moods. I have them, too, you know. Am I supposed to stay away from you when I'm angry or sad? Besides, none of this is your fault. You can't be everywhere at once, and you sure as hell can't anticipate what anyone else will do."

Ace nodded, not looking the least bit convinced. "I've got work to do."

More than a little concerned, Hope placed her hands on his chest and looked up at him through her lashes. "Will I see you tonight?"

Shaking his head, Ace stepped away from her and moved to the window. "No. I'm on patrol tonight. Go home and take it easy. I'll call you tomorrow."

Hope walked up behind him and rubbed his back. "But you're already tired. How are you going to work all day and then all night?"

He glanced over his shoulder. "I'm going home in a bit to sleep for a while and then I'll be back."

"I'll go to your house and—"

"No, Hope. I said I needed to get some sleep, something I won't do if you're there."

"But—"

"No." He turned to take her in his arms and kissed her forehead. "Are you going to be a wife who nags all the time?"

Wrinkling her nose, Hope put her hands on his shoulders and rubbed against him. "If I get out of hand, I guess you'll have to spank me."

"Go home, honey. I'll call you tomorrow."

Still unsettled, Hope left his office.

And the seed began to grow.

* * * *

Hope turned to look at the clock on her nightstand for about the fourth time. Groaning, she buried her face in the pillow, knowing she wouldn't be able to sleep until she talked to Ace.

Cursing herself for her insecurity, she reached for her cell phone. After turning on the low light next to her bed, she propped a pillow behind her and stared down at the phone. Running her thumb over the small screen she debated her decision, and knew she had no choice.

Damn it. He was driving her crazy. She knew she'd never get to sleep until she heard his voice.

She dialed his number, hugging a pillow to her chest while she waited for him to answer.

"Tyler."

"Ace? Hi, it's me. Um, Hope. Um...are you okay?"

"Of course. Why wouldn't I be? What's wrong, honey? Why are you still awake? Are you in pain?"

Hope turned to her side, still hugging the pillow. "No, I soaked in the tub before I got into bed."

"Headache?"

"I took some aspirin and it's gone, Ace. I'm fine. I called to talk about you." Pushing the pillow away, she sat up. "Did you get any sleep?"

"Yes. Hope, what's this about? What's wrong?"

Hoping her habit of speaking her mind wouldn't cost her to lose the only man she'd ever love, she took a deep breath and let her anger free. "That's what the hell I want to know. Don't you want me any more?"

Ace cursed. "What the hell are you talking about now? Just this afternoon I gave you the pendant to match my ring. Didn't I ask you to marry me?"

"But the necklace doesn't mean anything to you!" Hope swallowed a sob. "You didn't touch me."

"Of course I touched you." The weariness in his voice convinced her more than anything that her instincts were right.

"Look, Ace, I know something's wrong. If you've got a problem with me, spill it."

The heavy silence scared her more than she'd like to admit. The frustrated sigh following it didn't make her feel any better.

"I'm sorry, Hope. I knew I'd handled you wrong."

"You didn't *handle* me at all."

"Is that what this is all about? You got hit by a truck, Hope."

"I know that, damn it! I just need to feel close to you. You're making me sound like some sex-crazed—"

"What are you wearing?"

His silky tone wiped away a little of her apprehension. Frowning, she looked down at herself and grimaced. Well she could lie, couldn't she? Leaning back against the pillows, she smiled. "I'm wearing a sexy black nightgown. It's all lace so you can see everything. That is, you could see everything if you were here."

Ace's soft chuckled relieved her somewhat. "Liar. You're wearing one of those big cotton T-shirts you like to sleep in."

Hope shot up. "How do you know that?" Getting out of bed, she went to the window to peer through the blinds. "How do you know what I sleep in? Every time I sleep with you, I sleep naked."

"Of course you do. Never mind how I know what you sleep in." His voice took on a slight edge. "You lied to me, baby."

Hope shivered at his tone, her nipples pebbling against the big cotton T-shirt she wore. She licked her suddenly dry lips. "So, what are you gonna do about it?"

Another of those deafening silences unnerved her.

Ace sighed. "Baby, I'm on patrol. Get a good night's sleep and we'll talk tomorrow. Good night, honey."

After he disconnected she stared down at the phone, placing it carefully on the nightstand so she didn't give in to the urge to throw it. Mentally replaying the conversation, she tried to shake the uncomfortable feeling that talking to Ace had changed nothing.

* * * *

When Ace pulled into the parking lot of Desire's hotel restaurant two nights later, Hope could barely contain her excitement.

She waited for him to come around for her, just sitting there staring up at him when he opened the door to help her out.

Staring up at him, she could hardly believe he was hers.

Smiling, she reached out to grab handfuls of his hair to pull him closer.

He bent close, touching her lips with his. "Never, for one minute, doubt how much I love you."

Holding onto him, she shivered at the feel of his hands settling on her waist. Meeting his kiss, she poured herself into it, desperate to surrender to him.

All too soon, Ace broke off his kiss, his hands gentle as he lifted her from the seat, sliding her down the length of his body to set her on her feet.

"Are you sure you're all right? No more headaches?"

With their arms around each other, they crossed the parking lot. "Ace, I told you that I'm fine. Listen, the guy wasn't going that fast. I've had bruises before and I will again. Lighten up, will you?"

She reached down to grab a handful of his fine ass. "I think I already showed you, Sheriff, that I'm tough."

Ace grabbed her hand, holding it in his. "But you're not handling tenderness very well, are you?"

Uneasy, she looked up at him from beneath her lashes and poked his hard stomach. "I can handle tenderness. Just don't you dare back off because you're scared of hurting me."

Opening the door, he ushered her into the restaurant. "Don't be ridiculous. I thought we'd agreed that I was in charge."

Hope lifted a hand in greeting to several people she knew. "Are we eating in a privacy booth? I wore the dress with the buttons on purpose."

"No. Come on. You haven't eaten since breakfast."

Stunned, Hope blinked up at him as he seated her. "How the hell do you *know* this stuff?"

With a small smile, Ace took his own seat and opened the menu. "I know you better than you know yourself. Trust me to take care of you, baby. What would you like to eat?"

Something in his voice bothered her. She pushed her menu aside and leaned toward him. "Ace, I promise you that I'm okay. You're scaring me. What I really need from you is to know that things haven't changed."

Ace smiled indulgently, patting her hand as he looked back at the menu. "We're getting married soon, baby. Everything is fine and will get even better. Now, what would you like to eat?"

Chapter Fifteen

A week after the truck clipped her, Hope was going out of her mind. She knew that not being able to catch the guy who did it frustrated the hell out of Ace, but if he didn't make love to her soon, she would explode.

"What the hell's wrong with you? You're in love and engaged to one of the sexiest men on God's green earth and you're acting like somebody stole your favorite toy."

Hope looked up from the mess she'd made on her desk to glare at her sister. "If Ace doesn't screw my brains out soon I'm going to hurt him."

Charity blinked and plopped down into the chair in front of Hope's desk. "I don't get you. You're mad because he's not screwing you after you got hit by a truck? You're black and blue all over!"

Hope shrugged. "The bruises are almost gone." Sitting back, she sighed. "I know it sounds crazy, but he hasn't touched me in any sexual way since he gave me a massage. He's so gentle with me, it's as though he's afraid I might break."

"What's wrong with that?"

Hope sat up and played with a paper clip. All week she'd kept her fears to herself. She had to tell someone or she would burst. "The night of the accident, do you remember when he was in the bathroom with me?"

"Yeah. So?"

"Well, he was looking over the bruises and he got this really strange, almost defeated look on his face. Anyway, he asked me if *he* caused any of those bruises. We had some pretty rough sex the night before, I mean, it was fabulous—"

"Spare me."

Tossing the clip back onto her desk, Hope leaned back again, propping her feet up on the corner. "Anyway, he seemed really upset about it. I told him that we'll probably give each other bruises, but I'm a big girl. Hell, I get bruised all the time running into things. And I like rough sex. Sure, there are times when slow and easy might be nice, but I don't want him thinking that I can't take it. Damn it, Charity, I want Ace back. What he said that night is going to drive me crazy until we make love again. I can understand that he'd want to be careful for a little bit, but I need to feel close to him again."

"But he comes to take you to dinner almost every night."

"And I love being with him. But other than mind-blowing kisses, he doesn't touch me. I'm telling you, something's wrong."

Charity smiled and leaned back. "Then do something about it. I've never known you to sit back and wait for something before. Maybe he's waiting for you to make the first move so he knows you're feeling better."

Hope sighed and nodded, her stomach clenching. "I know, but I'm afraid, and it pisses me off." Making a decision, she stood. "After the club closes tonight, I'm going over there."

* * * *

Hours later and aroused from tonight's demonstration, Hope called Ace. He picked up on the second ring. "Tyler."

"I'm a very horny woman who needs a great deal of attention."

"Is that a fact?"

"Yep. I've been listening to a man begging his mistress to let him come for the last hour. I remembered what it felt like to be in that position and willing to do anything to come."

"Remember that, do you?"

"How could I forget? I know it's been a long time, in fact, it seems like forever, but I was wondering if you knew where I could get some relief. Somebody stole my vibrator again. I was thinking about buying another one."

"You'd better not."

Hope leaned back and closed her eyes at his dark tone. This was the man she missed so desperately. Relief weakened her, and she had to swallow the lump in her throat before speaking. "Or what?" Her heart skipped a beat when he didn't answer right away.

"Or you'll wish you hadn't."

Forcing a lightness she didn't feel, she laughed softly. "That didn't sound very intimidating, Sheriff."

"I'll intimidate you plenty when I see you. Are you done for the night?"

"Yes. You?"

"You caught me stepping out of the shower."

"So you're naked and wet?"

"I am. Are you home?"

Hope looked longingly at the white ranch house to the front porch with the two comfortable chairs and sighed. "No. I'm not at home." Walking toward the steps to the porch, she pictured a few flowers out front, the kind that her mother had. For the life of her, she couldn't remember the name of them.

"Where the hell are you?"

Grinning, Hope made her way quietly up the stairs, skipping the second one which she'd already learned creaked, and settled into one of the chairs on the front porch. "Hiding from you. What would you do to me if you found me?" She had to keep her voice low so he wouldn't hear her from inside, but the background noises she heard told her that even now he was throwing on clothes. Another drawer slammed.

"Sheriff? I've been a bad girl, hiding from you. You gonna spank me?"

"Damn it, Hope. I don't like you running around at night. Where the hell are you? I'm coming to get you."

"Why? You don't want to screw me anymore."

Silence reined, the deafening sound of it telling her that Ace had stilled. His weary sigh tugged at her heart. "Of course I want you, baby. Now tell me where you are so I can come and get you. I'll bring you back here and make love to you nice and slow, so slow you'll think you've died and gone to heaven."

"I won't break, you know."

"Where are you?"

"Sitting on your front porch."

When the phone clicked in her ear, she smiled and casually closed it and stuck in it the pocket of her jacket, looking up when the front door opened.

Wearing only a pair of jeans that he hadn't yet buttoned, Ace stood in the doorway with his hands on his hips, a small smile playing at his lips.

"Not a real good hiding spot."

Hope looked him up and down, from his wide shoulders, down his strong chest to his tight abs and beyond, and grinned. "I wasn't trying too hard." The bulge behind the zipper of his jeans seemed to grow under her gaze, holding her attention until she reluctantly looked away, following the long trail of denim to his bare feet. A Greek God would be jealous of the body standing in front of her. It was hard to believe sometimes that he finally belonged to her.

"How the hell can even your feet look sexy?"

Ace's smile grew. "I think getting hit in the head scrambled your brain. You coming in?"

Hope leaned back in the chair and propped her feet on the small table. "I don't know. What are you offering?"

Ace's eyes flared at the challenge, but immediately dimmed as he smiled indulgently. Coming forward, he lifted her high in his arms. "I'm going to strip you out of those clothes and devour you."

As he started inside with her, she laid a hand on his hot chest. "I might be agreeable to that." She reached up to kiss his jaw. "I've missed you."

Ace strode into the house, closing and locking the door before carrying her down the hall to his bedroom, kicking the door shut behind him. "I've missed you, too. God help me, but I don't think I can give you up now. I can't even sleep at night without you." He laid her on the bed and slid a hand inside her jacket, his mouth covering hers.

Hope threaded her fingers through his still damp hair, holding him to her, her senses whirling. She moaned into his mouth, arching as his hand covered a breast. His tongue explored her mouth as though kissing her for the first time. Already she trembled, the power of his kiss on her senses drawing her into the warmth of his love. She felt it with every stroke of his tongue, every slide of his lips on hers.

His hand left her breast to move over her stomach, gently caressing, his other hand sliding under her to pull her even closer. One kiss led to another and another, each one more devastating to her senses than the last.

Hope held on to him like a lifeline, tilting her head when his lips left hers to brush lightly over her jaw and to her cheek.

"I love these dimples." His soft, low tone, so different and yet so familiar, washed over her.

Turning her head to smile at him, she wrapped a leg around his thigh. "Hmm. I love you."

Ace lifted his head and brushed her hair back from her face. "I love you, too, baby, probably more than I should."

"Impossible." Swept up in a vortex of warmth and desire, she wrapped herself around Ace, impatient each time she had to let go of him so he could remove another item of clothing.

He slid a hand inside her jacket and around her to lift her against him. He removed her jacket slowly, his mouth never leaving hers. As he tossed it aside, she toed off her shoes, quickly hooking her leg around him again. He broke off his kiss to pull her sweater over her head, his mouth exploring the curve of her breasts as soon as he bared them.

Clumsily pulling her arms out of the sleeves, she impatiently threw it aside to sink her fingers into his hair again. She trembled in his arms, shuddering when his hands roamed her body with slow, firm caresses that molded her against him.

Her stomach muscles quivered under the hand he slid inside her pants. He took his time in unfastening them, driving her wild as he slowly worked them down her legs and off. She shivered against him, waiting for him to rip her bra and panties from her, dying to feel him against her bare flesh.

Instead, he unclipped her bra, drawing it from her so slowly she thought she'd go crazy. His lips covered every inch of skin he exposed, his warm kisses setting her on fire with need. Instead of making her wait as he usually did, he gave her what she wanted immediately, using his tongue and lips on her nipples, slowly sucking one and then the other into his mouth, creating a languorous heat that flowed over, and made her movements clumsy.

Stripping her bra completely off of her body, he tossed it aside, immediately gathering her against him. With a hand tangled in her hair, he tilted her head back to rake his teeth down her neck and over the slope of her shoulder while his hand covered her abdomen. His lips trailed down to her breasts as he turned her more fully onto her back and slid his fingers inside her panties to cover her mound.

Hope's moans grew steadily when his mouth closed over a nipple. She ran her hands over his shoulders, smoothing over the hard muscle and doing her best to pull him closer, gasping when his fingers moved lower to slide through her slit.

"You're always wet and ready for me, aren't you, baby?"

Moaning, she tilted her hips. "Always. You're wearing too many clothes. I want you naked against me." Frustrated that she couldn't reach his cock, she twisted restlessly.

"Easy, sweetheart. I told you I wanted to devour you." He quickly rid her of her panties and slid lower, his lips leaving a trail of heat down the center of her body as he made room for his wide shoulders between her thighs.

Hope bunched her hands in the pillow, gasping when he lifted her thighs over his shoulders and cried out at the first touch of his mouth on her slit. She moaned, thrashing from side to side as he used his mouth on her, gently but steadily driving her closer and closer to the edge. He didn't tease her the way he normally did, not at all. She couldn't even catch her breath as he took her higher and flung her over so easily it amazed her.

She heard the rip of foil as he lapped at her gently, and before she could completely come down, he settled over her.

Bracing his weight on his elbows, he bent to kiss her, his lips still tasting of her. Wrapping his arms around her, he lifted her as he slowly entered her. Once he filled her completely, he held himself deep, lifting his head to look into her eyes.

"You feel so good, baby. Are you all right?"

Running her hands over him, Hope dug her heels into his tight buns, silently urging him to move. "Of course I'm all right. God, it feels so good having you inside me. I love when you surround me like this. It feels incredible, like there's nothing else." Stilling when his hand tightened on her bottom, she waited breathlessly for his finger to touch her bottom hole.

Instead, he pulled her closer and began thrusting, slow, deliberate strokes designed to give her the most pleasure. The friction of his cock moving inside her, filling her over and over, had her far too quickly approaching another orgasm, his steady, sure movements not giving her a chance to keep up.

His firm hold kept her against him, his lips moving over her hair and forehead as he made love to her, his movements smooth and controlled as always, but his silence unsettled her.

"Ace, I can't keep up. I want to please you, too."

He murmured softly, the speed of his thrust increasing. "You do, baby. Just let me give you what you need."

All rational thought fled as Ace's powerful body surged into hers again and again. Her orgasm hit her hard, washing over her in a giant wave that left her breathless and clinging helplessly to him.

He gathered her against him as he thrust deep once last time, his low groan rumbling in her ear as he found his own release.

She ran her fingers through his hair, holding him close while shudders still racked her body. Even though he kept most of his weight off of her, it felt good to have him cover her this way, his body pressing hers into the mattress.

He withdrew and moved to lie beside her, pulling her slightly over him with the arm still hooked around her. "When do you want to get married?"

Snuggling closer, she propped her chin on his chest and smiled, still a little dazed. "I'm ready to take you on anytime you want, Sheriff, but my mother wants to organize a party. Is that okay with you?"

Ace's hand moved lazily up and down her back. "Your mother works hard enough. We'll have a party at the hotel. Tell her to tell Ethan and Brandon what she wants and I'll pay for it." He shook his head when she started to object. "Hope, you know damned well I can afford it, and there's no need for your mother and fathers to worry about the cost or the work. Tell them I'll feel better if they order what they want and enjoy the party. It's the least I can do for taking their little girl."

"But Ace—"

"I'll talk to them. Just buy yourself a pretty dress." Sitting up, he rubbed her stomach and swung his legs over the side of the bed. "We're not going to be able to go away, though, for a honeymoon, at least not yet. I can't leave town as long as this idiot's running around. You've already been hurt, and I don't want him to have a chance to hurt anyone else. I'm going to get this bastard no matter how long it takes. We keep running into dead ends and it looks like our hands are tied until he strikes again. When he does, I'll be waiting."

Hope came to her knees behind him and pressed herself against his back, running her lips back and forth over his shoulders. "We can have a honeymoon right here in Desire. I can't wait to try out the bigger butt plug you promised me." Lightly biting his earlobe, she smiled when he shuddered. "Beau has a lot of nice toys in his store."

Ace turned his head to kiss her lightly. "You have an objection to the way I made love to you tonight?" Looking away, he stood.

Hope scrambled to the foot of the bed as he headed toward the bathroom. "Of course not! I love everything you do to me."

Ace smiled. "Good. I'm going to be a married man. Gotta keep my woman happy." He went into the bathroom, closing the door between them.

Frowning at the closed door, Hope pulled the quilt around her shoulders and sat cross-legged to wait for him. Something was wrong, and it knotted her stomach. Not one to beat around the bush, she confronted Ace as soon as he came out of the bathroom.

"Ace, is something wrong?"

He smiled reassuringly and lifted her against him. "Of course not, honey. What could be wrong? Can you be ready in two weeks?"

"Absolutely." Lost in his kiss, Hope pushed her worries aside. Soon she would be marrying the man she loved more than anything. He'd finally made love to her again. What could possibly be wrong?

Chapter Sixteen

A few nights later, Hope reclined naked on the rug in front of Ace's fireplace, watching the light from the fire play over his features. She arched, inviting his touch, and reached up for him, smoothing her hands over his gorgeous chest.

"You know, Sheriff, I still haven't seen that new butt plug."

Ace ran a hand down her body, smiling faintly when she trembled. "I thought you were supposed to be learning patience." His fingers played over her stomach briefly before moving up to her breasts and used his talented fingers to send ribbons of pleasure racing to her slit.

Raising herself, she touched her lips to his chest and reached for his cock, parting her thighs in invitation. "In case you haven't noticed, I'm not really good with patience."

Leaning back, Ace smiled, his eyes darkening as they raked over her body. "I've noticed." Resting his arms on the sofa behind him, he waited expectantly. When she paused uncertainly, he raised a brow and smiled.

Disconcerted that he appeared to want her to take the lead, she readily accepted, considering it a perfect opportunity to do some exploring of her own. Coming to her knees, she kissed and licked her way across his chest, smiling against his warm flesh as his cock jumped in her hand. The only light in the room came from the fireplace, the light from the flickering flames dancing over his skin and making it gleam like copper. She wanted to taste every inch of it.

Arching into the hands that slid down her back, she let her hair brush his thighs as she slowly moved down his body. Stroking his cock steadily, she kept her touch light and teasing, wondering how long he would let her get away with it until he either pulled her hand away or demanded more.

With the heat of the fire at her back and Ace's heat in front of her, she was wrapped in a cocoon of warmth and wished she could stay like this forever.

She licked at Ace's hard stomach, thrilling that his tight muscles quivered beneath her tongue. He remained silent, however, not voicing his usual demands. His hands continued to move over her, gentle and sure but with none of the fierceness he showed before. Even then she'd known he held back, but now he held back even more. Determined to get a reaction from him and shake that iron control, she moved lower, stretching out on the quilt in front of him, presenting herself to him. Squirming, she purposely gave him a good view of her ass, hoping to get a reaction. She slid her hand lower, cupping his sack and massaging gently as she touched the tip of her tongue to the head of his cock, licking away the drop of moisture that appeared there. In this, she could please him and, to please her, pretend he demanded this from her.

His hands slid to her hair, his fingers threading through it, tightening slightly when she took his cock into her mouth, only to loosen his hold again. His deep groan reverberated through her, and she tightened her hands on his thighs as she took him deeper.

The hair on his thighs teased her nipples as she moved against him, sending little shocks of pleasure through her. She rubbed her own thighs together as need continued to build, the low ache that settled there growing with each passing second. Waiting for the reprimand to keep her thighs open, she hid her disappointment when none came.

Unable to stay still, she squirmed and began to suck Ace deeper into her mouth, her lips stretched wide to accommodate his thickness. Reveling in his taste and in the way his thighs trembled, she sucked him a little harder, stroking a fingernail gently over his sack.

Ace said nothing, running his hands over her hair and shoulders, keeping his touch gentle. He moved her hair aside to watch what she did to him but made no move to stop her or instruct her in any way.

To know that this big, strong man was all hers never failed to excite her. Being able to explore him this way, to touch him however and wherever she wanted excited her even more.

It also made her a little uncertain, perhaps even a little insecure, that he didn't seem as intense as usual and she had no idea what he was thinking.

Remembering something she'd learned at the club, she decided to play a little and see if she could get a reaction from him. Expecting him to take charge any second, she held on to his thigh with one hand and slid the hand that cupped him lower. Wondering how far he'd let her go, and wanting to give him the kind of pleasure he gave her, she gradually worked her finger toward his anus.

Ace let go of her hair to grip her wrist and pull it gently away. Sliding both hands under her arms, he lifted her, pulling her from his cock to sit on top of his thighs. "Why don't you come up here, baby?"

Hope wrapped both hands around his cock, running them slowly up and down his length. "I was playing."

Ace smiled faintly. "I noticed, but wouldn't you rather have my cock in your pussy instead of your mouth?"

Hope fantasized about being forced to suck him like he'd ordered before, to have him hold her there and order her to in that dark voice he hadn't used with her for a while now. "I like sucking you. Don't you like it?"

"Of course, but I'd rather be making love to you." He reached over to where several condoms lay waiting on the coffee table. "I want to be inside that tight, hot pussy and feel you come apart all around me."

Hope reached for the condom, but he'd already started rolling it on. "I wanted to show you something I learned at the club. Why did you stop me?"

"Because that's something I do to you, not the other way around."

A little put out but relieved to hear the steel in his tone again, Hope pouted. "You don't touch me there anymore."

Ace finished donning the condom and lifted her, lowering her inch by inch onto his cock. "Do you need some attention there, baby? Come here, sweetheart, let me take care of you."

Moaning as his thick length slowly filled her, Hope grabbed his shoulders to steady herself, her pussy clenching on him greedily. She breathed his name as he filled her, closing her eyes in bliss as his heat engulfed her inside and out.

Seated to the hilt, Ace wrapped an arm around her, running his fingers through her slick juices to gather them. "I'm glad you like having your ass played with. I have a lot of plans…Just relax your bottom, honey, and I'll take care of you."

Hope moved on his cock, gripping him desperately as she rode him, distracted by the fingers that played at her slit. "Ace, tell me. You have a lot of plans? Plans for my ass? I want you to show me each and every one of them. I like when you touch me there, Ace. I like everything you do to me." Each time he pressed at her there, she shuddered expectantly, holding her breath for the moment when he would penetrate her. She couldn't wait for him to fuck her there again. He'd done it so slowly the first time, gentle with her because she'd never done it before. But she wanted him hot and wild and hungry for her.

Ace had apparently decided to tease her a little, making her wait as he encouraged her to keep moving. "That's it, baby. Do whatever feels good." He poised his finger at her forbidden opening and started to press firmly. "Take me inside you, baby." He slowly worked his finger into her, his other hand stroking her back when she shivered. "That's it. Nice and slow."

Hope dug her nails into him as she moved up and down, fucking herself on both his cock and his finger. She loved the challenge and freedom of being on top, but losing herself in the feel of Ace all around her, she couldn't keep her rhythm. Just when she got the angle she wanted, she lost it. Her bottom and pussy kept clenching on him as though trying to suck him in, and she whimpered in frustration, moving faster. It felt so good to have him inside her this way, to have his cock moving over her tender flesh, but something was missing.

"Ace, help me. I don't know what to do for you. I can't get it right."

Ace crooned softly to her, his words muffled against her neck as he tilted her backward, supporting her with a hand under her hair. "Straighten your legs, honey. Wrap them around me." When she complied, he used the hand on her bottom to move her against him, sliding his finger deep into her anus and holding it there.

Holding onto his shoulders, Hope rocked her hips, aiding his movements. When she opened her eyes, it was to find him watching her, his eyes filled with pleasure and love but lacking the intensity she'd become so accustomed to seeing.

"Ace, does this feel good for you? Please, tell me what you want me to do." She tightened on the finger in her anus, once again marveling at the exquisite invasion.

Ace's strokes increased in speed, his cock providing a delicious friction against that sensitive spot inside her. Brushing his lips over hers, he nibbled gently at her bottom lip.

"You feel incredible, honey. You always do. Just do what feels good."

Hope had no chance to say anything else as he took her lips with hers, opening readily for his kiss. She kissed him hungrily, pouring all of her love and passion into it in an effort to feel closer to him. With her body on fire and her senses reeling, she tightened her hold on him in desperation. Her moans grew in intensity as he took her to the brink, his short, quick thrusts and the finger moving in her bottom sending her flying.

He'd already learned her body so well that he could catapult her into orgasm quickly, his touch exactly what her body needed to go over.

She moaned as she came, tightening all around him.

A few quick thrusts later, he joined her, his low moan vibrating against her chest as he gathered her against him.

Neither spoke for several minutes, and it irked her that Ace didn't even seem to be out of breath.

He held her closely, running a hand up and down her back. "You okay, honey?"

Holding on to him, she turned her head to kiss his shoulder, a moan breaking free when he slid his finger out of her bottom. "Of course. Why are you treating me like I'm made of glass?"

Ace kissed her hair. "Don't be ridiculous."

Hope pushed against his chest, leaning back to look up at him. "I'm ridiculous now, am I? I'm tired of you telling me I'm being ridiculous."

Ace gathered her back against him and held her, his hand caressing her back again as though to soothe her. "You're not made of glass. You're the woman's who's going to be my wife very soon, and I want to baby you a little. Would you deny me that?"

When he said it like that, she did indeed feel ridiculous. "Oh, Ace. I love you so much. I can't wait until we're married. I've waited forever for you."

Ace chuckled. "You're too young to have waited forever. Are you warm enough?"

Hope cuddled against him. "Very warm. I love you, Sheriff."

"I love you, too, baby."

* * * *

Over the next several days, the feeling that something bothered Ace continued to grow, making Hope restless and irritable. She hated this feeling of being...disconnected with him somehow. Although he'd been as loving and tender as a woman could want, she couldn't shake the feeling that things had changed between them, and she didn't know how to fix it.

She knew he'd been preoccupied with the person who seemed to like causing trouble in Desire. It infuriated him. Rafe and Linc weren't any happier, and the tension in the entire town could be cut with a knife.

The men had spent the entire week having meetings and getting together on the street to speak in low tones to each other while watching the women who went about their day-to-day business.

Moving around the kitchen, Hope couldn't keep her thoughts from returning to Ace. She couldn't help but compare the way he'd made love to her before the accident, before he'd asked her to marry him, to the distant way he'd been with her this past week.

The deep connection they'd shared was gone, and she desperately wanted it back.

She closed her eyes remembering the look in his when he'd taken her before. The way he'd practically devoured her—Jesus, she'd never experienced anything like it before.

And already it was gone.

The sound of the apartment door opening jerked her back to the present.

"They must have shifts scheduled or something. Is that Daddy Finn's vegetable soup?"

Hope looked up from the pot of soup she'd been absently stirring when Charity walked into the apartment. "Yeah. Who has shifts scheduled?"

Charity took off her jacket and hung it up on the coat rack, sniffing the air as she came into the small kitchen. "The men. I figured you would know about it. Every time I walk down the street, I see men just standing around on corners. It's making for a lot of interesting conversations." She got out bowls and spoons and started setting the table, laughing softly. "I just walked by in time to hear Kelly ask Blade what he was selling and offered him a hundred bucks for a good time."

Picturing the always cool and controlled Blade, part-owner of Club Desire, the club owned by Doms who taught other Doms, being propositioned on the street corner by his wife would be a sight well worth seeing.

Laughing, Hope turned to her sister. "I'm sorry I missed that. What did he say?"

Charity reached into the refrigerator for the pitcher of iced tea. "Well, at first you could tell he was shocked and was doing his best not to laugh, but then when Kelly started circling around him, looking him over, everybody else lost it. He used that cold voice of his, you know the one, and told Kelly that a date with him would cost her considerably more than a hundred dollars. Kelly pretended to think about it and reached out to feel his butt. She tells him, 'Okay, you have nice buns, I'll give you one-fifty.'"

Hope laughed so hard it brought tears to her eyes. "I can just picture Blade's face! What did he say to that?"

"He started laughing and hugged her, promising retaliation. God, you can see how much he loves her. Then he threw her over his shoulder and headed for home."

As Hope ladled the soup, she couldn't help but be a little envious. "I wish Ace would do something like that to me."

Charity used the mitts to pull the bread out of the oven and brought it to the table. "What are you talking about? I'm sure our good sheriff takes care of you. You're getting married to the man next weekend."

Hope looked down into her soup, stirring the vegetables around. She couldn't wait to marry him, but it bothered her that he seemed…different. Nodding, she looked up. "Yeah. Mom and Dads finally finalized the buffet at the hotel."

Charity broke off a piece of bread and frowned at her. "What is it? Did you and Ace have a fight?"

Hope sighed and shook her head. "I almost wish we had. Something's wrong, and I'll be damned if I can figure it out. He's lost some of the intensity already, like maybe he doesn't want me as much anymore."

Charity looked at her worriedly. "Do you think he's changed his mind?"

Hope shrugged, the knots in her stomach tightening. "He's very loving and sweet. He seems like he's impatient to get married, so that's not it." Hope sighed and stirred her soup. "He makes love to me every night, and it's incredible. I don't even have the chance to catch my breath. He just sweeps me away." Scowling into her soup, she clenched her jaw. "I think he does it on purpose."

Charity took another bite of her soup, frowning. "Does he talk to you?"

Breaking her bread into little pieces over her soup bowl, Hope nodded. "He's really pissed that he hasn't caught the guy who hit me, and he thinks it's the same person who turfed the field behind the men's club and shot out the windows in both clubs. He's trying to get approval to hire more deputies. Rafe and Linc will be leaving any day to bring the woman they're both in love with to live here."

"That means Ace would be working alone."

Hope nodded. "And even when Linc and Rafe get back with the woman they want to marry, they can't even be with her together if they're all taking different shifts. So, Ace is trying to get approval to accept applications for a few more deputies."

Charity nodded. "It seems the way to go. I can't imagine he'll have any trouble getting approval from the town council. Hell, we're the ones who'll be voting on it. He's not worried about it, is he?"

Hope shrugged. "He doesn't seem to be, but he does talk to me. He tells me about his day and asks about mine."

"Then what the hell's your problem? He sounds like the perfect man. I've seen the way he is with you. He treats you like a china doll and he's a perfect gentleman."

Hope looked up from her soup, her stomach churning in both anger and dread as Charity confirmed the fear that had been hovering at the back of her mind for days. "Ever since the accident, he's been careful with me, too careful."

Charity nodded. "Of course he would be. You didn't expect him to manhandle you when you were bruised all over, did you?"

Hope dropped her spoon into her bowl and sat back. "The bruises have faded, Charity. I just hope nothing else has."

Charity shook her head. "You said yourself that the lovemaking was great. If Ace is happy and you're happy, don't rock the boat. Give up your stupid games and make a life with the man you love."

Hope jumped up from her chair. "Damn it, Charity, just because you don't like games in the bedroom, don't think the rest of don't want them.

Can't you understand? Dominance in the bedroom isn't just a game with Ace. It's the way he lives. I accept that about him, hell I love that about him. My need to submit in the bedroom is just as strong as his need to dominate. I can't have him giving up a part of himself because he thinks I can't handle it. We both need that, Charity, and if he changes, he's always going to feel like he's missing something."

Sitting back down, she dropped her head in her hands. "So will I, and it'll ruin everything. We're going to end up resenting each other." Lifting her head, she wiped away a tear, rubbing her stomach where it burned. "Why can't he believe me when I tell him that I need the same thing he does?"

Charity put her own spoon down and took a sip of iced tea, sitting back in the chair to regard Hope steadily. "You're really serious about this? I mean you expect Ace to dominate you when you have sex? You really want him to spank you and God knows what else?"

Hope stood again, too restless now to sit and reluctantly amused at her sister's question. "Of course. You know, Charity, sometimes it's hard to believe that you grew up in the same town I did, not to mention the same family." Wagging her brows, she laughed at Charity's red face. "I plan to spend a lot of time getting into trouble just to earn myself one of his spankings. God, he's good at it."

Dropping back into her chair again, she wrapped her hand around her own glass of tea, running her thumb up and down the cool side. "I don't know what I'd do if he's already decided I'm too delicate to handle him." Looking up at her sister, she snorted inelegantly. "Can you believe that? Me? Delicate? Hell, I don't even know if that's it or not. He hasn't said a word, and every time I hint at it, or even bring up the subject, he asks what's wrong with the way we have sex now. It makes me feel like an idiot."

"Could you live with the way sex is between you now?"

Hope nodded. "Sure. I love Ace. But I can't live with him trying to change such a vital part of him for me, especially when it's not necessary. I feel like I only have a part of him, Charity. I can't live with that. I want it all."

Charity paused with a spoonful of soup halfway to her mouth. "Then go get it. I can't imagine it would be too hard for you to earn yourself one of those spankings."

The fire in her stomach disappeared, replaced with an excitement that she hadn't felt since the morning the truck hit her. Grinning, she hurried to finish her soup.

"Oh, I think with a little help I can do better than that."

* * * *

Hope grinned at Sebastian's cool look. "Do you have a sister somewhere that I can hire for my club?" She could have sworn his lips twitched but didn't know for sure. She'd tried to get past him several times over the years when she'd been curious about the club, but he was damned good at his job. After that she'd tried to get in just because they told her she couldn't.

Sebastian looked down his nose at her, but the twinkle in his eye ruined his look of superiority. "Miss, you know you're not allowed admittance, and don't try to tell me you're here to see Mrs. Royal because she's not on the premises."

Hope did her best to look insulted. "I've heard the stories about how Rachel got in. Give me some credit. I wouldn't use a story that's already been done."

Crossing his arms over his chest, the ever-proper butler lifted a brow. "Of course not. What story did you plan to use tonight? It better be good. The sheriff's not going to be pleased that you showed up here."

Hope grinned. "You just let me worry about the sheriff. Can I talk to either Blade, Royce, or King?"

"Miss—"

"Stop calling me Miss. You know damned well what my name is. Hell, you bandaged my knees when I fell off my bicycle."

Sebastian continued as if she hadn't spoken. "Miss Sanderson, you know very well that the Masters are very busy."

"Yeah, well the club's not open for the night yet, and they don't have any classes this month. I know Blade's probably not here yet, but the other two are. I need to see one of them."

"The Masters—"

"Who is it, Sebastian?" King Taylor's deep voice came from somewhere behind Sebastian a few seconds before he flung the door wide and smiled when he saw her. "Hope! Hey, honey. Congratulations on your engagement. I'll be there with bells on." His smile fell. "What are you doing here? You're not trying to get into the club again, are you? Does Ace know you're here?"

Hope stuck her tongue out at Sebastian's back as he moved away and King filled the doorway.

Literally.

Although not as tall as Ace, King had more thick muscle than any man she'd ever met. She'd heard years ago that his father used to call him a weakling and King had really taken it to heart. Nobody in their right mind would ever say that to him now.

Hope smiled at the wariness on his face. "I need to ask a favor."

King's eyes narrowed. "What kind of favor? And is it going to get me in trouble with the sheriff?"

Since she'd known him most of her life, his hard features didn't scare her, but she knew he could be pretty intimidating when he had to. Like Ace, he couldn't be called handsome, but something about him had women lining up in droves to be with him. That strong exterior with the teddy bear heart would be irresistible.

"No. But you can call him in few minutes and rat me out. That's what I want to talk to you about."

He held out a hand to take hers. "Come on in, but I reserve the right to call Ace if I don't like this."

"If you do this favor for me, you'll be calling him anyway."

* * * *

Sitting in his office, Ace spoke to Rafe, who'd come in to relieve him. "I'd hate like hell to think this guy's going to get away with what he's done."

Rafe drank the last of his coffee and got up to refill his cup. "It looks like he will unless he does something else and we catch him."

Ace tossed a pen onto his desk with more force than necessary. "I hate this. I'm going to find this son of a bitch. Stay alert. Anyone new in town is to be watched. If they don't like it, they can leave."

Rafe put his cup on the desk and lowered himself into the chair again. "That's not gonna be real popular for the businesses here."

Clenching his jaw, Ace turned to meet Rafe's eyes. "I don't give a damn. My priority is to protect the residents of Desire. It's something I haven't been very good at lately."

Rafe nodded. "I'm glad you got the approval to hire more deputies. It's hard to keep the town covered twenty-four seven with only the three of us. With you getting married, it'll be nice to have a day off to spend some time with your wife. Linc and I can handle it while you're on your honeymoon."

Ace shook his head, forcing down the guilt he felt at not taking Hope somewhere nice like she deserved. He'd have to do his best to make it up to her. "We're not going on a honeymoon until I catch this guy."

Rafe looked like he wanted to say something but changed his mind and nodded. "We'll catch him soon."

"Yeah." Every time he pictured Hope lying on the ground after being hit, he wanted to pound something. Damage had been done to property, and he didn't have a single suspect. Used to being in charge, he hated this feeling of helplessness.

Rafe reached for his cup. "He hasn't done anything since he hit Hope. Maybe it shook him. It sure as hell upset him enough to call."

"Maybe. I'd rather he didn't cause any more trouble, but it pisses me off that unless he does something else and we catch him, he just might get off scot-free."

Rafe's expression hardened. "I know. One of the reasons Linc and I came to Desire, besides wanting to live where ménage relationships are accepted, was how safe the town is. We want to start a family here, and since we'd both worked in law enforcement, we wanted to do our part. This guy comes by and spits in our faces and walks away."

Ace sat back and steepled his hands over his stomach. "It has to have something to do with the clubs. He didn't do anything to any other business in town."

"Maybe he just hasn't had the chance. The clubs are the largest businesses here, and since they're not on Main Street, he might've figured he wouldn't have as many witnesses."

"True, but we have nothing else to go on. I can't just sit on my hands and wait for this guy to cause more trouble. I've already talked to Royce at the club, and he's going through his files for anyone who's filed a complaint."

Rafe stood. "How about Hope? She hasn't been there long enough to make any enemies."

Ace scrubbed a hand over his jaw. "I know. Logan Securities vetted all of their members." It still pissed him off that she hadn't come to him. "I'm going to talk to them about anything that might have turned up in their background checks. I'll have to talk to Hope, too. Maybe she's gotten threats she hasn't told me about." His jaw clenched. If she'd kept something like that from him...hell. He'd have to hope a lecture worked.

Rafe paused before walking out the door. "Uh oh. Are you sure that's the kind of conversation you want to get into a week before your wedding?" Chuckling softly, he left, closing the door behind him.

Ace allowed his lips to curve, his smile falling as soon as the door closed behind Rafe. Before she'd been hit by the truck he wouldn't have hesitated at all to deliver a sound spanking to get her to tell him everything. He leaned back, closing his eyes on a groan when he pictured her face as he invaded her ass the first time.

The ecstasy on her face when he stretched her ass and used the nipple clips on her.

The sounds she made when she came after he'd made her wait for her release.

Her eyes when he'd talked about fucking her ass.

The sight of her ass wiggling as the ginger root took effect.

The feel of her tight ass clenching on his cock.

As it had since she'd been clipped by the truck, the images were immediately replaced by the sight of that same ass covered with bruises and his terror that he'd put some of them there. The discoloration of her creamy skin, the obscenity of her cute little bottom being red and bruised made him sick to his stomach each time he pictured it.

He assured himself that he could get used to vanilla lovemaking. The pleasure in making love to her would be enough, but he couldn't deny that he missed the incredibly strong orgasms he had when he dominated her. He'd seen the surprise and delight on her face and knew she'd never experienced that kind of pleasure before either.

Fuck. He missed it and missed the extraordinary connection he experienced with her at those times. When he'd dominated women in the past, there'd been a special closeness, but with Hope, the woman he loved, the strength of the bond stunned him.

He'd looked forward to nurturing that closeness and leading her into a lifetime of submission, creating a bond with her that would be unbreakable.

With that gone, he felt an uneasiness that just wouldn't go away.

Since his shift had already ended, he stood and headed out, wanting to get to Hope as soon as possible. He drove home thinking about her and her attempts to get him to dominate her again. Nothing would make him happier than accommodating her.

His cock stirred. Maybe in the future. If he could ever get those images out of his head.

Once he got to the house, he hurried inside. The quiet had never really bothered him before, but now that Hope had been here, the house seemed to cry out for her presence. It would be nice to have her to come home to after working all day. When he worked the night shift, it would be nice to come in and shower and crawl in next to her warm, soft body and feel her cuddle up to him.

Anxiously looking forward to their lovemaking tonight, he raced through his shower. He'd just finished and dried off when his cell phone rang. Thinking it would be Hope, he rushed toward it, disappointed to see it came from Club Desire. Keeping his disappointment from his tone, he answered.

"Tyler."

"Hey, Sheriff. I've got a little bit of a problem, and I think you're the perfect person to take care of it for me."

"King? What is it? Did he come back?" Fuck. Holding his phone to his ear with his shoulder, he started grabbing clothes to get dressed.

"No, nothing like that. I have a problem with a woman who says she's a sub and has the perfect right to be here. She's in Blade's old playroom and refuses to leave."

Ace fastened his jeans and grabbed the phone from his shoulder, a little stunned. "Doesn't Sebastian usually take care of that for you? I'll come over, but I don't understand why you just don't throw her out." He looked at the clock and mentally groaned at the time this would take him away from

Hope and couldn't resist teasing. "What's the matter, is she bigger than you?"

King chuckled. "Very funny. No, she's just a tiny little thing, but damned if she doesn't have a mouth on her. She says she won't leave with anyone but you."

Ace reached for a T-shirt, starting to get a funny feeling in the pit of his stomach. "Who is she?"

"It's your fiancée, Sheriff."

Ace dropped on the bed. "Hope?"

"You got more than one?"

"I'll be right there."

"Thought you might."

Jumping to his feet, Ace disconnected and jammed the phone in his pocket to finish getting dressed. What the fuck was Hope doing? Shit. All those damned hints. He should have known she was impulsive enough to pull something like this.

He finished getting dressed and, grabbing his jacket, raced for the door. He'd seen the room she was in before, and picturing her in it now had his cock as hard as a fucking rock. Somehow he had to get her out of there before he gave into the urge to use some of the equipment there and teach her a lesson she'd never forget.

Minutes later, he pulled into the parking lot and found an empty space. Throwing the gear shift into park, he realized he was muttering to himself, mostly cursing, and forced himself to take a deep breath before getting out.

He would just talk to her calmly and get her out of there. Once he had her back at his place, he'd make love to her and satisfy this raging need.

Who was he kidding?

He wanted to spank her little ass for doing something like this and fuck her long and hard from behind. If anyone needed an ass-fucking to learn who was in charge, it was Hope. His groin tightened, his cock pushing painfully against his zipper just thinking about it. He got out and hurried across the parking lot and up the front stairs. Maybe he should take her to dinner first and cool down.

Sebastian opened the door before Ace even got there. "Good evening, Sheriff. We've been expecting you."

Ace clenched his jaw. "Where the hell is she?"

Chapter Seventeen

Hope picked up another item and held it up. It looked like some kind of a chain, maybe nipple clamps but the ends were bigger.

"What's this?"

King snatched it out of her hands and stuck it back in the cabinet, closing the door with a decisive click. "Stop touching everything. God only knows how Ace is ever going to get you to behave. I doubt even Kelly comes in here and picks things up."

"You said this used to be Blade's private playroom. He probably has one in his new house now, so he doesn't use this anymore."

King folded his muscular arms over his equally massive chest. "You'd have to ask him."

Too nervous to sit, Hope continued to wander around the room. "Do you and Royce have a playroom?"

King leapt forward and slapped her hand when she started to reach for one of the butt plugs that had been lined up on a shelf from smallest to the widest. "Of course we have a playroom. Stop touching things."

Hope stuck out her tongue at him and moved away, sliding her hands over the cool leather of the large table in the center of the room.

"Do you share it?"

Narrowing his eyes, King took a step forward when she reached for one of the straps that hung at the corners. "Since we share women, it would only make sense to share a playroom."

Hope hurriedly dropped her hand and moved away to eye the mirrors that filled one wall. "Don't you get jealous when Royce is touching the same woman you're making love to?" She strolled slowly away to another wall lined with hooks that had a variety of devices hanging from them.

King followed her, apparently ready to stop her if she reached for one of the small whips she studied curiously. "I don't make love. I have sex. And, no, I don't get jealous. We work well together."

"Work? That doesn't sound like fun."

"Oh, it is."

"Don't you and Royce ever want to get married and settle down with one woman?"

His deep laugh held a hint of sadness. "Can you imagine a woman who would take on not one, but two Doms? It happens, but it's rare. We haven't met anyone that we would even consider marrying. She'd have to have a lot of spunk."

Hope wrinkled her nose at him. "Sorry, I'm already taken."

King chuckled. "I wouldn't touch you on a bet. Ace must need his head examined to think he can tame a wildcat like you."

"I'm starting to think the same thing."

Hope gasped and spun at Ace's deep drawl, smiling impishly. "Sheriff. What are you doing here?"

King started from the room, patting Ace on the shoulder on his way out. "Thank God. She's all yours."

Ace took his eyes off of her only long enough to glance at King. "Yes, she is. Thanks for the call."

"Anytime." Shooting a look over his shoulder, he smiled faintly. "Bye, Hope. I hope you know what you're doing."

Ace didn't speak again until King left the room. His eyes narrowed, holding hers as he advanced, closing in on her with each step. "What exactly *are* you doing, Hope?"

Lust burned low in her belly at the determination on his face as he kept coming closer. "I'm trying to get my man to notice me." Waving a hand, she grinned. "I thought this might be the perfect place to get his attention."

His eyes flared when she took a step back. "Why would you feel that you don't have my full attention?"

Suddenly feeling incredibly vulnerable, Hope shrugged. "I miss you."

Ace came to a stop. "What do you mean, you miss me? I'm always here for you, baby. We're getting married in less than a week."

She hated this insecurity. She couldn't live this way. "Are you sure that's what you want?"

"Of course that's what I want." His eyes hardened into two dark chips of ice. "Have you changed your mind? Have you decided that being married to me isn't what you want after all?"

Hope took a step closer. "I want you, Ace. I love you." Going for broke, she took a deep breath. "Why don't you make love to me the way you used to? Don't you want me that way anymore?"

"Don't be ridiculous."

Hope's temper snapped. Both relieved to finally be getting this out in the open and scared to death of losing him, she trembled, trying hard not to show it. "Again I'm being ridiculous! Listen you…you…idiot! I'm not the one that went into this and changed the rules without notice. You're making me crazy. If you've decided you don't want me anymore, just say so, damn you. If you're worried about what the people here will say, I'll tell them all that I dumped you."

Ace closed the distance between them in two strides. Grabbing her by the shoulders, he lifted her to his toes. "Idiot? I'm making *you* crazy? You've been wiggling that ass at me every chance you get when you know damned well how much it turns me on, and I can't do a fucking thing about it. Not want you anymore? I go around with a fucking hard-on thinking about the things I want to do to you. I'm the damned sheriff, and I can't keep my mind on my fucking job because of you."

Hope gaped at him. She'd never seen him like this. Ever. "Ace, I—"

"I'm *always* in control. Always. You can't be the size I am and lose control, and I made up my mind a long time ago that no woman would have the power over me that my father's wives have over him. And what do I do? I end up tying myself to a pint-sized brat who turns me inside out at every opportunity."

Setting her on her feet, he turned away from her, rubbing a hand over his face. Keeping his back to her, he put his hands on his hips and hung his head. "Everything is fine with us, Hope. I love you. You love me. We're getting married. The sex is good. Everything'll be just fine. Don't make a big deal out of nothing." His monotone told her that everything was far from fine.

Furious, Hope turned, looking for something to hit him with. Racing to the wall, she grabbed one of the butt plugs and flung it at him.

Ace spun, obviously sensing a threat. The stunned look on his face as he ducked might have been funny at another time, but right now she was too mad to appreciate it.

"You threw a butt plug at me?" He ducked as another butt plug sailed past his head and started after her.

Hope didn't trust the gleam in his eye and quickly ran around the table, keeping it between them. "Irony, huh? You're acting like an ass so…"

Fire shot from Ace's eyes. His jaw clenched repeatedly as he advanced. "You're about to get fucked in yours."

Taking an involuntary step back at his tone, Hope lifted her chin, determined to have this out right now. Fear of losing him made her hesitate for a split-second, almost backing down.

Until she looked into his eyes.

In them she saw the love she'd anxiously searched for, but also saw raw possession, white-hot in intensity.

The combination took her breath away.

It convinced her more than anything that she had to go for the brass ring. *This* was Ace. This was the man she loved and she wanted it all.

In an instant, the look disappeared, but she'd seen it and she wanted to see it again. She wanted to stoke the fire until it burned out of control and he took her the way they both needed.

Lifting a brow, she gave him her most arrogant look. "Really? I don't think so. I think I could pretty much get away with doing anything I want."

His eyes flared again. "Think that, do you?"

Hope grinned, a smile designed to really tick him off. "Of course. You're so much in love with me you'd let me get away with anything."

Ace's eyes hardened. Standing with his hands on his hips, he looked every inch the dominant male. He slowly moved around the table toward her, forcing her to circle the table to keep it between them. Lust flared briefly when she moved away. "Is that what you think love is? Being so blinded by what I feel for you that I don't see to your protection? That all I do is coddle you? I told you already that I'm not that kind of man."

"Could have fooled me. Isn't that what you think love is? You tell me you love me and then treat me like a doll you're afraid of breaking. I'm a woman, Ace, in case you haven't noticed." Eyeing him warily, she almost got caught when he feigned toward the right. She had to move quickly to escape him and knew she'd only been able to do it because he allowed it.

He was playing with her, so he must have had his own agenda, one that she seriously hoped matched hers.

"Oh, I've noticed." Stopping suddenly, he shook his head, the look of defeat and sadness in his eyes knotting her stomach. "I can't get it out of my head."

Hope blinked and took a step toward him. "Can't get what out of your head?"

Ace sighed and braced his hands on the table to lean closer to her. "All those bruises. You're so damned little, and when I remembered the night before and what I'd done to you, I was scared to death that some of those were from me. I love you, Hope, probably more than I should. You're going to rip the heart out of me, and there isn't a damned thing I can do about it. I know you said you liked it a little rough, but for the life of me, I can't do it."

"Oh, Ace." Shaking her head sadly, she covered his hands with hers. "I don't know how else to convince you that I can take it, especially if you're scared. I love you. I know you'd never hurt me. But neither one of us can go on denying something that's such a big part of us. Sure, I love making love the way we have been since the accident, but there's something inside me that wants to be *taken*, too."

She took a step back, her face burning. "I want you to take all of the choices out of my hands. I want you to take me, use me for your pleasure. I want to scream 'no' and you ignore me. I want you to make me come when I say I don't want to. I want you to turn me over your knee and spank me." She smiled at the flash of something unbearably hot in his eyes. "I know that's what you want, too. I don't mind a bruise or two, hell, I might just bruise you. I trust you completely, Ace, with all that I am. Your love for me and your ingrained caring for women won't let you hurt me the way you're afraid of." Reaching out to touch his hand again, her heart leapt when he turned his to cradle it.

Hope blinked away the tears stinging her eyes. "Please, Ace, don't hold back from me. I want *all* of you. I need you to want all of me. I accept that you want to dominate me. I need you to accept that I *need* to submit to you. I know what I want, Ace, and I've been honest with you about it. Please don't make me feel ashamed for asking for what I need."

Ace gathered her close, pulling her across the table and into his arms. "Oh, baby, I never meant to do that. I'm so sorry. Hope, you're just so damned little. If I ever hurt you..." Lifting her, he kissed her deeply, his arms tightening around her as he swept her mouth with his tongue again and again, tangling it with hers until her head spun. He lifted his head, his eyes full of love and passion. And something that alarmed her. Indecision.

Hope pushed lightly against his chest until he released her, hating to see him so vulnerable because of his fear for her. "You haven't. You won't." She unbuttoned her shirt as she moved away, putting the table between them again. Sliding the shirt from her arms, she tossed it to him and slowly turned. "Look, no bruises."

Ace caught the shirt that hit him in the chest, his lips twitching as he looked her over. His eyes held hers for several long seconds, relief, love, passion, and a hint of fear mingling into a look that melted her heart.

Finally, he smiled, his eyes hooded. "I don't believe you. Let me see the rest."

Hope toed off her sneakers and reached for the fastening of her jeans. "Put your hands on the table. I don't want you jumping over here while I'm tangled in my jeans."

"Excuse me?"

Thrilling at the steel in his tone, Hope hid a smile. "Do it."

"No. Give me the jeans."

Hope grinned. "Maybe you should take off *your* jeans. I could fuck your ass with one of the dildos on that shelf over there. Hey, would that make you my bitch?"

Ace smiled coldly. "You really are looking for trouble, aren't you?"

Toying with the zipper of her jeans, Hope fluttered her lashes. "You know where I can find some? I've got this room for as long as I need it. Since it's Blade's, they don't book it. Hey, I have an idea. Maybe you can go downstairs and find a Dom that'll do us both."

The look on his face was priceless and dampened her panties in an instant. "Give me those fucking jeans right now before I rip them off of you."

"I don't trust you."

"I always knew you were smart."

"You gonna spank me, Sheriff?"

"And then some."

"No, I don't think you want me badly enough. Is your cock hard?"

"You're gonna find out."

Hope took a chance and stripped off her jeans as quickly as possible, a little surprised that he didn't take the opportunity to come after her. "I'm not losing the socks."

"The socks you can keep. Give me those jeans."

"They won't fit you."

"Give. Me. The. Fucking. Jeans."

Hope threw them at him and pouted. "Why didn't you come over here while I was taking them off?"

Ace grinned coldly. "I knew you were expecting it. Besides, I'm enjoying the striptease. Lose the bra. I want to see those nipples." He turned his back to her, tossing her shirt and jeans onto a bench and went to the cabinet that stood against the wall.

Hope watched curiously as he opened it and perused the contents.

"Very nice. Blade has good taste." He picked up several items that she couldn't see, only to put them back on the shelf, the sound of metal clinking piquing her curiosity, until he finally found something that satisfied him. Turning, he jiggled what sounded like some sort of chain in his hand. Looking under the table, he grinned. "Perfect."

Hope followed his gaze to a series of metal hooks and chains imbedded into the floor. She'd seen them in the club she'd gone to before, and knowing what they were used for, began to get a little nervous, which only added to her excitement.

Glancing over at her, he raised a brow. "You don't have that bra off yet?" He pushed a lever at the side of the table, sliding the edges apart until a space about a foot wide appeared near one end.

Intrigued and more aroused by the second, Hope couldn't tear her eyes away as he moved to the other end and flipped up a cushion that had been hidden underneath. "Guess what I'm going to do to you."

Hope sneered. "Aren't you afraid you might bruise me?"

Ace reached behind him for a whip that looked similar to the one he had at home but hadn't used on her in too long. "The only pain you're going to feel is going to be your nipples, your ass, and your clit. This whip is designed to sting, not bruise, and you'll feel the effects of it for quite a while. It'll make what I'm going to do to you that much more satisfying. For me, that is."

"Ooooh, Sheriff, you're scaring me."

Ace chuckled. "You're not at all scared, but by the time I finish with you, I think you'll have second thoughts before thinking you can get away with challenging me again." His eyes narrowed. "Lose the bra."

Hope pretended to consider it, playing with the front clasp, careful to keep an eyes on him. "Or what?"

"Or I'll rip it off."

"You'd have to catch me first."

Ace vaulted over the table before she could blink, leaving nothing between them. "Take one step and that bra and those panties will be ripped off of you. I don't like you wearing the damned things around me anyway. Take the bra off and give it to me. Now. I won't tell you again."

The steely tone caused a shiver through her, his voice deeper and darker than she'd ever heard from him before. Caught up in the fantasy he brought to life, Hope slowly undid the bra and just as slowly removed it. She tossed it to him with a seductive smile and ran her hands up her body to her breasts, cupping them and pinching her nipples, effectively hiding them from his gaze. "This feels so good. I think sometimes I could come just from having my nipples played with." Although she'd masturbated several times in her life, she'd never touched herself in front of anyone else. Having Ace watch her now, knowing that she teased them both, added an element to it that had never been there before.

His eyes darkened, narrowing even more. "Did I say you could do that?"

Need built at an alarming rate at the look in his eyes as she touched herself. Sharp little pinpricks of awareness travelled through her body to her slit, where her juices had already soaked her panties. She pinched her nipples a little harder, moaning at the exquisite pleasure. It excited her to stand before him wearing only her panties, while he remained fully clothed the vulnerability heightening her senses. Keeping her eyes on his, she shook her head as she continued to play with her nipples.

"I didn't ask."

Ace's jaw clenched, his eyes laser sharp. "Do you really have any idea what you're asking for?"

Hope ran a hand down her body, sliding it inside her panties to touch a finger to her swollen clit, her knees buckling at the sensation. "The question is, Sheriff, do you?"

Ace pounced—she could think of no better word for it—somehow closing the distance between them in a heartbeat. He yanked her hand from her panties and pulled her against him, lifting her against his chest. He'd moved so fast she barely had time to blink. He looked down at her, his eyes hooded as he carried her back to the table.

"I know what you're getting."

Hope grasped at air as he placed her on the table and quickly flipped her to her belly, momentarily panicking that she would fall. She should have known better.

He handled her with ease, placing her facedown on the table with her breasts in the opening he'd made a few minutes earlier. With a hand on her back to hold her down, he ignored her kicking and screaming to secure a strap around her waist to hold her in place. "You can scream all you want. These rooms are soundproof. Only I can hear you and after the little show you just put on, I'm not listening."

His firm hands on her body always gave her a thrill, but now the thrill became more intense as he adjusted her body to his liking, fastening her wrist in a strap above her head and testing to make sure it held before moving around the table to the other. His almost clinical touch stirred something inside her, knowing he felt anything but. Once he finished with her hands, he moved to her legs. Making sure to position her abdomen on the cushion at the end, he effectively raised her bottom several inches.

Hope kicked her feet, even managing to connect a few times while pulling at the straps on her arms. "Untie me, damn you."

He overcame her struggles with alarming ease, strapping each of her legs to the leather-covered table right below the knee and again at her ankle.

"No."

It took some effort, but she managed to rub her thighs together. Her pussy and clit throbbed mercilessly, her thighs already coated with her juices. "That was stupid. You strapped me down with my legs together. Looks like you're not fucking me after all." Her laugh got cut short when something clicked and her thighs were pulled apart, the pieces of the table separating with her legs attached securely to them. "How did you know it did that? Have you fucked anybody on this table?"

Ace ran a hand over her bottom, and she could feel his gaze at her slit, now open and raised for his pleasure. Her clit, pussy, and ass were now completely vulnerable, and strapped down as she was, she couldn't turn her head far enough to see anything. Her slit became so sensitive and needy that even the air moving over it was unbearable.

"Stupid. Idiot. You've called me some bad names, baby. Taunted me, defied me, argued with me, and downright disobeyed me. You sure are racking up some punishments, aren't you? And, no, but Blade and the others showed me these rooms when they opened. I haven't been here since." He ran a hand over her bottom. "But I have a very good memory."

She couldn't stop trying to wiggle her bottom but couldn't move very much at all. She needed to rub her clit against something, but all the wiggling in the world did no good since Ace had made sure there was nothing to rub against except air. When he disappeared from view, she looked around frantically but couldn't see him.

"Ace? Where are you?"

Her question got answered a moment later when pain shot through her nipple. "Oh! Ace, it hurts."

"Breathe, baby. You remember how to do it." His voice came from under the table.

She heard another click but became too distracted with her breathing to try to figure out where it came from. Just when the pain became bearable, her other nipple suffered the same fate. Moaning into the leather, Hope pulled uselessly at her restraints.

"Careful, baby. You're going to hurt yourself." Ace's voice came from just beside her ear, and she turned toward it involuntarily. "Your nipples are attached to a chain. The chain is attached to a hook in the floor. If you try to lift up, it'll pull those cute little nipples."

Of course Hope had to try it for herself, wincing and crying out at the tug on her nipples when she raised herself barely an inch. Moisture flowed from her at the erotic pull to her slit, and unable to resist, she did it again.

Ace slid a hand over the cheeks of her ass. "Of course, you're going to love the way it feels." Bending, he ran his lips over her shoulders, working his way down her back to her bottom. "Now let's get to work on the rest of you."

Hope shivered as he moved down her body. "Ace, take the edge off. Make me come." Each tug at her nipples only made the need worse, but she couldn't stop moving.

Ace disappeared behind her, and she heard movement but couldn't tell what he was doing. Without warning, he spread the cheeks of her ass wide and inserted something about an inch into her forbidden opening.

"Ace! What are you doing? Oh, God." She clenched on the item, whimpering when a large amount of cold lube shot into her.

"I've got to make sure you're lubed really good, baby. You're gonna get an ass fucking you'll never forget."

"Yes! Do it. Fuck my ass, Ace."

Ace chuckled coldly. "You're gonna have to wait for it. You haven't been whipped yet. I think we should start with your tight little hole. What do you think? Doesn't matter. Let's see how loud you scream."

Hope barely had time to process his words before the whip came down hard on her tight opening. She screamed at the sharp sting, which was immediately followed by a white-hot burning that brought tears to her eyes and made her jump, pulling the clips attached to her nipples.

Before she could take another breath, Ace used the whip on her upraised bottom, not as hard as he could have, but hard enough to sting. And kept using it. The whip came down repeatedly, hitting every square inch of her bottom, interspersed with strikes to her inner thighs.

Her ass just kept getting hotter, the stings awakening her flesh like never before, only to become so hot she felt as though her ass was on fire. Her cries filled the air as he continued, each strike taking her closer and closer to the edge and chipping away at her defenses. When the whip landed on her bottom hole again, she screamed, trying to breathe through the pain as he went back to work on her ass and thighs. Before he'd finished, two more strikes to her bottom hole had it burning almost unbearably and clenching desperately with the need to be filled.

"Beautiful." Ace ran his hands over her bottom and inner thighs, reigniting the heat. "You'll stay hot for quite a while. Each time I touch you, it'll bring it back. Not so mouthy now, are you?"

Covered in sweat, Hope slumped against the leather. Weak and trembling, but more aroused than she could ever remember being, she became aware of the whimpered moans that continued to pour out of her and that she was helpless to stop. Tingles raced through her, hot and sharp, from her nipples to her clit to her ass and pussy and back again. She'd never been more aware of her body, and her body had never been so highly tuned to sex as in this moment.

Ace's voice sounded low in her ear. "That's it, baby. Breathe. You've got the most beautiful ass I've ever seen in my life. My cock is aching with the need to be inside that tight ass and taking what's mine."

"Ace, oh, God. I think I'm coming. I don't know. It doesn't stop. Help me."

Running his hands over her back, he crooned to her, caressing her gently, only to occasionally run a hot hand over her bottom or inner thigh, making it burn once more and strengthening her awareness.

"Let go, Hope. Don't try to fight it. I won't let you. I want it all. You're going to submit completely, surrender everything you are to me. I won't be denied tonight." The dark cadence of his voice vibrated through her, sending a prickling over her skin. "Now I'm going to whip your clit, baby. And you're going to love it."

The need to fight him surged within her. "No. Don't. I can't take it."

Ace's lips touched her hair as his hand reached beneath the table to tug at the chain, sending jolts of lightning to add to the burning at her center. "You know you need this, baby. I'm not going to stop, no matter what you say. You stirred up this need in me on purpose, and I won't stop now until we're both satisfied."

Trembling, Hope rubbed her cheek against his jaw. "Help me. Don't let me stop. I'm scared." She moaned as his naked chest touched her back. A sound from beside her told her he reached for something she couldn't see. Seconds later she felt something cool and hard against her bottom hole, which immediately began to push into her.

"All you have to do is trust me, baby. There's no stopping what I'm going to do to you now."

Hope cried out as it pushed into her, fighting it even knowing she couldn't stop him. "No. Stop it. Take it out. It's too big."

Ace kept pressing. "My cock's even bigger. This'll help stretch you a little more. You'll be glad I did this when I fuck your ass. Now be a big girl and relax that ass so I can fill it."

"It burns." The sharp pull on her nipples reminded her to stay still, but it just kept getting more difficult. Her bottom stung already from the whip, making the burn of being stretched even hotter. She gulped in air as Ace pushed the plug the rest of the way in, blowing out a breath in relief when she felt the base press against her.

"Regret pushing me yet?"

Her bottom gripped the plug tightly, making her feel even fuller. "Never."

"You will. Your bottom tingles now, doesn't it? When I push my cock into you, you're gonna really feel it." Ace ran a hand over her bottom again, seeming to know how sensitive and hot it had become because he kept his touch lighter than normal. The fact that he knew everything she experienced increased her arousal, his knowledge and confidence strong aphrodisiacs.

She wouldn't be able to hide anything from him, especially if he knew what she would feel before she even felt it. She couldn't stop clenching on the plug, whimpering at the fullness in her anus and at her almost painful arousal.

"Now, let's see how long I can make your clit whipping last before you come."

Hope groaned, the throbbing in her clit becoming worse at his words. "Ace, I don't know if I can do this."

Ace bent to kiss her shoulder and reached down to slide a finger into her pussy, nipping her when she tightened on it. "Of course you can. Remember, you have no choice. You said you trust me." His voice deepened as he moved his finger in and out of her, pressing on the plug with each inward thrust. "You said you're all mine. I've never before taken a woman who belonged to me completely and who'll still belong to me when we leave here together. I want all of you, Hope, and before we leave here, I'll have it."

"But, Ace, oh, God, you already have me—"

"Not yet, baby, but I will."

Not completely understanding him gave Hope a moment's trepidation, but she had no time to dwell on it as Ace straightened, withdrawing from her and moved away. She felt him standing between her splayed thighs, felt the brush of his clothing as he moved. No longer able to hold back her moans, she waited breathlessly for the first strike to her tender clit, having no idea how she would stand it.

She pressed her legs against the leather, using the leverage to rock her hips as much as possible, amazed at the incredible ache that had settled there. She could only imagine what she looked like, her ass in the air, her slit spread wide as she wiggled. She no longer cared.

Hope only cared about relieving this torment. She blew out the breath she'd been holding, the movement pulling the chains at her nipples and eliciting another deep groan. It ended in a gasp when something pressed into her pussy, making her feel even fuller.

"I think you'll like this little egg. Have you ever had one in your pussy before?"

Her cries sounded pitiful to her own ears, growing louder when the egg began to vibrate. A sharp blow to her clit nearly rendered her senseless. The sting and almost immediate burning sent sharp sizzles through her and caused her to clench on the objects filling her. A series of small waves washed over her, one right after the other and stealing her breath.

"I asked you a question." His finger danced lightly over her clit, stopping when she cried out at the sharp swell that pulled her in its grip. "Oh, no you don't. Not yet."

"Let me come, damn you. Oh! I started to come. You son of a bitch." Pulling frantically at her bonds, she tightened on the egg and plug but couldn't recapture the feeling. "Bastard, untie me."

Two more hits to her clit and she was lost. "Answer me."

Hope cried, begging for relief, the endless and painful throbbing of her clit keeping her poised on a razor sharp edge that she just couldn't go over. She fought like a wild woman, her hoarse cries sounding animalistic and tortured.

"Yes. Please. Help me."

"No, baby. You're still fighting me."

"I'm not. I swear I'm not." She groaned as his hands caressed her inner thighs.

"Of course you are. Give into it. I won't stop until I have your total surrender."

Out of her mind with pleasure and need, Hope rubbed her face against the leather, unsurprised that it had become wet with her tears. Whimpers and sobs mingled. "I don't know what you want." Her clit burned, such an exquisite torture, the sharp tingles centered there nearly driving her out of her mind.

Ace touched her clit, his touch not hard enough to give her what she needed. "You will."

Hope bucked again, fighting to rub herself against his fingers and sobbing when he moved his hand away. "Ace. Please! I'm begging." Her insides tightened and quivered, teetering on the edge of orgasm for so long she could barely breathe.

Ace tapped her clit with the whip, renewing the sensation. "I know. This isn't about what you want, remember? It's about what I want from you."

Twisting restlessly, Hope screamed through two more strikes to her clit. He didn't hit her hard, but as sensitive as her clit had already become, it was more than enough to shatter the last of her defenses. Shaking uncontrollably and gulping in air, she slumped, unable to fight it anymore. No matter what she said or did, she couldn't get any relief. Whimpering at the fingers dancing over her clit, she closed her eyes in surrender, unable to do anything but accept whatever he gave her.

Acutely aware of his every move, she'd become totally oblivious to everything else around her. All that mattered was Ace.

"Your clit looks beautiful, baby. Red, swollen, and shiny with your cream." He circled his finger around it once more, eliciting a low moan from her, before tugging at the egg inside her. "I like using this inside you. When we go out to eat the next time, I'm going to make you wear one of these the entire time."

Not knowing if she should answer him or not, not sure if she could, she moaned as he tugged at the egg, positioning it right at her opening.

The ripples that went through her were like little orgasms that just kept coming. Her body clenched at the egg and the plug, never-ending tremors racing through her. She felt Ace move beside her, felt his presence there even though he hadn't touched her at all.

"Good girl." After a sharp tug on her nipples, he ran a hand down her back before moving to stand between her thighs. She didn't even flinch when the whip struck her clit again, absorbing the sting and following heat with a whimper.

"That's it, baby. No more fight left in you. Be a good girl and come for me before I take your ass."

A slick finger moved against her clit, unerringly giving her the exact touch she needed to go over. A huge tidal wave of sensation washed over her, and she had no choice but to let it take her, no longer having any strength left. She whimpered through it, closing her eyes against the strength of it as tears of release ran down her face.

"That's my good girl."

Hope shivered when he turned off the vibrating egg and withdrew it from her pussy, but she couldn't hold back a moan when he worked the plug out of her, leaving her anus clenching helplessly at the emptiness.

A thick finger firmly pressed more lube into her anus, stroking gently, her bottom hole no longer fighting his invasion. "You're all mine now, aren't you, baby." He withdrew his finger and reached for a condom. "This time you'll take all of my cock in this ass. Stay nice and loose for me. Let me in." He poised the head of his cock at her opening and began to push into her.

Unable to hold back a cry at the pinch and burn of it, Hope shivered. Chills raced down her spine, the relentless pressure at her opening forcing the muscles to give way.

"Good girl. Your ass is so tight, honey. You're killing me." His deep, rough tone sent a thrill through her, bringing tears of joy to her eyes once again. Her ass was in the perfect position for him to take her at will, and the feel of his thick cock pressing steadily into her was almost more than she could bear. It stretched her more than she thought she could be stretched, filled her more than she thought she could be filled.

And he just kept giving her more.

She just let go, too weak to attempt fighting him, she lay there, helpless and vulnerable, as Ace's thick cock steadily pressed into her anus, filling her relentlessly with his heat. The dominance of the act fulfilled a need in her, a need stronger than she could have imagined. She couldn't stop him. She had no defense against his invasion of her most vulnerable opening.

She belonged to him without reservation.

Giving herself over to him, she lay there, amazed when he gave her more. She'd never even considered that this level of submissiveness existed, her only thought to give him pleasure and to turn herself over completely into his care. She hadn't realized just how much she longed for his total possession until he surged deep, impossibly deep, and she felt his sack against her bottom.

"Mine."

If she hadn't been so attuned to him, she doubted she would have heard him, his growl deep and almost unrecognizable.

It felt so foreign, so naughty and decadent to be filled in such a way. Lost in a world where nothing existed except Ace's voice and the hard heat filling her anus, Hope shook, the chills up and down her spine never-ending.

His hands tightened on her hips, and he started thrusting, each thrust proclaiming his ownership. "This ass is all mine now, to use as I please, whenever I want it. You're mine, baby, and I'll never let you go."

Hope drifted in another place, a place where nothing mattered but pleasure and pain combining to become one and the same. Taken as never before, vulnerable and used for his pleasure, she absorbed all of it, existing only for his command.

"Come."

A deep swell came from somewhere within her, tumbling her along as it held her in its possessive grip and consumed her. Her anus gripped the thick heat, her body surrendering to its master, milking him until his almost inhuman growl told her he'd joined her. She slumped against the hot leather as ripples raced through her, her mind a blank slate.

Her submission was complete.

She'd never felt so fulfilled.

Chapter Eighteen

Ace leaned over Hope's trembling body, struggling to get enough air into his lungs. He'd never in his life come so hard that his entire body shook. His legs felt like cooked spaghetti, and he wondered briefly if the top if his head had blown off.

He couldn't just stand here, though. Hope would need him now.

Withdrawing from her, he grimaced at her faint moan. He quickly took care of the condom and moved to her side, kissing her hair and shoulders as he rid her of the straps and reached under her to remove the clips as gently as he could, leaning close to absorb her shudder.

"You were magnificent, baby. God, I love you. Come here. I need to hold you." Gathering her in his arms, he sat with her on a nearby bench, wiping the damp hair back from her forehead. He held her close, bending to touch her lips with his, a little startled that she didn't open her eyes.

"Baby, look at me."

His relief that her eyes opened was short-lived when he saw the tears in them. Fear was like a knife to his belly. "Oh, God, baby. I hurt you. I swear it'll never happen again. I'm so sorry." Burying his face in her throat, he rocked her, his mind racing. How badly had he hurt her?

Hope's hand in his hair had his head snapping up. "You're kidding, right? Oh, Ace. It was unbelievable. I never knew it could be that way."

Slumping in relief, Ace smiled tenderly, his love for her filling his heart until he thought it would burst. "You sure you're okay?"

"Better than okay." Her hand dropped back to her side. "Except I don't think I can walk out of here. I can't believe how incredible that was. Promise me you'll do it again."

Ace laughed softly, filled with a joy he'd never hoped to find. "On our wedding night. For tonight, though, I'm going to take care of you."

Cradling her against his chest, he rocked her as gently as he would a baby, running his hands over her until her trembling stopped. He laid her back on the bench to dress her before quickly donning his own clothes again.

"I want to go to your house."

"Yes, baby. We're going home."

Hope cuddled against him, making him feel ten feet tall. "Home. I like the sound of that." Reaching up to caress his jaw, she smiled, melting his heart completely. "I love you, Ace."

Love and possessiveness grabbed him by the throat. He didn't know what he'd done to deserve her but vowed to spend the rest of his life keeping her happy and safe.

After dressing both of them and between caresses and slow kisses, Ace carried Hope down the stairs of the club, smiling at her attempt to keep her eyes open.

Sebastian met them at the bottom, his expression cold, but his dark eyes twinkling. "I trust, Sheriff, that you're going to take care of this little troublemaker."

Ace smiled down at Hope, filled with love so strong it took his breath away. "Absolutely. She's all mine."

Sebastian nodded. "So she'll cause no more trouble?"

Hope grinned. "You know me better than that."

Ace narrowed his eyes, his lips twitching in an attempt to hold back a grin. "If she does, I'll take care of her."

The butler inclined his head as he opened the door. "Yes, Sheriff, I believe you will."

* * * *

Hope couldn't wipe the smile from her face.

Watching Ace drive back to his house, her smile grew with caress, as though he couldn't stop touching her. Once they arrived, he carried her straight through, barely acknowledging his brothers' grins. He strode with her to the bathroom, where he quickly undressed her and hustled her into the shower while he shucked his own clothing before joining her.

Hope moaned under his hands, her body still ultra-sensitive. She basked in his gentle attention as he washed every inch of her body before hurriedly washing himself.

"Let the warm water run over you for a bit. I'm going to go send Law and Zach out for some food." He bent to kiss her again, his smile indulgent. "I gotta take care of my woman."

It only took a few minutes before Hope got lonely. She got out and dried off, wrapping a towel around her and went in search of her fiancé.

Ace stood waiting for her just outside the bathroom door. "I sent Law and Zach for food. I was coming back to dry you off. Next time, wait for me. Come here. I want to see your clit."

Alarmed, she took a step back. "Ace, it's so sensitive I don't think I can—"

"When I said I would take care of you, I meant it. You're mine now, Hope, and you'll deal with all that entails. Lie down."

Even after all he'd done to her, her body responded immediately to the steel in his tone. Amazed that her clit already tingled in anticipation, Hope obeyed him, for the first time noticing the tube in his hand.

Ace helped her onto the bed, positioning her so that her legs hung over the edge and knelt between her thighs, shouldering them apart and very gently bent to kiss her clit. "You were such a good girl today. I was very proud of you."

Hope fisted her hands in the bedding. "You know damned well what it does to me when you talk like that. Damn it, Ace, I'm too sore."

"That's what the ointment's for. I'll make it all better, baby, I promise. You just lay back and relax."

He licked her clit, his warm mouth closing over it to suck it gently. Keeping his touch light, he used his tongue all around her from her clit to her pussy, lifting her legs to lick her sore bottom hole before raising his head.

Amazed at the sensation, Hope found herself close to coming again, but didn't know if she could stand it. She whimpered softly in her throat as Ace moved to sit on the bed next to her hip.

He squirted a generous amount of ointment onto his fingers before tossing the tube aside and using his other hand to separate her folds. "Once I massage this in, baby, your clit will feel much better."

He gently rubbed the cool ointment onto her clit, the slick gel thick enough to ease the friction of his fingers moving over it, his touch deliberate enough to make her come again almost ridiculously fast. While still coming down from her orgasm, Hope thrashed her head from side to side as Ace lifted her legs and rubbed another thick layer of ointment all around her bottom hole.

Spent, exhausted, and weak, Hope hardly moved as Ace bundled her into a thick robe and carried her to the kitchen.

Law and Zach had already come back and had started to set out the food. Zach leaned down to kiss her cheek. "Hey, honey, you look wiped out."

Hope grinned as Ace sat, keeping her on his lap. "I am. Your brother wore me out today."

Law filled a glass of iced tea and started to hand it to her, but Ace took it from him and held it to her lips himself. The look of surprise on Law's face nearly made her choke on her tea. He bent to kiss her forehead before helping Zach put out the rest of the food.

"Well, I guess Law and I better get that house built in a hurry. When you get back from your honeymoon, we'll be gone."

Ace grimaced. "We won't be going on a honeymoon just yet. Not with this bastard still on the loose." He bent his head to kiss Hope's damp hair. "I'm sorry, honey, but I promise that when we catch him, you and I are going away to wherever you want to go."

Hope snuggled into him. "My vote is someplace warm where we don't have to wear clothes."

Chuckling, Ace took her plate and silverware and pushed them aside. "Deal. Your mom's pot roast is amazing. Can you cook like this?"

Stunned when he held a forkful of her mother's roast to her lips, Hope nodded. "You betcha, but Charity's better at it." She opened her mouth obediently, curling against him in acceptance at this new and delightful display of dominance.

Ace leaned close, his warm breath on her ear making her shiver in delight as his hand moved over her bottom, out of sight of his brothers. "I already found out what you're good at, darlin', being my woman, and that's more than enough for me."

THE END

www.leahbrooke.net

ABOUT THE AUTHOR

When Leah's not writing, she enjoys her time with family and friends and plotting new stories.

Also by Leah Brooke

Desire, Oklahoma 1: *Desire for Three*
Desire, Oklahoma 2: *Blade's Desire*
Desire, Oklahoma 3: *Creation of Desire*
Desire, Oklahoma 4: *Rules of Desire*
Dakota Heat 1: *Her Dakota Men*
Dakota Heat 2: *Dakota Ranch Crude*
Dakota Heat 3: *Dakota's Cowboys*
Dakota Heat 4: *Dakota Springs*
Alphas' Mate
Tasty Treats Anthology, Volume 2: *Back in Her Bed*

Leah Brooke writing as Lana Dare

Beaumonts' Brand
Amanda's Texas Rangers

Available at
BOOKSTRAND.COM

Siren Publishing, Inc.
www.SirenPublishing.com

Breinigsville, PA USA
17 November 2010
249518BV00005B/111/P